Fool

Fool

a novel

FREDERICK G. DILLEN

Introduction by Nancy Pearl

The characters and events portrayed in this book are fictitious. Any similarity to real persons, living or dead, is coincidental and not intended by the author.

Text copyright ©1999 by Frederick G. Dillen
Introduction and Reading Group Guide copyright © 2012 by Nancy Pearl

All rights reserved.

Printed in the United States of America.
No part of this book may be reproduced, or stored in a retrieval system, or transmitted in any form or by any means, electronic, mechanical, photocopying, recording, or otherwise, without express written permission of the publisher.

A Book Lust Rediscovery
Published by AmazonEncore
P.O. Box 400818
Las Vegas, NV 89140

ISBN-13: 9781612183688
ISBN-10: 1612183689

Introduction

I was doing my regular gig on Steve Scher's morning show, *Weekday,* on KUOW 94.9 FM in Seattle many years ago when a caller asked me how many pages she should read before she gives up on a book. Thus was born what has come to be known as Nancy Pearl's Rule of 50:

> Life's too short to read a book you don't love. If you're 50 or younger, give a book 50 pages before you decide whether or not to keep reading it. When you turn 51, subtract your age from 100 and that's the number of pages (which, of course, gets smaller every year) to read before you bail on a book you're not thoroughly enjoying. When you turn 100, you are free to judge a book by its cover, whatever the attendant dangers of doing so are.

The Rule of 50 (which ended up in a similar form on Starbucks Grande cup #169 in their "The Way I See It" series a few years ago) has long been a dependable guide in my reading life. I appreciate it more and more with each passing year, but sometimes, when I start a new book, I can tell almost immediately—certainly within the first few pages, and sometimes as quickly as the opening paragraph—whether or not I'm going to fall in love with it.

No matter how cautious I am in other areas of my life (not that there's much to my life besides books and reading), I admit with no shame that when it comes to reading, I not infrequently find myself tumbling head over heels into an all-consuming and satisfying relationship with a novel or work of narrative nonfiction. I should point out here that (in accordance with The Rule of 50) I only read books that I am passionate about, or at least thoroughly enjoying (by page 33, in my case). I long ago gave up slogging through a book in the hope that it might get better. But, as a kind of corollary to the Rule of 50, I also realized that even if I wasn't enjoying a particular reading experience, it could be due to my current mood, so that giving up on a book didn't mean that I couldn't go back to it and try it again a few days, weeks, months, or even years later. It took me three attempts, over the course of two years, to finally see what almost everyone else saw—evidently immediately—in George R.R. Martin's fantasy series, Song of Ice and Fire. Count me in now as a big fan.

My love for Salman Rushdie's *Midnight's Children* didn't develop at once, either. I remember trying to read it at least twice before I was able to appreciate it. Now, of course, including *Midnight's Children* as I do among my very favorite novels, I am extremely grateful to the Random House sales rep who recommended it to me in 1981 when I was working at Ken Tracy's late and much lamented Yorktown Alley Book Store in Tulsa, Oklahoma. I wish I remembered her (or his) name, so I could offer a belated thank you.

But I don't even remember why I first picked up Frederick Dillen's *Fool* in 1999, the year it was published. I have no recollection of anyone recommending it to me, and I was unfamiliar with the author—I hadn't yet read his debut novel, *Hero*. But I discovered, to my delight, that *Fool* was one of those books that had me at "hello." I felt that first delicious inkling of book love before I got to the end of the first page: my heart started beating a little faster while my reading slowed. By the time I got to page three, I was well and truly hooked.

But hooked by what, exactly? Answering this is something I think about a lot. Pretty much whenever I'm not reading, playing Angry Birds or Plants vs. Zombies, or trolling the shelves of libraries and book stores looking for something to read, I think about what makes someone connect with a particular work—

that whole mysterious business surrounding the question of why we like the novels that we do.

It's clear to me, based on my experience as a bookseller and a librarian, that the specific plot details—what the book is about—have little to do with the pleasure that a reader takes in a book. If a bookstore customer or library patron told me that he or she loved Chad Harbach's *The Art of Fielding* and wanted another novel *just* like it, I wouldn't suggest another novel about a midwestern college baseball team with a gay subplot. Instead, I'd look for other novels with characters so well-conceived that they seem absolutely real; characters so alive that when the novel ends you feel bereft of their presence in your life. (Three good suggestions here would be Pat Conroy's *The Prince of Tides, The Brothers K* by David James Duncan, and Matthew Quick's *The Silver Linings Playbook*.) It's the feelings or emotions that you experience while you're reading a book that you remember, not the details that make up the plot.

So I'm happy to tell you what *Fool* is about: Barnaby Griswold's life changes almost overnight when he's found to have acted perhaps slimily (but not illegally) by selling short a stock; his wife leaves him, his daughters ignore him, his friends desert him, and he earns the eternal enmity of the investors who lost loads of money because of what he did. How does middle-aged Barnaby cope with this avalanche of disasters?

I have to tell you, though, that I'm afraid this description gives you little or no sense of what it is about the novel that drew me to it. Even adding the adjectives "humorous" or "witty" somewhere in the above description wouldn't particularly illuminate what it is about the novel that makes it so special.

Now try this one:

"'For Christ sake don't become a fluffmeister,' are the last words Barnaby Griswold's father ever says to him. Yet a fluffmeister is Barnaby's default position in life, as much as he may try to be an athlete, a lover, or a pilgrim."

Gets much closer to the heart of the novel, I think. Cherl Petso, one of my former students at the University of Washington's Information School wrote that description, or annotation, as we call it in library-land, after she finished reading *Fool*. It tells us almost nothing about the details of *Fool*'s plot, yet it certainly conveys to me the essence of what makes the novel so good: the humor ("fluffmeister") combined with a tinge of sadness ("the last words Barnaby Griswold's father ever says to him") and the knowledge that we're going to encounter a novel that describes a journey to self-understanding ("as much as he may try to be an athlete, a lover, or a pilgrim") and probably acceptance ("a fluffmeister is Barnaby's default position in life"). In fact, reading over Cherl's annotation right now makes me want to pick up the book—which is sitting next to the computer I'm writing this on—and start reading it again.

The reasons why we love a particular novel range from the exalted ("It changed my life") to the prosaic ("It was a page-turner") and everything in between. I've never read a novel that I can honestly say changed my life, although there have been many times that I've looked at the world a bit differently after finishing one. So my reasons for adoring *Fool* probably fall somewhere in between those two extremes. Here are the reasons I noted when I reread *Fool* for consideration in the Book Lust Rediscoveries series:

> I love how Frederick Dillen uses commas to keep a thought going, and going, and going, instead of chopping it up into pieces with periods.

> I love the scene involving a riding lawnmower.

> I love the quandary Barnaby faces during a game of cards with his former mother-in-law: "what to do when you can please people no matter how you fluff."

I love his relationship with Ada, his former mother-in-law.

I love Happiness, Ada's caregiver.

I love that Barnaby and Marian spend an afternoon at the zoo in Oklahoma City. It was at that zoo, in fact, that my younger daughter Katie was bitten by an emu.

I love that a large portion of the book takes place in Oklahoma City and that Barnaby takes Ada out to dinner at a restaurant called the Corner Box where the majority of the diners are senior citizens. There was a restaurant just like it in Tulsa (I don't know if it's still there, but I rather doubt it), and when my parents and in-laws came to visit, we would often take them there for the early bird specials. Believe me, Dillen's description is spot-on.

I love Barnaby in all his imperfection and ultimate humanness, and for all his imperfections and humanity.

I love the word "fluffmeister." I'm hoping that I'll have had at least one chance to use it in conversation by the time you read this. (You'll have to read the book to find out what it means, exactly. It's a question ripe for discussion with your fellow *Fool* readers.)

Fool will, of course, affect each of you differently; no two loves, or lovers, are alike. But I hope you'll find as much pleasure in reading it as I did.
I hope you enjoy *Fool* as much as I did.

Nancy Pearl

To my wife Leslie and to my daughters Abigail and Tatiana
With thanks to Joe Regal

In celebration of A.D. (1936–1999)

Fool

ATHLETE

Barnaby Griswold loafed and drank his way through good schools, but those were the days, God bless them, when the world made room for boys from families with the right balance of propriety and financial resource. Not that Barnaby didn't take any lessons whatever from his education, but the real work of his youth had been to learn once and for all that he was intelligent only to the near side of cunning and that the fundamental truth of his life lay in foolishness. Books and study and logic and meditation were all fine for other people and for respectable decoration, but Barnaby was a fool no matter what his father had hoped and no matter how Barnaby had tried, briefly, to turn out otherwise, no matter how Barnaby continued occasionally pretending for his father whose last words to Barnaby were, "For Christ sake don't become a fluffmeister."

Those words reverberated as intended, but they were too late. The words that took precedence were "Know thyself," words uttered, for all Barnaby knew, by one of his own ancestors. Barnaby was a fool, and he had learned it early. What was more, and more important, he had learned that the world reserved an agreeable place for fools who were prepared to stand up and claim their entitlement. He thought of that entitlement as a happy welfare with better neighborhoods, fun really. He had made his living as a fluffmeister, and it had been a good living. More and more, in fact, Barnaby wondered if his father had objected to his career not because of the despicable reflection on any individual who chose to labor in the vineyards of fluff, but because the work paid well enough to suggest a world and life that were out of kilter. Barnaby's father, who abhorred disorder and secretly distrusted life, insisted that fundamentally the world and life were good and right, insisted that it behove (behooved?) every decent man, gentleman or no, to insist likewise. Barnaby, on the other hand, who enjoyed things, knew there was much to be had in celebrating a deal, in New Jersey say, even a terrible deal, with appalling new friends and one of those green-and-eggplant sunsets.

Now, on Sunday of the Labor Day weekend, on the shore well north of Boston, on the old Richardson court at the crest of Winott Point with thirty-five polite Pointers for audience, the matter at hand involved whipping Dicky Kopus until he bled, until he ran away home.

Why? Because Barnaby's life as he knew it was over. Technically it had been over for some time, as everyone watching understood, but after today, there would not even be a home to which Barnaby himself could run away. In circumstances like these, men resurrected their lives by winning something physical, especially men like Barnaby who had never won at the physical things as children. If you wanted the good life back, you had to become a champion. Not an easy dictum, but true, and let there be no doubt about what Barnaby wanted. The good life, his own good life specifically, was central to his very nature.

"Play tennis, Barnaby," called a grown man's voice from among the fans, and Barnaby waved and smiled and called back, "Play tennis, Barnaby," and everybody laughed.

Unfortunately, however, Barnaby had just double faulted to lose an important game.

More unfortunately, Kopus had won the first set and now, with Barnaby's double fault, had gone ahead in what might be the final set. If Kopus held his own serve in the next game, he'd win the match.

The only blood so far was Barnaby's, from where he'd scraped his knee trying for a lob. When the scrape happened, Kopus apologized as if he was responsible for Barnaby's big feet and spastic coordination. Then every time they'd changed ends since the scrape, Kopus had asked if the knee was holding up.

"You sure?"

"It's fine, Richard. Just a scratch."

In fact it did hurt, but the worse part was that before drying, the blood had run down his leg and made a black mat of one side of his sock, which let Kopus offer condolence and concern with an extra load of horseshit sincerity. With his thick eyebrows up and with the welts of his low forehead plowing fleshy compassion, Kopus's sincerity could be appreciated by the audience even if they couldn't hear the practiced dialogue that came along with the package.

Though they could hear very well. Everybody, even the old ladies, just sat as always on the grass of the slope up from the edge of the court to the driveway. True, the owner of the court, the ancient patriarch Richardson, sat in the shade on the porch of the big house, beyond the drive, but he couldn't have heard anything even if Dicky Kopus had shouted it at him face-to-face, and God knew Kopus was a shouter when he wanted to be. Also a racket thrower, though there wouldn't be any of that during the finals of the Winott Cup, not with a couple of once-removed Winotts watching, with Jerry Childs, the new tennis association martinet, sternly pretending to officiate.

Cheating, yes. Kopus was a famous cheater, and he had set things up early in the match by calling two unimportant serves from Barnaby out, which they were, and then seconds later shaking his head and loudly congratulating Barnaby and admitting untruthfully but with great fraudulent good spirit that the serves were in. All to convince the audience that Dicky Kopus was a man who could be believed in the event that, late in the match, crucial shots from Barnaby, good shots, had to be called out.

The bad news was that Kopus hadn't had to cheat.

Barnaby was giving it away.

And now they had to change sides, and Barnaby would have to receive Kopus's serves facing toward the harbor. The lawn rolling downhill behind that end of the court brought the screen of trees lower than the height of a toss for serve, and at the end of summer, today, you could lose the ball in the sky. Which made it all the more irritating that Barnaby had double faulted when he himself had that advantage. Double faulted, for Christ sake, to set Kopus up for the match.

So Barnaby smiled and waved and called, "Play tennis, Barnaby." He looked at the ball he'd just served into the net, as good as handing the championship to Kopus, and he started a loose-jointed, happily dejected walk toward the sidelines, toward the end of his ruined and still unrestored life, toward the crowd which, despite its prurience, finally moved with the first gatherings of blankets and searchings for wandered children, the first concrete thoughts of cocktails before the big party down at the stone beach below the Winott boat hut. Barnaby Griswold was through, and at some point for ladies and gentlemen, decorum suggested one look away.

But then?

Barnaby did understand that limping would be bad form. He headed toward the grass and the crowd, toward the end of the net and toward the watercooler and the two aluminum-and-plastic-web chairs there where he and Kopus could sit during their change of sides, and he imagined his father saying, "If you're going to lose, lose. For Christ sake don't limp."

So he gave a slight but noticeable limp. He made it to his chair, and he sat down heavily enough for all to see the weight of his forty-six years and of this match (not to mention the catastrophic rest of things). Among the faces of the audience, as Barnaby turned his back on them to sit, the ghost of his father's face was frozen in shame, and Barnaby himself, in a pretense of shame, stared down at the red plastic, push-pump watercooler that sat between his own expensive sneakers and the net post.

He didn't look at Kopus to see if Kopus had registered the limp. The point was to avoid Kopus's eyes. The point was exactly eye-averted shame of the first order. Kopus himself, needless to say, would manufacture a limp to explain away any meaningless Thursday afternoon doubles loss before Memorial Day, but Kopus knew that Barnaby would not. Kopus knew that for Barnaby to double fault and then put on a limp, in the finals of the Winott Cup, and then sit staring at the watercooler before the last game, Kopus knew that was giving up and crying about it, all of it, in the most humiliating way for Barnaby. Kopus knew that in some circumstances Barnaby needed to maintain an honest posture and a gentleman's elevated demeanor. Kopus knew that right now Barnaby was in every respect a broken man. At least Barnaby hoped Kopus knew.

And here Kopus came, unable to resist, swimming with his swarthy, mackerel face into Barnaby's line of sight, bending over ostensibly to thumb a cup of water out of the cooler but really to look up into Barnaby s humiliated eyes.

"Tough double fault," was what Kopus said. "It's the knee," was what Kopus said. "You hadn't fallen on that knee," he said, "we'd be playing even."

Rather than at the scrape on Barnaby's knee, though, Kopus looked with big, seedy eyes up into Barnaby's eyes, and could not keep from grinning. Kopus was Barnaby's age and was not without abilities; he had built a one-man storefront insurance agency into a North Shore octopus of money, leaving a trail of bodies in his wake. Truth be told, Barnaby would not have wanted to meet Kopus in one of Kopus's alleys at night. But subtlety? No.

"Well, Richard," Barnaby said, looking away in abasement so utter that the ghost of his father got up from the grass behind them and left altogether, "let's get this last game over with."

Kopus stood and comfortingly, patronizingly, patted Barnaby's shoulder, and then strode onto the court to gather balls for his serve.

Barnaby sat a moment more, looking, letting the moment sink in. The net was new, but otherwise it wasn't a great court. There were cracks beginning at the lines, and in the doubles alleys there were a couple of long fissures where black paving actually lifted up through the faded green surface. The whole thing tilted down in a northwesterly way at the biggest of the two enormous maroon-leafed trees on the side away from the house, and beyond the tree at the lane and the vined, ferny pitch into the swamp. Were they some kind of elm? Those red leaves? A depression in the court that collected the last of the leaves during the winter was blotched and stained forever, or until ancient Richardson died and somebody bought the place and resurfaced. But the depression was outside of play after all. And the fencing around the court was an old rope mesh, one of the great anachronistic delights in Barnaby's world. The rope had been a delight, really, since the summers it provided distraction for a much littler Barnaby during his early wooden-racket lessons.

Nobody would ever cut a thing like those maroon trees; the trees would stay, but one day someone would put in a real fence of chain link.

It was rope for now, though, and beyond the rope was the crowned and pebbled lane shaded by pea vine reaching up from a swamp that probably hadn't changed since the ice age pocked the murk in there with loaves of granite. Sixty years ago, when there was the swank, gay colony on the Point, Big Bill Tilden had stopped in to play and dabble and whatever, maybe on a day just like this. It would have been a clay court then. Red clay. Chinese elms? Chinese maples?

God, but Barnaby loved this court. He was going to miss it more than he could ever have said. He could have knelt and put his forehead to its warmth. He was going to miss his life, and he wished to Christ he could put his forehead to that. As if it had not been four years coming, he could still imagine he was only daydreaming and would now wake up with everything as it was supposed to be, with everything his again. Oh, to close his eyes and kneel and press his forehead down anywhere.

No. Don't get into that frame of mind. For Christ sake. Not with the match on the line. Up. Do not kneel down.

Barnaby made himself stand and limp out onto his new side of the court. Yes. All right. Keep the God damned focus. Think champion. Do you want your good life back or not? He knew the answer to that, all right.

He also knew that he had gotten under Kopus's skin. So now all he had to do was hit the ball. Barnaby Griswold smiled with cheery desolation at the crowd which had stopped gathering its blankets to watch him, decorum be damned, as one watches fresh blood in the moments around a highway slaughter. He smiled invitingly, hopelessly, across the net at Kopus who was already doing him the favor of not quick-serving.

Barnaby bent his knees and made what few people would have recognized was more than a halfhearted bounce of anticipation.

In his old life, in his real life, in the life he lived joyously until not so very long ago, Barnaby ate. Of course he ate. But he always drank more, and his theory was that the booze kept the weight down. Horseshit of course, but good for a laugh. Weight-alcohol inversion, basis of the Griswold diet.

Basis anyway of occasional saloon friendships and, more than five years ago in New York, back when Barnaby Griswold was Barnaby Griswold, basis of forced entry into the Old Ladies Bank deal, which was not Barnaby's last deal but might as well have been; it was the deal that finally did everything for him and to him.

Five years ago the oil boom had been on so long everybody thought it was the truth, and Barnaby had had a lunch at La Cote so futile that he hadn't even gone to the sidewalk with whomever they were. Or else the lunch had been so successful. Or else he'd walked them out and come back to the table. Anyway, he was at the table by himself finishing the third bottle of probably a Montrachet and watching the long, narrow, cosmopolitan darkness of the place empty out when he became more aware of the Oklahoma boys.

Differently aware. Everyone had heard them enough to be more than just aware.

Why hadn't Barnaby gone on to see what was happening at the River Club, or dropped into the office to get some quotes and a clean shirt and make dinner reservations? Well, there was the wine naturally. And it may have been a slow afternoon. It may have been a slow week, judging by the time he burned subsequently. But no, it was more than that too; it was profound machinery at work, and he knew it. He was surprised he hadn't realized what was up during lunch, though he may have realized even then subliminally. There was a surge running in the sea that floated Barnaby Griswold; there was a wave building, the kind of wave that built beneath a deal, and it was not building as if the deal were a small one. These two Oklahoma boys didn't just have their ominous little hands in money; they had their hands in money that involved Barnaby Griswold.

There was no hesitating if you hoped to survive purely by your instincts and keep your girls in private school, and so Barnaby took his bottle of wine in one hand and his glass in the other and heaved to his feet. Yes, there was absolutely a wave; it was already carrying him, and even as he steadied himself on it, he could see that the boys' table down the aisle supported two orders of dessert crepes and two orders of dessert soufflé, seventy-five dollars in desserts alone, and through their third tablecloth seeped evidence of a lot of cuisine and lubricants gone under the bridge before dessert. "God bless it all," Barnaby said with quiet solicitation to the expensive air around him in the emptying restaurant.

The boys' waiter had retreated, Philippe it would have been in that part of the room, and from the farthest end, from the direction of the kitchen, Michel was advancing. Somewhere Philippe was praying to one cordon or another that Michel wouldn't lower the boom before the boys tipped.

An elegant barracuda with an unremarkable, off-brand name but full funding came at Barnaby, leading one of the new Brazilian kids it looked like. Barnaby had tried to pitch her once, and she had pretended to think he was picking her up and had gotten her hand down inside his pants while the two of them waited outside for cars. Her boy, Thai rather than Brazilian in those days, had looked toward Central Park and talked in unin-telligible rapture about urban landscape. It hadn't frightened Barnaby. Even if you've lived your life as the large, ridiculous fellow to whom girls and love are allergic, you don't drink several bottles of wine at lunch to get scared. But the barracuda was not just good-looking; she was also smarter and braver and more ruthless than Barnaby ever was even in his dreams, and he had had the sense never to pitch her again. What was her name? His father might have forgiven her anything because she was so ravenously other than what Griswolds were. Barnaby would have liked to hear in so many words why he himself could not be forgiven, though of course he knew; he was supposed to be a Griswold. More to the point, he would have liked, out of respectful curiosity, to get a look at the barracuda's portfolio.

Now he stood back and spread his arms, bottle in one hand, glass in the other, as if she needed that gesture and the space it provided to get past him and away to the street. He balanced back with his thighs against an empty table behind him, and the table moved and he slopped wine out of his glass. He hoped that Philippe's busboy had not set up the table for dinner yet. He hoped it really was an empty table. He listened for evidence about that. He stood up straight and nodded, bowed, at the barracuda as she passed. She did not notice him. The Brazilian kid nodded and then took the nod back.

It must have gotten late, because in the elaborate dimness back along the other side of the room it looked like a very chic couple was talking to a tiger from the wallpaper, and the tigers rarely appeared until lunchtime had come and gone. Great-looking tiger this afternoon. Well, how could a tiger ever not be great? (Such splendid creatures; awfully good friends, really.) Which made it three-thirty.

Barnaby leaned into motion and paced the few long steps to reach the boys' table before Michel could get there and can them, and fortunately Michel had to stop and speak with the tiger's chic couple. But the boys had definitely passed a threshold. They were shouting something down the windowless tunnel of the room toward the kitchen.

"You men are from Oklahoma," Barnaby said. "And if you can forgive my intrusion, I would like to tell you the happy secret to eating all those desserts comfortably."

They both looked up at him, both lifting their chests and pressing their fattened necks against the backs of their shirt collars with military importance. Their suit coats were well open to show off the investment-banker suspenders they'd picked up at Paul Stuart. The older one's stomach rose over his chest to his chin. The younger one said, with what did not sound like a welcoming attitude, "Who the hell are you?"

The older one pointed a finger at the desserts and said with deep seriousness, "FedEx it to Oklahoma City. Got to fly back this afternoon and we may not have room on our plane. Never eat it now. Couldn't possibly eat another bite of all this shit now."

"Alcohol," Barnaby said. He stood above them and smiled at them like an oversized weatherman with a good report for the weekend. "If you drink sufficiently you can eat more than you want and still run like an absolute fucking gazelle all your life. Forgive my language."

"What the hell makes you think we're from Oklahoma?" the younger one said.

That younger one would be a challenge, and Barnaby loved a challenge.

To the older one Barnaby said, "Your waiter's Philippe, isn't it?

But let me offer this bottle of burgundy into the situation at hand. May I?"

"Philippe. Good man. We can use him. Already told him to come on down and take over our dining room at the Petroleum Club." But then that older one noticed his young colleague's attitude and began to bridle as well. "You the owner here? There a problem?"

Barnaby laughed. "I've tried to buy it, but they tell me they can't afford to lose me as a customer."

"What the hell is that supposed to mean?" the young one said with such endearing venom that Barnaby beamed.

Barnaby gave all of his pleasure to the young one and said, "I have a wife."

"There's a relief."

Out the corner of his eye, Barnaby sensed Michel's approach.

"My wife's from Oklahoma City," Barnaby explained, and they both raised their eyebrows like Englishmen judging a stranger's familiar sunburn in the Sudan. Barnaby liked almost everybody, but he found himself liking these guys in particular. "Winifred Briley. Her father, now deceased, was a distinguished physician, chief of staff at St. Somebody or other." They didn't register the name, so that put them promisingly (most things were promising for Barnaby) off the map. If it could have made any sense, he would have said car dealerships.

"Mister Griswold. These gentlemen are your friends. Charming."

"Yes they are, Michel, and we're just now working everything out. Can you give us a minute?"

"Give us a minute, Michel," the older one said in exactly the weighty tone of voice he would use when he instructed the angel of commerce to allow Barnaby a very substantial amount of money. It wasn't a tone of voice that you wanted to ignore, even from a fellow like this who looked precariously older than his probable fifty years. Barnaby thought to suggest his own very good cardiologist.

The younger one could have been almost Barnaby's age, but his weight swelled under the skin of his face like baby fat; he managed to look like a fraternity boy who'd eaten too much because life away from home made him irritable.

Michel backed off a yard or so, and the fraternity boy said in his high, brittle, crotchety plains whine, "Old buddy, who the fuck are you?"

Somewhere, indeed probably everywhere, were people who would not like these boys, but Barnaby could never count himself among such people. He had to acknowledge that the young one gave off sulfurous vapors of wreckage and recrimination, but that was only cause to remember happily that most friendships for Barnaby were brief. Barnaby set his glass down on the Oklahoma table and held out his hand. "Barnaby Griswold. How do you do."

The young one looked at Barnaby's hand without moving to shake it, and then said, "Does a name like that make you an eastern snob?"

"Barnababy?" the older one said, as much in honest confusion as in adolescent meanness.

And that, Barnababy, was an echo Barnaby hadn't heard since the teasings of boarding school. Barn-a-baby, Barn-a-baby. How splendid for a nickname to surface after thirty years and grease the wheels of this moment.

Barnaby smiled and nodded at the older one.

And, "Barnababy, Barnababy," the young one said with such a full, instant freight of meanness that, grease or no grease, Barnaby felt as if he were back in the dealership where Win had bought her German car. When Barnaby had occasionally had to bring that car in for service, he'd found that ordinary politeness inspired furies of disdain in the Teutonic service manager. To get the car serviced at all, Barnaby had had to learn to beat his fist on the counter and shout for attention in a voice of murderous command.

"Barnababy Griswold," the young guy declared, "is a clown's name."

So Barnaby spread his feet and unbuttoned his suit jacket. He stared at the young guy who looked ready to get up and fight. He stared at the old guy who stared back in confusion gone to outrage. Then Barnaby set his bottle of wine firmly on the table beside his glass and balled his fists and put his fists onto his hips. He was a big man. Bigger than either of these men. He swayed over their table.

He said, "You think Barnaby Griswold sounds like a clown?" And then, though he hated to do it in La Cote, especially with Michel vibrating only yards away, he shouted.

"Well wise up about clowns."

And once he'd shouted, he leaned abruptly down to within a threatening few inches of this vicious Oklahoma boy and let his voice go to a growl that would have satisfied any of the several tigers watching silently from the wallpaper with bloodthirsty interest. "Around here," Barnaby said, "the clowns are in charge."

Kopus was so sure Barnaby had folded that instead of a first serve, he offered a straight-ahead second serve, a forehand no less, and Barnaby stepped in, bent his knees, locked his focus on the ball, and stroked through. Barnaby hit a winner.

Kopus was so surprised he didn't even reach for it. Then he gave Barnaby a "Don't start fucking with me" glare. Barnaby may have suckered him for one point, but there sure as hell were going to be no more marshmallow serves. Barnaby hurried into position for the next point, and Kopus picked up the loose ball and quick-served without any rhythm or windup and followed the serve to the net. Not Kopus's usual style, coming to net behind a serve, but Barnaby had gotten under his skin, and Kopus wanted to finish it off.

There wasn't time to think, always an advantage for Barnaby and his knees were bent from some earlier life. Also the background on Kopus's toss was better from this angle. Barnaby could see. And, Kopus was not exactly a fat boy, but he had a lot more stomach than speed, regardless of running backward along the Point Road between the harbor and Barnaby's house at times Barnaby was likely to see him. It took Kopus a good two shots to work his way to the net.

Barnaby picked up the flight of the ball and took it on the rise and stroked a rocket back up the middle. And, oh Christ, there was Kopus trapped, naked and flat-footed, fluttering his racket in no-man's land. It did not look good, and mixed with applause for Barnaby's shot was laughter at Kopus. Kopus, who was never ashamed to look bad to win, was nevertheless someone who did not like to be laughed at when he lost. Well, who did? But this was Kopus, the Point's second-generation immigrant. Kopus, the distasteful, new-dough invader, a laughing stock in front of Jerry Childs, the new climber, and everyone else on the Point, all of whom including Childs thought they were better than Kopus, all of whom made up, Barnaby assumed, the largest gears turning the machinery of Kopus's hatred as well as his oily cloak of charm. Kopus turned toward the pasteled proprieties of that little hillside in the sun and looked ready to throw his racket into the midst of them.

Barnaby wasted no time getting into position again, because Kopus had picked up the loose third ball after the first point and had it in his pocket. Kopus could spin into another quick serve and would keep the point even if Barnaby were yards away from being ready. This was not the time to look at the hillside and see who was happy for him, see the bare legs that told about summertime and rustic, tasteful privilege and all the things that warmed his heart when his heart needed warming.

And Kopus did it, stepped behind the baseline and spun without windup, without even a look across the net, into his jerking, broken-winged swat.

Barnaby could not see the toss in the empty background, saw the contact, lost the ball in flight, and then saw it land three inches long.

"Gee. No, Richard. I'm sorry. That one's out." He had known it would be out. Kopus had wrenched at it. Kopus was too angry and was losing composure. He had served as hard as he could and pulled himself out of his best motion. Not that Kopus was graceful in the best of times.

Then Kopus cranked into his second serve, and Barnaby bent his knees and knew with a giggling giddiness that Kopus was slamming wildly, that Kopus…

Yes.

"No," Barnaby shouted. "Out." He was too loud and too happy, but he couldn't help it. Kopus had double faulted in the match game, double faulted when he had the advantage of the blind background, double faulted to love-forty. Out of the quicksands of loss evermore, Barnaby's good life was rising. On a distant horizon, there were the towers of his own shining city again. Banners and trumpets and hope.

Now he had to be sure not to blow it. He had to get ready for the next point. He had to bend the God damned knees. Watch the ball.

At love-forty, Kopus hit a safe, composure-regaining serve, and Barnaby stiffened in his knees. With too much time to think, with the game in his pocket, Barnaby seized up for God sake; he puffed the serve back, giving Kopus a floater to put away. And a voice in Barnaby's stomach screamed, Barnaby Griswold, homeless without a nickel. And the quicksand rose and Barnaby Griswold's future emptied forever.

But Kopus rushed and swung with a hard, flat, crazy person's swing. Talk about not bending your knees. Kopus hit Barnaby's puff ball almost to the back fence.

The set was tied. Oh, into a tiebreaker when Kopus had had it wrapped up and then blown his own serve with the lousy background at his back.

Barnaby was certain again, in the truest way of his nature, that hope justified itself no matter what, and so he allowed himself one quick, hopeful glance at the hillside.

No, his father had not returned.

His father had known from conception that Barnaby was a wrong genetic slurry, and the most rigorous expectation even from bag races at birthday parties was that Barnaby would try hard and fail with decent self-respect. For a while the expectation had also been that in the next sons the slurry would take a more favorable posture, but his poor mother's frail, no-longer-young belly had failed to produce, and Barnaby, left out in full sun, grew into his father's horror.

At least his father had been able to die knowing that Barnaby's sort of life found the rewards it deserved. Two years ago, shortly before he died and just before the admonition against fluffmeistering, an admonition they both knew was long since beside the point—two years ago, not much more than three years after Barnaby had met the Oklahoma boys in La Cote and embarked on the Old Ladies Bank deal, not long in fact before Barnaby's public apology—two years ago, his father had in fact offered Barnaby an unconditional blessing. By then everybody knew the full extent to which the Old Ladies Bank deal had exploded Barnaby's business life and personal life and whatever other sort of life Barnaby was ever again likely, or unlikely, to have. And so the blessing was supposed to have settled things between father and son.

Of course it hadn't settled a thing, not for Barnaby who had to carry on and who wished at least that the shell of his darling, pathetic dead mother could be on today's sunshined hillside to see Barnaby humble nasty Dicky Kopus. He also wished for forgiving appearances by his ex-wife and his two Barnaby-abhorring (or Barnaby-oblivious, anyway) daughters. Because, as it was, the slope up from the court offered no soul who liked Barnaby any more than Barnaby liked them.

Why was it that Barnaby's friends (waiters and bartenders aside) had always been either people he'd just met or people he would never see again? Why was it that he had neglected his mother like everybody else?

There was no need to ask why Win and the girls were not around.

Barnaby Griswold was lonely in a place where he and a thin line of Griswolds before him had summered for a hundred years.

Wasn't there a pretty girl? Love would be such a comfort. Wasn't there a girl anywhere who could love Barnaby Griswold?

No, and why would there be? Pretty girls had never in his life so much as looked at Barnaby, and very few other girls had looked for more than a minute either.

As it happened, there was a pretty girl, just beside the court, a girl with a halo of frizzed hair, but there was nothing she could possibly want with Barnaby.

God, but he wished this was not his last summer. He wished with all his heart that it was a real summer and that he could know again that nothing mattered.

He tried to imagine his daughters smiling at him, and as if he were himself an idle spectator, he glanced across the net at Kopus who was pacing and breathing and pumping himself up for the tiebreaker like one of the legion of vicious tennis punks on television.

Kopus was a man of the time. Not so different, but for the aspect of taste, from Barnaby.

Only Kopus had never gotten caught. And when Kopus did whatever he did outside the light of probity with which the Point lit itself, when Kopus killed someone or other, there was probably not much metaphor involved.

It was Barnaby who'd gotten caught. Guilty or not, it was Barnaby who'd lost the bundle. It was Barnaby. It was Barnaby. It was Barnaby.

Holy shit.

It was the tiebreaker.

What was he doing?

The fucking match was on the line, and he was not paying attention.

Champions fucking paid attention during tiebreakers. They did if they wanted their good lives back.

He came to the baseline and bounced a ball once and stared across at Kopus. He bared his teeth for Kopus to see. He sucked in his breath with a quick, fearful rush, and then let it out with an aggressively audible, "Yaaaah." He did not spit, but he did allow a line of drool to escape the corner of his mouth as he bent over before rocking into the motion of his serve.

Kopus saw it. Kopus knew who (whom?) he was up against.

Barnaby tossed the shiny, furred yellow ball up into the blue sky above Winott Point and unwound his torso in the beginning of the reach to smack that furry sphere half to death and into Kopus's misery.

He wondered, though too late now to do anything about it, if he'd sufficiently bent his knees, if he'd bent them at all. It all felt a little stiff, and as he strained upward, the line of drool laid itself along one earnest, rosy, sweaty cheek back almost to Barnaby's ear.

The older, heavier one said, "I'm Tom J. Baker, and if you'd known my father and known Baker Chevrolet in those days, you'd call me TJ Junior. Since we're just getting to know one another, and here in New York, you can plain call me TJ. We believe in first names in Oklahoma. And this gentleman across the table from me is Peter Potter."

Which should have sounded like the name of a banker on the eastern seaboard but was in fact said all the way through like a single Christian name. Peterpotter. Or, as it came out, "Peterpotter Dodge, Peterpotter Chrysler Plymouth," and around the lots, "Mr. Peterpotter." It was enough to make Barnaby remember what it had been like getting used to his own name.

And that younger one, Peterpotter, who looked like a sour fraternity kid waiting to get in a sucker punch at the edge of team fights, Peterpotter stood and put his remarkably little hand on Barnaby's shoulder and said, "Sit down, sir. I want you to hear what we're planning to do this afternoon. TJ, I think we ought to tell our friend Barnaby about our idea. Maybe he'd like to join us. Barnaby, you ever gotten to drive the plane on a flight to where the wind comes whistling up your ass?"

Barnaby had not, but the meat of the idea involved something else anyway. TJ and Peterpotter were since just that morning in possession of an eighty-million-dollar unrestricted line of credit from Chase Manhattan, and on their way out of the bank they had each wanted a cheap cigar. At a newsstand on the street, where they'd found the cigars, they'd asked in fun how much the whole stand would sell for, and the guy who took their money from behind the dirty magazines had said, "How about I sell it to you one cigar at a time? Those are sixty cents apiece. Plus tax."

So they'd bought the whole stand for real, for spite, and hired the guy to watch it until they picked it up on their way to the airport.

Really. They were such easy men for Barnaby to like.

What was not easy right away was imagining how a newsstand might fit into a car. Barnaby had never noticed that there was such a thing as a newsstand and smoke shop that folded up, and he wasn't sure that TJ and Peterpotter had correctly noticed it either. But once they were all convinced that no stand worth taking home as a souvenir could possibly be small enough for a car, then it all worked itself out. A pickup truck, probably, to do justice to a deal like this Chase Manhattan thing, would also be too small. So a one-ton flatbed, the boys said, and if the stand was much bigger than that, hell, they'd have to start thinking about a bigger plane.

Anyhow. Details. By that time every customer was gone; even the tigers were gone, and Michel's gangster cousins had come in from Long Island in their truck to drop off some contraband or other, and so Barnaby and TJ and Peterpotter rode off at rush hour sitting on the bare, small, open, platform of in fact the cousins' one-ton flatbed. The flatbed platform was made of wooden planks that were enclosed by an open fence of four-foot metal-sheathed stakes which rose in rattling looseness along the framing perimeter. Outside the stakes was a New York river of car tops and other small trucks.

The truck and its platform, its bed, were up; Barnaby could have crawled over on the yellow roofs of taxis to the sidewalk, to the teeming shoals of people so thick in their release from the day's work that Barnaby could smell sweat and breath even in the middle of the traffic. He could hear the noise of all the feet and the voices along with the tires and the horns. Everything was going crosstown under the watchful shine of a spring sun that lit and shadowed buildings in a tall, crowded, antically busy harmony with the noises and the smells.

Yes indeed, Barnaby was out in the middle, riding the bed at the back of a truck. Barnaby felt like a New York afternoon prince in the most splendid position to see and be seen; it felt like more than any man deserved.

Should he have known it was too good to be true? Should he have made, when he was still in his own territory, one serious appraisal of Peterpotter?

No, a grand procession can only be the best sort of omen, and when something of the best sort doesn't work out for the best, that is the fickleness of the gods. Or of God rather. Though he recognized his pagan impulses, Barnaby preferred to think of himself as an upstanding Christian within whom resonated the hymns of his boarding-school youth, hymns that would play through the voices of children and a few thrilling trumpets when he could afford to give the school something marvelous like a new library.

But the more important point right now was that as Barnaby sat on that heavy wood planking of the truck's bed and stretched his legs and put his hands out behind himself for support, he could feel the warmth of the planks along with the splinters in his palms. He could feel the warmth against his spreading ass through the good, lightweight wool of his suit trousers.

Warm? Dry? For Christ sake.

It was spring.

After a winter that would not stop and a springtime calendar that had brought only rain, the sun was out. Yes, it might have been out for some time today without Barnaby's realizing, but out only today; yesterday he was certain he had worn his rain-coat, in rain. For a desolate instant he understood he had been carrying that coat at the beginning of this day too, and he looked around as if the coat might be hanging from one of the stakes that surrounded the truck's bed. He could not have described the coat, but he felt he had liked it, that it had served him well, and that he would know it if he saw it.

He felt a belch and released it, the tiniest, most fleeting contribution to the noise of this moment in the world. Joyous.

Around the bed TJ and Peterpotter tried to grip their fingers into the cracks between the planking as if they thought they could really fall off any vehicle during a Manhattan rush hour. As if, for God sake, they had never ridden on the back of a truck in their lives. Barnaby wanted to believe that an Oklahoma boyhood for future car dealers must have involved the back of a truck at high speed on dirt roads, but in today's world one learned to set beliefs aside quickly. Let them go.

Taking the precaution of resetting his hands so that they were free of real splinters, Barnaby sprang to his feet, and in doing so tore a gaping hole in the calf of his right trouser leg. It did not faze him. Spring was in the air, and the sun was out, and as they turned off the cross street to head downtown on Fifth Avenue, Barnaby lost his balance, shot out a hand to break whatever the fall would be, and by miraculous chance caught hold of one of the stakes. Oh, this was a day. A taxi below him honked at his salvation.

Barnaby, holding to his providential stake, sent his attention like Jove to the cowering, grimacing, holding-on-for-dear-life figures of Peterpotter and TJ.

"Up," he shouted. "Get up."

Hadn't they seen him get up safely? He looked for their benefit to the stake that had become a staff of steadiness and command, and they did not look. Or they looked about to vomit. Barnaby shucked that corner of belief he'd tried subversively to maintain that Oklahoma boys really did grow up drunk in the backs of trucks. Then, with a surge of sympathy, he realized that certainly if these boys had been drunk in the backs of trucks, those trucks would not have been awash in a canyon of putrid air, air shaken to vibration by thousands and thousands of screaming vehicles traveling fitfully at five miles an hour.

Barnaby himself loved such air and understood the screams as approval not really for him but for a world of which he was a happy part and which he too applauded.

He let go his stake and gestured with both hands up at the glorious spring sky and its five o'clock sun, which actually had just gone behind what might have been his own office tower. No, actually it wasn't. Of course it wasn't. In any case this was no time to be thinking about his office. Here were two fine men from Oklahoma who did not understand and who were missing a parade.

On an exuberant impulse of genius, Barnaby stripped off his suit jacket and hung it over his stake.

And TJ and Peterpotter saw his suspenders. Suspenders much like their own. Suspenders upon which, for all anyone knew, much depended. Suspenders which suddenly gave heart to TJ and Peter-potter so that they threw off their fear and nausea and sprang up and grabbed on to stakes of their own, and once they had their balance, they too took off their suit coats and were proud in the martial decoration of financiers' braces.

"It's spring," Barnaby shouted across the open truck bed from his stake to their stakes.

"Spring," TJ and Peterpotter shouted back.

And it was. A few blocks behind, Central Park was coming into leaf. Somewhere were crocuses and forsythia. On the other side of the truck, another taxi made another cheering beep, this time for TJ and Peterpotter's rising, and TJ and Peterpotter smiled. Now they were beginning to understand. Now they were the boys Barnaby had imagined them to be, and he gave them his city as he had promised to do.

Had he arranged this truck? For just a second he forgot exactly what they were about, but it was only a second. Who cared? He raised a hand and saluted with delight to all the clogged flow of Fifth Avenue, and a few happy souls on shore, along the packed sidewalk, saluted back in one way and another. Of course they did. Barnaby made large, theatrical motions that were the hailings not of a star or a hero but of any ordinary man who finds himself on a great wave. Oh, this was more than the wave beneath a deal; this was the crest of one of life's golden surges, and Barnaby hailed everybody else on the crest.

TJ and Peterpotter hailed and saluted, and there were more answers from shore, and there were more honkings because what else did a taxicab driver have to salute with after all. Barnaby took his jacket off the stake and flared that over his head. A flag, by God. It was spring, and spring demanded flags. He beat his jacket in circles over his head and faced back at his office, sure that his secretary was looking, hopeful beyond reason that she knew where his raincoat was.

He saluted a policeman mounted on a horse, and the policeman did not salute back.

The policeman looked across above the tops of the cabs directly at Barnaby and was not pleased.

The light had changed and traffic was stopped, and the policeman and his horse came out at Barnaby. There was no shout of instruction or warning. This was a silent cop on an errand of enforcement, a cop for whom perhaps the workday had just begun; Barnaby could sympathize with that, but what about spring for goodness sake? Barnaby wished he had not managed to tear his trousers. He remembered that the objective was to collect a folding newsstand and smoke shop and get it out to a private airplane for these men from Oklahoma, and he hoped that his exuberance had not ruined their chances.

Barnaby hoped for much, but the policeman's expression as he threaded his horse to the truck was not promising. Waving from the sidewalks had stopped. Honking had stopped. No, the city had not stopped; Fifth Avenue had not stopped, but on this block spring was in peril and everyone knew it.

When what should appear?

A carrot.

One of Michel's three dishonest cousins was holding a carrot up out the window and back at Barnaby, a carrot in its native state, with actual dirt on it and a green stalk looping long and feathery out the top of the knobbly orange shaft of the thing. A carrot when you needed a carrot. What a people, the French.

Barnaby let go his stake and bent his knees for balance. That the truck was stopped seemed to make balance problematic, but two free hands were necessary, Barnaby was sure, for a carrot and a policeman and a horse. Barnaby focused on the horse, a horse with reliable, compassionate eyes, a horse with character. Oh Christ, what a day: a horse and a carrot. He couldn't help himself. He held the carrot aloft; he brandished the carrot triumphant, and both sidewalks erupted with a roar of cheers drowning out all the throb of motors, and then the horns blared up, not trumpets but thrilling just the same in their twining with voices. It came to Barnaby that local farms could not have produced the carrot this early in the season, and so the dirt was soil from God knew where and that made him think of liberté and Lafayette and the American bond with the French, things people didn't think of often enough, things he himself had never thought of before even in school when such thoughts were assigned, he supposed.

Here was the horse. Eyes as big and wet with memory as tennis balls lost in the swamp. Also hungry, those eyes.

Barnaby did not look at the policeman. Never push it. Good businessmen and good Christians will give you the same advice on that. Never rub it in.

Barnaby brought the carrot down from aloft, and where there had been cheering and honking, there was silence. The roar of life from other blocks, other avenues, came from a tinny distance that might have been as far as Mars. Barnaby offered the end of the carrot to the lips on that hinging, nostriled mouth, a mouth very close to Barnaby suddenly, a mouth that seemed to have a life of its own and a beginning interest in one of his suspenders—was that an Oklahoma connection? But then the carrot was sniffed, and the lips flopped over it like a retired trumpet player at a martini, and half the carrot was gone.

Barnaby did not look at the policeman; he thrust the carrot, the half carrot, back into the air, and the cheers and the horns resounded once again.

The light changed and the truck lurched. Barnaby brought the carrot down for balance, and the horse, quite understandably, mistook the gesture for an offer and snatched the rest of the carrot from Barnaby, and stayed there between lanes of rolling-again traffic with the feathered green of stalk weaving out the side of his mouth.

Good-bye. Good-bye.

After he won the tiebreaker, and won it easily, he stood beside the court not to look but to be looked upon. Against insurmountable odds, he was dead even in the match, and with the one set left to play, momentum was on his side. Let those who had ever thought to write off Barnaby Griswold, in tennis or in life, think again.

Up on the shingled porch of the old Richardson place, companioned by the dangerously overgrown granddaughter Jerry Childs had married to join the tribe, yes, ancient Richardson looked vacantly out into the sky above the court. Given the whiffs of reputation that still adhered, maybe he imagined he like Barnaby was on the court, surveying the hillside for young ankles exposed beneath the folds of linen dresses, spotting the firm flesh of a shoulder offered beneath the gauze and umbrella of a girl known for appetites. Fine. Barnaby wanted ancient Richardson to be undressing the summer women of his youth.

But Barnaby wanted the rest of the hillside at today's finals to be looking at Barnaby, and this was no careless exercise of vanity. This was how champions took possession of an arena. This was how tigers announced themselves to the other eyes of the night. So that everyone would understand what had happened and who was winning. And everyone on the hillside was indeed looking at Barnaby and understanding very clearly. Even the pretty girl with her frizzed wildness of hair, though she might not know Barnaby was presumed finished, washed up, in realms outside of tennis. Actually, she probably did know. Everybody knew. Barnaby lifted his chest. As he had all along meant to do, he was winning back his life, and he couldn't have cared less that his father chose not to watch. Because everyone else's preparation for departure had ceased utterly. Everyone else was rapt before Barnaby Griswold's phoenix.

He did wish that his own two daughters were here to witness the perspiring reissue of their father's life. Also to represent the succeeding rank of Griswolds; that was important even if the girls had already gotten most of what money they'd ever need from his old life. And all right, he did wish they would root for him. Was that so wrong? Hadn't gladiators always, regardless of how they behaved at home, hoped to hear their children's loving voices cry down into the battle, Go for it, Daddy. Kill 'em.

Barnaby went ahead and put his daughters on the hillside and drank in their admiring approval, winked at them from where he stood in the dusty, bloody arena.

Should Win sit with the girls? Or would the girls insist on being apart from their mother so that they could be more available to the possibilities of the final weekend of summer? Either way would have been better than the last of the Winott Point Griswold males playing his last match on the Point by himself. Win could still hope for Barnaby to pull through, couldn't she? His own wife, ex-wife as it was now. He remembered the feel of holding her bony hand, the feel of the skin over her knuckles. Was it wrong to wish for skin you were welcome to touch? It had been Barnaby who held the girls upside down when they were tiny and taught them to laugh. Surely that counted.

The sun was far into the humid afternoon, and it was still Labor Day hot. Barnaby loved that.

He breathed deeply and allowed all the generations of hillside audiences, Richardsons, odd Winotts, Swifts and Goodwins and Bryans, Griswolds of course, and now even the eager Childses and the Kopuses, to meditate one last moment upon the new, gymnasium-earned, chest-of-athlete that swelled valiantly beneath Barnaby's own sopping shirt.

Then he turned and settled into his chair and imagined his dead father standing at the bottom of the country lawn that went down toward the harbor. With his hands behind his back, the ghost of Barnaby's father surveyed his own steaming battlefield, the first Griswold to have lost everything, the archaically principled, senior partner of a distinguished Boston law firm that had lost cachet and lost the good clients and lost the good associates, that had finally lost its very nameplate, to the graceless inattention of a speeding world in which Barnaby for a while had learned to flourish. Was it possible that despite everything, Barnaby was his father's son? They were alike in having both failed to be good stewards of what they'd made. Barnaby's father was horrified at the similarity. Barnaby was horrified.

Because it was not true. Barnaby was making his back, right now.

Into the relentless aftermath of his father's battle, the ghost of Barnaby's mother went with ever-so-careful steps, down the crabgrass, to give his father the disappointing news: Barnaby had won the set. Barnaby now needed only to win the third set to win the Winott Cup. Wouldn't Barnaby's father come back up to the court and encourage his son?

Barnaby didn't stick around for his father's answer. As he sat there in his court chair beside the net post, he chose to watch out the back of his head the pretty girl with the halo of frizzing hair. She had seen him limp, and she had laughed, he thought. Because the limp had worked? He could not truthfully have said he'd registered her features, yet he knew she was pretty in the way one knows those things. There had unquestionably been a grinning, mischievous range of teeth after the tiebreaker, and when a man wins a tiebreaker all smiles are for him as a matter of course. She had long, bare arms with a slight shine of golden hair on them that was paler than the hair on her head. And the hair on her head, reddish hair, kept Barnaby, even in his imagination, from quite seeing into her face.

Was it true that Barnaby had never loved Win? Had he really just thought to trade mortgage payments and tuition payments for occasional dinners at home? Yes, but he had always understood love to be beyond someone like himself. In any case, he had kept his part of the bargain. As time went on, he had even bought all his dinners out.

But that wasn't what he meant right now. Right now things were coming apart, and he needed love. That wasn't it either. Things were changing. And he could change. He could offer love.

Barnaby was forty-six years old, and, God forgive him, he decided he loved the girl behind him. He could not bear the thought of growing old as alone as his parents, and he sat up straight. He prepared himself to turn around and kneel and propose marriage.

Thank Christ that Win and the girls were not actually here to spoil things.

And Dicky Kopus whacked his racket loudly against the red plastic watercooler.

That quickly the pounding of love was turned into alarm.

Kopus leaned down and whispered, "Come on, you crook. We have to play before the cops repossess your fucking racket."

Kopus strode away into his own side of the court, leaving Barnaby with a heart that pounded now beyond alarm to fear.

Despite himself, Barnaby glanced for police.

Then he ran on the court for safety, and Kopus cheated and won three games so fast that Barnaby didn't know what had happened.

Barnaby found new but not-yet-likely corners of endeavor that were being staked out by more or less capable people with ambition. If he could work with those people, talk sympathetically with them, eat and drink with them and reach an understanding about providing an appropriate profile and connections, which he usually could do, then he did that. Barnaby ate and drank with everybody until he and the owners and the accountants and so forth were all very clear about what it was the company did and how and what were the prospects and why. It was a delicate process, and sometimes a long process, which was why one developed strategies for physical survival like the Griswold diet. To take a concept, even one that has begun to function in a primitive way as a business, and to turn that into a posture that displays in an instant all the inherent virtues of marketability and underlying worth, of decoration and substance, that process was not fluff.

It wasn't even fluff, entirely, when you knocked on doors to find a susceptible underwriter.

No, the fluff started to mix when the issue was imminent and when you went to your friends like Tom Livermore who ran the Crenshaw Foundation and you ate and drank with them, though God knew Tom never drank more than one glass of sherry. It was Barnaby who drank, and enjoyed drinking. Barnaby drinking was part of the fun. When they went from saloon to saloon, Tom brought his one sherry along with him. If they sent their cars home, Tom carried his sherry with him in cabs to Christ only knew where. And then, if Barnaby had a product, or the presentable posture of one, then Tom Livermore and maybe a few other thoroughly real sorts of people came on board early, and the word got out. Barnaby himself in fact took the word out as zealously as St. Paul after his left-side stroke at Tarsus. Which was the same stroke Win's mother, Ada, would have. Actually, Ada would have the stroke, a little one, again and again, but Ada's moment was different from Paul's moment, and of course Ada's Oklahoma was different from wherever. Was it left side? Getting the word out, anyhow, was essential labor, and if the Johnny-come-latelies who couldn't afford to buy in early thought of Barnaby as nothing more than a tout, well, tough. When the issue opened, if the temperature in the oven was right, things rose. Egg whites. A meringue. The fluff fluffed. And in that fluff, the good Lord willing, was a dollar for Barnaby.

Marinas were a case in point. Who would have imagined a chain of marinas? Except one day suddenly everyone who spilled a drink on Barnaby had a yacht of some kind and was boring the party with worries about where to berth and where to whatever else. Enter a ne'er-do-well with a résumé of expulsions from respectable schools and respectable families and with money from New Jersey garbage-industry skimming and with connections to sail lofts and engine types and with a dream of a chain of marinas in which to live life. A part of Barnaby was sorry to have sold as soon as he had, but it didn't take much perspective to remember that only so many people, even in the high season of buyouts, were ever going to have yachts, and sooner or later a lot of those folks were going to lose their money or realize what a pain in the ass a yacht was for fifty-one weeks a year.

So, no, it wasn't as if Barnaby were without perspective altogether. There were in fact people, Tom Livermore among them, who turned to Barnaby when the market was hard to read.

Barnaby was a divining rod, and a good one, but he used his gifts at the beginning of things in very small companies.

With a different background, with a different part of the puzzle than the beginnings upon which he was accustomed to work every day, he might have understood the significance of Peterpotter and TJ sooner. As it was, he had only the voice of indeterminate instinct, which told him to stay close to those happy Oklahoma boys even though he knew rather quickly that there was nothing for him in their start-up oil outfit. He was happy for them with their wad of money and their enthusiasm, but the world was already awash in speculative drillers. He could, with effort, imagine them doing something besides losing it all, but unless he was an out-and-out burglar, and he was not, there was no obvious part of that eighty million from Chase with Barnaby's name on it.

Which made the plane ride only more difficult.

After their marvelous parade, and then after loading the stand, which was not easy but not without amusement, and then after the ride the rest of the way to Newark Airport, which was frankly a matter of endurance—after all that, a plane ride with Peterpotter and TJ could have seemed superfluous.

Did he really have to get on the plane?

It was not as if Barnaby wasn't a man who was good for the long haul. That much he had inherited from his father: stick it out. But to have endured the sobering discomfort of the open-air commute to Newark Airport without knowing the reason why, and then, then to board a plane and head out into the actual desert with no vision whatever of a deal, that had more to do with theology than Barnaby liked.

He boarded, nonetheless.

And the cigars, the cigarettes, the merchant's apron while holding for takeoff, were entertaining.

There were seats that swiveled and enough room to swivel them even with the newsstand underfoot.

There was, comfortingly, a pilot on the other side of a door to the cockpit. And, just as comfortingly, Peterpotter and TJ showed no interest in opening that door.

There was some contagious exuberance on actual liftoff.

Fair enough.

Once they were airborne, however, it did seem to Barnaby that there should be a quiet time in which you laid your head back and closed your eyes. A nap was what honored the headache following a parade, not to mention the aches attendant on wrestling pieces of a newsstand and smoke shop into an airplane without the help of teamsters (because no one should ever have to be told not to pay Frenchmen before a job is done).

"What's the matter, Barnaby? You don't like girls?"

The moment they were airborne and stabilized, Peterpotter had gotten out all of the newsstand's dirty magazines. Peterpotter had regained the self-assertion that for a while the truck and the traffic and the size of New York had drained from him. As though it were a sovereign ship, stepping aboard the plane put Peterpotter, and TJ with him, back onto Oklahoma soil. Well, Barnaby liked everyone to feel at home, and Barnaby himself had always felt a perverse affection for Oklahoma, but did Peterpotter and TJ know how long a flight it was to Oklahoma City in a small plane with two fueling stops?

"Hell, we've got enough booze on board to get us to China and back," was the answer, and it occurred to Barnaby that planes rather than trucks might have been the venue for these boys' adolescence.

So be it.

You pulled up your socks and you plunged into the dirty magazines like a twelve-year-old schoolboy among other twelve-year-olds on the train home from boarding school for Christmas. You went page by glossy page identifying anatomy. It was the closest any of them would ever get to medical school, and the thrill was there if you shouted and pretended.

"Look at that!"

With more cheap cigars for atmosphere.

After the unsettled first landing for fuel however and during the bilious takeoff that followed that landing, Barnaby was momentarily taken aback by Peterpotter squashing a sugar-powdered little roll of devil's food cake and whipped cream into the back of one of Barnaby's hands. Barnaby was a devout, eye-shut gripper of armrests in small plane takeoffs, but he opened his eyes for the devil's food.

TJ, already wearing his own badge of devil's food, giggled, and Peterpotter blurted in a cracking voice of pimpled anticipation, "Didn't your fraternity have any food fights, Griswold?"

What a question for someone to whom Manhattan had long been a battleground of meals.

What's more, despite being tired, Barnaby was still powerfully committed to these boys.

But no. A literal food fight was not for Barnaby. He smiled, granting permission, approval even, of Peterpotter and TJ. But he did not reach for the pile of cellophane-wrapped snacks himself. He unfastened his seat belt, but he stayed in his seat and nodded encouragement at the joyous Sooner squeals as Peterpotter and TJ went beyond their first formal mashings to full-flung war upon each other with frosting-filled cupcakes and little pielettes and fruit-filled turnovers. Peterpotter and TJ naturally applied these things to Barnaby every bit as much as they did to one another, and Barnaby was a very good sport; he resisted the urge to shield himself with centerfolds. But no, he was not persuaded to participate, and if anybody thought he was shirking, so be it. Barnaby had spent too much of his life on airplanes mustering other illusions. He also believed that the nature of airplanes, the suspension of life so far above ground, deserved an inviolable measure of respect. Frankly, he worried that a food fight could take air out from under the wings of a small plane.

Meanwhile, cherry became the favored weapon for both Peterpotter and TJ because of its livid stain when applied to broadcloth or thinning hair. Peterpotter ate the cherry where it adhered to him, and ate the chocolate as well. TJ ate the beef and sausage jerky for some reason. Barnaby, in yet another testament to the Griswold diet, was not hungry. Instead, as things finally wound down, Barnaby felt like either throwing up or else opening a window to clear the cigar smoke, but the night outside the windows had gotten black and empty enough to make anyone glad the windows didn't open. When Peterpotter vomited chocolate goo and cherry stain into the litter of magazines, Barnaby decided to keep his own nausea to himself.

Earlier, there had been talk that at the second set-down for fuel (in Memphis?) everyone might want to head out and hee-yah the late clubs. Or was one of the women in the magazines from Memphis? In any case, after the vomit, there was no more talk of hee-yah.

The approach of the second landing became instead an occasion for seat belts again and for nervous sweat. The vapors from so much smear of chemicaled dessert (not to mention the throw-up) fostered a mortal sureness that the plane would crash. The black of American night out the windows seemed suddenly to Barnaby not just a premonition that he had come too far beyond his own pale; it seemed actually a mouth already swallowing him.

Nor was Barnaby alone in mortality.

"Oh, please Lord, don't let me die," Peterpotter cried as the plane shuddered down in tight banking circles designed to bring three people alone in all the world right then through the clammy, breathless anteroom of death. Down they went, hurtling to the hard earth and the flames none of them would feel except as they felt it all now.

"Don't let me burn," Peterpotter cried.

With the rational membranes that remained under his control, Barnaby wondered if there was any nitroglycerin on board for TJ who, in ominous silence, sweated through his shirt so prodigiously that his suspenders curled from the soaking.

"Take Griswold," Peterpotter cried, pointing. "He's the one from New York. He's the one too good for a food fight. Take fucking Griswold."

Barnaby did not glance again over at the pretty girl with the halo of copper hair. Jesus, he was forty-six and she was probably a kid. He did glance over, and he couldn't tell if she was a kid or not. Well, past her teens anyway, for God sake.

Barnaby gave her a glance full of "No more fooling around," and then found himself wondering with which clan she was affiliated because he had never seen her before. Though he knew as well as anyone that girls could grow into whole other butterflies overnight. Yesterday she might have been twelve.

With love in his heart, Barnaby turned to Kopus who had already spent a full allowance of cheating.

Barnaby bent his knees, and he won his serve, and he broke back, and he won his serve again.

Bam. Just like that. Three games apiece. All even.

Barnaby had always (to put it kindly) been growing into his size, so he had never made any of the varsity teams at boarding school, but he had played for intramural teams, and his father had visited school more than once to watch as Barnaby whiffed on a big clearing kick from beside the goal at his own end of the soccer field. His father had given up weekends to watch Barnaby catch a blade and fall down on the ice while a five-foot, 120-pound wing skated past him alone across the blue line with the game to be decided. Always Barnaby's father had stood (as Barnaby imagined he stood now, amidst all the other seated fans on the slope), with the rigorous spine of a man who has seen his son play and is prepared nonetheless to acknowledge a connection to the boy.

Now, however, Barnaby had trained and was fit and his strokes were grooved. Now Barnaby was an athlete on the varsity, and he was going to win the championship; he was going to win back the good Griswold name.

And as Kopus gathered balls on the other side of the net, Barnaby looked again to the copper hair that sun and damp heat had frizzed into a divine announcement of what Barnaby hoped would be his long-term future in matters to do with affection, matters where he had always been so naked. He didn't want to be naked anymore. Please, he didn't want to be lonely.

And yes, there she was.

But she was not looking back at Barnaby. She was turning and getting up, and she had long beautiful legs and a perfect ass in her short pants, and she was going away.

She was leaving.

Didn't she know that everything had changed and that his tide was coming back in besides?

Was there time to yell after her before Kopus served? What would he yell?

My name is Barnaby Griswold. Should he yell that as loud as he could?

His father (who never owned a German car but did serve in the war) had told Barnaby during the summer he was thirteen that Barnaby should announce his name clearly and then most people would understand how he wanted to be known. Those who didn't understand, he would have to fight if he wanted to live the rest of his life with any self-respect. Who knew what a life of self-respect was supposed to mean, but the boarding-school boys had in fact called him Barnababy, Barnababy every day of the previous school year, of first form year. And on the first day of second form year he walked toward all the same boys and saw that the worst and stupidest of them was about to call out the name again. So Barnaby made his hands into fists and held them out from his sides and walked hard, with his necktie over his shoulder and his sport jacket flapping, directly at that stupidest boy, ready to fight, but calling loudly beforehand, "My name is Barnaby!"

Except the boy was even stupider than anyone knew and called back, "Baby Farm, Baby Farm."

Baby Farm?

Everybody laughed, and Barnaby was so startled himself that he tripped over his own feet, and as he fell down he caught one of his fists in a side pocket of his jacket so that it took a long time for him to hit the ground, and when he did hit ground he couldn't help rolling around on his back. Everybody laughed so hard at that that it was agreeable. They weren't laughing from hatred. They were laughing because Barnaby was funny, and so he rolled on his back some more until he could hear them not laughing as much, and then he stood up and said to the stupid boy, "It's supposed to be Barnababy, you asshole."

That was funny too.

When he turned to all the other boys, they were going away. They knew who he was, and he had made them laugh, and now they were leaving. They were going on to lunch, which was only fair, and so he hurried after them with, strangely enough, his real name established and Barnababy forgotten.

And that day and for the rest of his life he had always eventually caught up with those other boys. They had always had somewhere they had to go, often somewhere for lunch, and they had waited there for Barnaby.

He just had never caught up with the girls.

No matter how he had tried, he had never ended up wherever it was the girls had to go.

Girls left Barnaby's vicinity, and no matter how he wanted to follow, they never waited.

They couldn't wait even now when Barnaby had changed into someone so overflowing.

Just like a hundred girls a summer when he was a kid, and long past a kid, this girl was going away with the rest of his life, and today, on the last day of his last summer, it seemed like she was the very last girl.

Win's mother, Ada, was hardly a girl, but Barnaby felt he had enjoyed her in the past, and as luck would have it, the plane did not crash. So when Barnaby got to his hotel in Oklahoma City, he called Ada.

And she was amused. She said, "I've been expecting you." She assumed Barnaby had arrived to join the children of friends in stealing other people's money, which of course Barnaby hoped would turn out to be the case.

Frankly, he hoped Ada could tell him just how the children of her friends were doing it and where Peterpotter and TJ fit in. He especially hoped she could tell him where he himself might fit in.

Truly, he'd always regretted not spending more time in Oklahoma with Win's parents.

Though it was also true that he'd been too busy to visit during the occasion of Dr. Briley's final illness some years before.

The fact was, alas, that Barnaby lived his life in his deals, so who could be surprised if there had not always been time for him to come along on the very few visits Win made back to the home ground she despised?

Nonetheless, he described to Ada the progress of luncheon and plane ride in some detail, and when he was done, Ada said icily, "I don't believe one word of it."

And then she laughed.

Did Ada have a taste for outrage that Barnaby had never bothered to suspect? When Barnaby told her it was all the truth, she laughed again in a rich and throaty laugh unlike anything he'd ever imagined from her. Was she also a flirt?

Well, what satisfaction to discover other worlds in a mother-in-law, and he told Ada that.

Ada stopped her laugh and said, "I've always loved a fool."

She said it in a voice of bored, judgmental intelligence, a voice that drove Win crazy and that was just like Win's except that under Ada's tone was the possibility of humor and the hope of pleasure.

"No kidding?" Barnaby said, ever hopeful himself.

"Before I married, the love of my life was a fool."

The delivery was still bored and judgmental, but the words themselves were revelation. They were what Barnaby had often imagined as, despite so many discouragements, the way women ought to speak of people like himself.

"So you always knew that I was a fool?"

"I certainly did."

"And not just from my looks?"

"Oh, Barnaby. There's more to a fool than just looks. Charles, the fool of my youth, looked like a senator."

If he had been in the room with her instead of on the phone, Barnaby could have seen that she was teasing, but on the phone her delivery was almost perfectly without inflection.

"When did you know about me?" he asked.

"The moment you opened your mouth."

Barnaby might have been waiting his whole life for women to tease him. He had been waiting his whole life. "Why did you never tell me?"

And now her voice became all dreary disappointment and southern diction. "You so rarely came calling. Women of my generation need to be called upon."

He laughed more, and his laughter got Ada to laugh again, and from all of that pleasure came a felicitous sense that life was on course in Oklahoma.

What did not come, unfortunately, was any clue as to why he, Barnaby Griswold, was in Oklahoma. Ada vaguely knew the names of Peterpotter's and TJ's car dealerships, and had met at one time or another TJ's parents when they were still alive, but for her, as in fact for Barnaby, much of the interest in Barnaby's adventure was the very nature of Peterpotter and TJ as car dealers. Not everyone knew car dealers, and who could imagine car dealers with eighty million dollars, and who could imagine them, once they had it, doing anything other than throwing food?

So there was some disappointment that Ada could not tell Barnaby what sort of a deal he'd hooked into. On the other hand, she could tell him precisely where in Driscoll Hills to get his trousers rewoven quickly and well.

The real disappointment, as always, was calling home.

Because Barnaby understood himself as a generous man. He had to. Witness all the energy he gave to his professional life, all the abundance of affectionate attention (and you can't fake that the way you can fake figures) he gave to successions of clients and near clients and possible associates of clients, all the beating his body accepted in these duties. Really, he had given the physical vigor of his youth to entertaining the Peterpotters and TJs of this world. The plain fact was that Barnaby was too generous for his own good, as his cardiologist had been telling him for some time, and yet when he called home, Win translated his every breath into a litany of selfishness.

As soon as she answered the phone, Win was angry to the point of ultimatums. Barnaby told her, "But I just had a long and marvelous conversation with Ada," and Win was angrier still. What sensible woman could be angry that her husband and his mother-in-law liked one another? What wife wouldn't be delighted that her husband had tried to pump his mother-in-law for business insights and then stayed on the line to chat? Unless that wife couldn't get along with her mother any better than she got along with her husband. No, Barnaby apologized profusely to Win on all counts, but it was very clear that he was not the bad guy in this story.

Nor had he been missing for thirty hours. "Thirty? Come on. A busy man's failure to appear at the Nightingale-Bamford School dance recital does not start wheels turning at the Missing Persons Bureau."

When he called his secretary, she said she hadn't noticed any unusual absence on his part at all.

What was more, his secretary as a matter of course had found his raincoat. Which was the sort of thing that confirmed it all for Barnaby. A good carpenter lived in his carpentry. A good scientist, one supposed, lived in his science. A good fluffmeister lived in his fluff, and it took only something as simple as a raincoat turning up unexpectedly to remind Barnaby what a right place that was to live. In fact, with news of the raincoat, Barnaby recovered his conviction that he was profoundly at work. Even as he bid the East Coast good night, he recovered altogether his conviction that somewhere in the jubilantly tasteless vicinity of Oklahoma City, there was a substantial deal just for him.

"Griswold," Kopus called from the other side of the net.

Barnaby turned, and Kopus quick-served him, and Barnaby was so completely caught off guard that he was pure reflex and slammed a backhand up the line for a winner.

But after that backhand, Barnaby realized with terrifying immediacy that he really might win this championship and now was the time. Which was different from training years for the competition, different from dreaming of victory, different from being afraid of losing. Much different. Hard to breathe different.

And Kopus, despite his better balance sheet, must have felt some of the same thing.

Because abruptly now both of them began playing afraid to miss and afraid to hit out. They, both of them, played complete puff ball.

Christ. Grown men patting balls back and forth. And yet when Barnaby tried to pound an approach shot and come into net, he was so stiff that he hit the rope netting behind Kopus on the fly, and he could see Kopus decide right then not to try another hard shot himself for the rest of the day. The points went on and on. Other people left from the hillside, a few, the hostesses Barnaby figured, though he only sensed the departures. He kept his attention so riveted on the court that he could not straighten his arms entirely. The sun was lower, but it was still hot, and Barnaby let the sweat run into his eyes. They pushed balls back and forth to one another like old ladies, and Barnaby would have been glad his pretty girl was gone if he had let himself think about her. His knees were bent, and he could not straighten them. He walked like Groucho Marx, and the world was a tiny, brittle, near-motionless event inside the lines of this court.

And then somehow, as if the tennis balls rather than the players finally arranged things, Barnaby was one point away from breaking Kopus's serve. One point from getting to serve for the match himself.

Barnaby's shirt and shorts were soaked, and yet he was cold. He had goose bumps up his arms and legs. He tried to wipe his eyes clear of salt sting and could not loosen his neck and shoulder enough to get his sleeve up to his face.

He got into position to receive Kopus's serve, and out of the corner of one eye he saw, darkened by the shade of the smaller of the great red-leafed copper beeches—that was the name of the tree—he saw, in the shade at this end of the court, right outside the rope netting beside where he stood, the silent, attentive halo of his beautiful girl's copper hair.

He'd thought she'd left like every other girl he'd ever imagined.

But she hadn't. He could not look more than the instant of recognition, but she was here. Things had changed after all. Barnaby had changed, and because of that, someone had decided to stay with him.

Kopus served.

Barnaby bent his knees for real, and took Kopus's patted serve on the rise and stroked through it. He hit a bullet return and was amazed at himself. What a shot. He was one game from the match. He was going to win the championship. He turned toward the beautiful girl.

And on pure reflex, Kopus slammed Barnaby's return back.

And as soon as Kopus connected, Barnaby knew he could not hit the ball again himself. He had lost his connection to the point, even if he could reach the ball. But he also knew that the ball would land near the line on the far side above the shaded lane and the pitch down into the swamp, the side away from everybody sitting on the honest hillside that sloped down from the Richardson porch.

Which meant what?

Cheating.

Kopus's ball was hit hard, and yet there was time to swivel and take a long leaping step and a half. There was time to reach back with his racket as if he actually meant to swing at the ball. There was time to bend forward and study where the ball would land, time to study that his leg and foot precisely blocked his father's line of sight, time to realize with a giggly elation that virtually everyone else was blocked too.

There was time suddenly, fearfully, very consciously, to wait.

Do not call the ball out before it lands.

Here it came, for one instant a perfectly still yellow sphere with every hair of fuzz distinguishable, a today's world of tennis ball that still smelled of its rubber before contact with the faded, gray-white, two-inch line of weather-worn paint, which separated one swath of powdered green asphalt from another, which separated the singles court from the doubles alley, which separated one man from championship and another from dismay, which separated Barnaby from all he wanted now and forever.

He had decided to cheat before he was born.

Was he sorry for Kopus? Yes, because Kopus would never expect this of Barnaby. Kopus knew Barnaby as someone of the old school for whom the tennis court was a repository of principles. Which was how Barnaby knew himself. It was one of Kopus's advantages; Kopus cheated at tennis and Barnaby did not. Except that now much more than tennis was at stake. Everything was at stake.

The next instant, the tennis ball was a blur not dropping down but racing across, skidding so fast that Barnaby, who stared with fixity at where it should land, could not even be sure it was in. It had to be in for him to cheat. Christ, maybe it was out. But this was no time to wonder.

"Out," he shouted.

If you're going to cheat, shout; everyone understands that. He stood over the spot, staring at where it would have had to land to be out, and maybe it had landed there.

He had meant to cheat, had planned to cheat, wanted to cheat and didn't care. He was a cheater, whether he wanted to think of himself that way or not.

He looked out through the old rope fencing that he loved for its persuasion of a gracious past that was gone, and there was the only girl who had ever not left Barnaby. She was half hidden in the dappling of shade, but she was there, with her glorious hair and her long limbs as neat as a real athlete, with her hands on her hips and one hip cocked to the side, with her face still not visible except for the shine of her eyes.

From the hillside behind, there was applause for a good, fair point.

From across the net came no noises of contention.

But his lovely girl looked right at Barnaby and knew him for what he was.

At the Sooner First City Bank, Peterpotter and TJ had mortgaged all their car lots to the limit in a boom-drunk Oklahoma City and then spent everything on a handful of mineral rights that were at the speculative height of boom prices. They took the mineral rights to New York along with geologists' reports, and hit pay dirt at Chase Manhattan.

Folks who didn't have a half-dozen car lots to leverage, or who preferred not to bother, also went to Sooner First City, which until a few years before had run a quiet, single-branch retail trade just outside Driscoll Hills between an old cafeteria and a vast, newish parking lot from a mall that had yet to fully expand. The cafeteria was where a certain brand of elderly and prosperous ladies, once their junior-league duties were well in the past, had for a few generations, mother following daughter, gone to lunch.

The cafeteria had a real name, but the men around Sooner First City had been calling it the Old Ladies since Sooner First City had been bought by a squad of new-breed bankers who were frustrated by the glacial ways of downtown institutions and were determined to keep as much of the oil boom money as possible inside the state. Some of the bank's most active trade came from children of the cafeteria's elderly well-to-do; in fact a good deal of that trade was leveraged off those rich old ladies' money. The new bankers themselves never ate lunch at the cafeteria, or the Old Ladies as they called it, but in apparently no time at all the new incarnation of Sooner First City had become known as the Old Ladies Bank.

To be pointed out in the right circles (actually, almost any circles in those days) as an executive of the Old Ladies Bank came to be a very fine thing. The Mercedes sedans that the bank kept strung out in the parking lot to a width greater than the building itself all had license plates that read a staid SFC for Sooner First City, but the private Porsches had plates like OLB RAH and OLB GO and OLB $.

Barnaby, needless to say, was delighted when Peterpotter and TJ introduced him to the bank. He was not entirely at home with some of the trappings, the occasional boots and the string ties, but he was so thoroughly at home with the spirit of the place that when he walked in there, he felt like his own world had won. Because as small as the actual building was, this was a real bank in the busy heart of a very real, very substantial industry. It was enough to make him feel sorry for his father.

There was so much business that officers took turns writing loans out of the custodian's closet off the one stairwell, flushing out millions of dollars of high-interest paper while squatting beside the mop bucket and scribbling on their knees. The loans by now were not even just to dental corporations going into the oil business; there were guitar players starting thoroughbred horse farms, and there were movie syndicates by the dozen, and never never never any review of business plans. It was like one of those hilariously forgiving, third-rate boarding schools for stupid and misbehaving rich children, a school entirely of undeserved A+s, the sort of school Barnaby was always surprised to have missed. If you went upstairs at the Old Ladies Bank you could hear the laughter echoing from downstairs, and if you were downstairs you could hear the laughter shouting out above. The only place a discouraging word might ever be heard was on the stairway if someone thought you were cutting into the express line for the custodian's closet. But the line moved fast. And at the end of every happy day, the day's loans were all bundled and repriced for profit and shipped upstream to Continental Illinois and to a couple of regional Michigan banks where the bundles were, as far as Barnaby could tell, received and paid for with delirious appreciation.

In a reflective moment, it occurred to Barnaby to go take a look at those upstream banks and see if that was where his angle lay, but, no, he knew he was at the source of things right where he stood. He could have gotten a considerable loan himself on the basis of his laundered clothes and the testimony by Peterpotter and TJ as to his prowess in a food fight, but the interest rate was not cheap, and he did not have a feel for the future of llama ranching, and most of all he always did prefer to use other people's credit. Still, when on his fourth evening in town he went to the Old Ladies Bank mid-quarterly celebration, and the president, the young guru of Oklahoma's go-go bankers, made an entrance naked but for a baseball hat with wings that flapped, then for just a moment Barnaby thought llama ranching might be the thing. Since it was after hours, he joined in the exuberance of the party, and the moment of weakness passed, and he watched the quiet exit of two Morgan Bankers he recognized from New York. No surprise that those assholes couldn't get into the feel of things. He watched a woman from Chase Manhattan, who must have chased directly after TJ and Peterpotter, try to prove she could play in the mud with anybody if there was a chance of stealing a little action from the Michigan regionals. He watched a Seattle banker who had come with his own winged hat and was already taking off clothes well beyond his necktie.

The next day, out of a need to feel he was doing research, he insisted Ada come to the Old Ladies cafeteria with him for lunch.

Ada loathed the Old Ladies and told him so in no uncertain terms and then said she would come with him anyway because it was a mother-in-law's duty.

"Have the foie gras," she said with a gleeful sneer as they pushed their trays past ranks of pot pies and biscuits.

But Barnaby liked pot pies.

More, he liked meatloaf. He liked tapioca and elderly women and rigorous mysteries of decorum. He liked the faint smells of fossilized wax and of somebody else's hard work. It was all enough to make him feel cared for and safely again within one of the institutions that had guarded the perimeters of his youth. Yes, instead of a lawn there were Cadillacs pulled up to the long, tinted picture window, and beyond the Cadillacs was all the two-story, plastic and stucco offal of a commercial thoroughfare, but this was Oklahoma after all, and the prices in the cafeteria, to say the least, were terrific.

Had he been a young Oklahoma entrepreneur, Barnaby could have found reasons to eat his every meal at the Old Ladies.

Had he been a common thief of a different variety than his own training made possible, he might have known how to quickly remove all the rings that weighted so many of the fingers in the place, and then he could have retired. Because there were jeweled clusters four and five to every customer's hand in the place except for his own large, modest hands, and except for Ada's almost equally large, equally modest hands.

Prompted to consider Ada's hands in this fashion, as she carried her tray away from the register, Barnaby recognized that Ada was in fact admirably large all over, substantial rather than fat, with a considerable bosom swelling her torso out between the regions of her chest and her stomach, there under the front of her white silk blouse and her timeless suit jacket. And today, on a questionable errand of business in alien territory, much as Barnaby found himself comforted by the cafeteria, so too he was comforted by the discovery that—what with his own high-riding stomach and her low-riding bosom—Ada's shape could be akin to his own buoyant shape.

Next to his sometimes erratic posture, her good posture was less akin. Her posture and the severe elegance of her cheekbones and even the nakedness of her hands (which had a sterner meaning than his own ringless hands) mitigated against comfort in a way that his father's presence might also have mitigated, but still

Ada's shape was like an old friend. Certainly Barnaby was more comfortable with Ada than he would have been with the other matrons, whose swollen and very particularly colored heads of hair were flora incognita for Barnaby.

"I may forgive you for bringing me to lunch here," Ada said when they'd sat, "but it won't be anytime soon."

She said it, and her spine was rigid, and her mouth was turned down in displeasure, but her delivery was more readable in person than over the phone. The shape of her body, a shape Barnaby knew, was poised for adventure despite the accomplished charade of sufferance. She was in fact pleased enough with the displeasure around her mouth to show it to Barnaby a second time. She was a grown woman, a woman old enough to be his mother, a woman with real dignity, and she was not about to become giggly at the good fortune of lunch in a cafeteria, but Barnaby had an eye trained for detecting inclinations to fun in real cynics. Barnaby knew Ada was glad to be out with him, and that made Barnaby feel as gallant and expansive as if it were a date.

He grinned at her with his expansive gallantry and with an understanding that he was the only man in the place, and she said, "Never try to charm in a cafeteria," and turned haughtily away. She smiled despite herself when he laughed, but her smile went at some coyly distant prospect which only she could have identified.

"I thought this was the place to be," he said, removing his plates and tools from his tray as Ada had done and admiring the gravy in his mashed potatoes.

"The best place to have lunch would have been my kitchen table," she said, still looking away, but now clearly looking in order to see who among her acquaintances and enemies in the room had noticed that she was at lunch with an attentive younger man.

Her kitchen table might or might not have been what Ada would actually have chosen, but it was absolutely what Barnaby's father would have chosen, and Barnaby wondered if Ada and his father were not a good, if ever unrealized, match.

And abruptly now Ada brought her attention back to her plate and dug eagerly into her shepherd's pie, a dish she had chosen, as she'd made clear in the line, for its lesser degree of repugnance than other possibilities.

She chewed and swallowed and turned to glare at Barnaby, and said, "Terrible," and dug in for another mouthful.

Leaving alone the wax beans in one quadrant of his own plate, Barnaby tried his meatloaf, mashed potatoes, and gravy all in one bite, and found them to be exquisite. He wondered if Michel might consider a meatloaf special on, say, Thursdays.

He wondered, marveled, at the hands at the other tables.

"The meatloaf," he said, "is very good, and the hands in this place are astonishing."

Really. Around the room, every hand's glittering elderly fingers were so separated by stones and bands that they looked like skeletal demonstrations in the Museum of Natural History. To swim with those fingers would have been like paddling with a fork.

But no one in the room looked like a swimmer, and more power to them for that. Rather than swimmers, they were talkers, and from every side of Ada and himself came repeated echoes of the name *Old Ladies Bank*. What with those ripe echoes and all the jewels and Barnaby's own chemistry, there was a powdered, brown-gravied reek of greed in the air, a scent distinct from but very much related to what you could smell in La Cote on many afternoons. Barnaby knew that Michel would not be keen on the connection, but Barnaby was; it had become central to his faith in humanity that wherever he went he found the world to be of a piece.

"Ada," he said. "Do you have any money in the Old Ladies Bank?"

And as soon as he said that, he was aware of radar at near tables coming alert to a mention of the namesake institution.

"Certainly not," Ada said. "And I don't plan to." Then she laid down her fork and beamed at Barnaby. "Are you going to ask me to put my money in there? Oh, I'm so glad. I'm the only person I know who hasn't been asked."

Barnaby held up his hands and shook his head and said, "No, no," aware as he did so of the radar at the near tables now withdrawing interest.

Ada sighed largely, mostly in pretense, and said, "Just as well. I couldn't have done it anyhow."

And the near radars went off entirely.

But Barnaby's radar, irrational as always, turned on.

He knew that Ada's father had been a respected banker in the state, and he knew that Ada had some common sense. He knew that she didn't have any go-go children in town managing her money. She had a liberal trust the doctor had established at one of the responsible banks downtown. There was no reason she would have put anything in the Old Ladies Bank, or borrowed there, or anything else there.

Yet Barnaby asked Ada quietly, beneath the cover of alien radar, "Why couldn't you have put your money in the Old Ladies Bank?"

And Ada answered him quietly, earnestly, without irony.

Win would later suggest that here was the first of Ada's strokes, but it didn't seem so at the time.

Ada said, "In early days when we lived out in Wesley and Dad was the good banker in town, several men he knew came to him and asked him to join with them in an oil venture. They had good geology reports and they were good men. Dad knew them all and liked them. He said at the time that if he were ever going to speculate, this would be it. But it was a speculation. He would have had to put up some money of his own, and perhaps even bank money if things went bad. His name as a banker would have been a kind of guarantee on a speculation, and that wasn't how he thought a banker's name ought to be understood. And so he didn't do it. He believed they would hit oil, but he didn't do it.

He had a young family, and he believed in responsible behavior. He turned those men down, and they got somebody else to go in with them."

"And?" Barnaby said.

"And so I would never be involved with a bank everybody talked about. Nobody talked about Dad's banks. Dad wasn't a go-goer. People trusted him. I wouldn't for a minute trust anything with a nickname like Old Ladies Bank."

"No," Barnaby said. "But what happened? Did they hit oil?"

"Oh, it was a big strike. It became a well-known field. Plenty of the rings in here came from that field. But that never bothered Dad a bit. And now all these women's children and grandchildren are depositing and borrowing and everything elsing with that go-go bank as fast as they can. And making money hand over fist, so they say. Well, I don't care. Dad wouldn't have had anything to do with it, and neither will I."

And with that it all came clear.

Yes.

Barnaby's father would have approved of Ada's sentiments and of her story. Barnaby's father would have approved of Ada's father. Personal responsibility, professional integrity, discipline, good sense, right behavior. That was where Barnaby's father lived.

And now his father's actual voice rang out.

His father's voice entered the Old Ladies cafeteria and said firmly to Barnaby, "Sell short."

What?

Was that something he would ever hear from his father? Barnaby's father had never sold short in his life, would have understood shorting as speculation in misfortune, a moral wrong: promising to deliver, at a given price on a given date, a stock or commodity you didn't have and then hoping to buy it more cheaply than the given price before the delivery date came around. It was a sensible enough way to gamble for pessimistic souls, for people who recognized down markets and wanted to take advantage. But that wasn't Barnaby. Barnaby's whole nature, and the business he'd built upon that nature, went to the other possibilities, to the gay balloons of heliumed inflation, to a market going up.

Which was why he had been looking at the obvious and not seeing the obvious strategy.

Which was why Ada's story, and his father's approval of the story's conduct, came through like advice from on high.

And the timbre of the voice in which that advice was delivered was absolutely his father's.

"Sell short."

Sell short.

"Put your money on catastrophe. The world will not long tolerate an Old Ladies Bank."

Yes, that was his father, biblical in moments of urgency. So struck was Barnaby that he said aloud, "Yes, Daddy. Thank you."

When he looked back and remembered, maybe Win was right. Maybe that was the day someone might absolutely have known Ada had begun to have her strokes. Because she simply nodded as Barnaby talked aloud to an absent father between bites of tapioca. Before that, she had told her story of fortune missed in early-day Wesley without any ironic remorse. And Win subsequently let him know that the story of the oil field was an old chestnut always told with irony and remorse. But that was Win. And all of it was only in recollection anyway.

In the actual moment there arose the occupation of so much else.

Even if the price of oil held where it was, there would be a shake-out around the Old Ladies Bank, and it wouldn't be a small shake-out. Even if the price of oil went above the current astronomical levels, the Michigan banks would feel any failure of the Old Ladies Bank. Continental Illinois would feel it, judging from what Barnaby had seen in just four days.

But the price of oil might not hold.

It would not hold.

And here the helium flooded into Barnaby's lungs and from there into the world, so that the world floated free of every dismay and out to the blue sky above a summer ocean.

The price of oil was going to collapse.

Inspiration, revelation, genius, grace of God. Triggered by advice from his father. Here it was.

Barnaby pressed the fish-eyed pebbles of the Old Ladies gluey tapioca between his tongue and the roof of his mouth and knew.

The price of oil.

No, Barnaby had not just remembered seeing hard data no one else had seen. No, he did not know the Saudi oil Prince what's-his-name. Though Tom Livermore knew him, and what good had it yet done Livermore? Well, that was off the point. The point was that Barnaby simply knew, knew with every fiber of his own being, knew cosmically, knew beyond all data and insider tip-off. Barnaby knew oil was going down in the way only he could most certainly know, in the way which answered and sprang from his own essence. Foolishness. The Morgan Bankers left when the go-go guru appeared in only a baseball hat with wings because the Morgan Bankers were prigs who got frightened by naked people. Well, Barnaby had no quarrel with naked people, but now he saw the other truth. Those wings on that hat, even if the go-go guru could make them flap, were not enough to keep anyone suspended aloft. The foolishness in and around the Old Ladies Bank had transcended itself; that was what sweet Peterpotter and TJ had been trying to tell him from the start, and when foolishness transcended itself, it had to fall back to earth just like anything else, and it had to fall on its own foolish terms. That was the key. Where did the greatest, most foolish splatter of the Old Ladies Bank foolishness lie?

It lay in the collapse of oil prices.

Oh, Humpty-Dumpty from the Chrysler Building, and Barnaby was the first to know.

Unless it was happening even as he sucked his last lovely spoon of tapioca beside the first of Ada's strokes.

"The honor of the Harolds," Ada said, invoking her maiden name and her own father's righteousness in a voice too loud and too genuinely censorious to belong to someone with Ada's humor.

But Barnaby could not pay attention to Ada, because the price of oil was going to fall, and Barnaby had to take his short positions before it did fall.

He could not pay attention to any scruples about leveraging his own credit now either. This was the big one and he wanted as much of it as he could get.

He could not even pay attention to Peterpotter and TJ when after lunch they gave him a thousand-dollar cowboy hat and announced that he had won, retroactively no less, a senior executive position in their company as liaison to local oil banks and Wall Street. Could this ever look like insider trading? No, of course not. He put on the hat and laughed at the absence of salary and smiled for a picture with the go-go guru president of the Old Ladies Bank. Was he offered a position at the bank as well? Who knew? All the while in his head he was doing nothing but lining up his ducks.

Three o'clock, on the dot, he gave the hat to a cashier, threw someone's take-out burrito up the stairs to the line for the custodian's closet, and went full speed back to the Waterford to begin his calls.

Barnaby had to change sides and keep playing. He had to serve out the match.

And he did.

He shut away everything else and had no awareness even of sitting in his chair on the changeover.

He threw up the toss for his serve and hit it hard, and Kopus whacked it back into the net. He threw up another and slammed it, mindless, and Kopus slammed it back into the net again. He was going to win. He slammed another, and Kopus slammed it back, over the net, and Barnaby watched it land a foot long.

Triple match point, and he slammed in another. Cheating made you better even when the cheating was past. He'd never served like this in his life.

The fourth serve, Kopus patted at and got back, a floater, and Barnaby froze, swung, almost fell over, and missed entirely. Forty-five. Kopus patted another back, and Barnaby froze again, swung crazy and lined it off the end of his racket on a backhand into the crowd on the hillside. He thought they oohed at that, but he could not hear them. Forty-thirty.

One match point left and he slammed another serve in, and ran in at the net behind it. He ran as hard as he could, and he could hear his breathing like a dragon inside his ears, and Kopus puffed another one over, and Barnaby was there, and there was no time to freeze. He slammed at the thing like a murderer, and he hit it square and hard and drove it straight down into Kopus's court and the God damned thing bounced right on up and out of the court, over the rope fence behind Kopus. He saw the yellow fuzz of it disappear and wondered for an instant if he'd hit a bad shot. But his shot was good. It had hit in Kopus's court and Kopus was already coming to the net to congratulate, and Barnaby had won.

Won.

Barnaby turned and looked at all the chimneys above all the roofs that piled up into the sky above ancient Richardson. Barnaby had won the final point, and a current of every energy coursed through him. God damn son of a bitch, he had won, and as if he were angry, he knew that he would drink from the Winott Point Championship Cup and no one could stop him. His name would go on the cup, and it would be there forever, and fuck them all because he really had quit the booze and he really had gone to the gym like a stalactite martyr and he had said he would win it and he did win it. Let his father suck his teeth and look at that line of his son's name proved in thumbable silver. Except he was not angry. He was blessed and he was grateful, more blessing and gratitude than anyone could contain, so he slung his racket away over the rope fence at the end of the court toward the crabgrass lawn and the slope at the harbor. Up. The racket sailed up like a fiberglass gospel of milk and honey for everyone, up higher than any chimney and out into the air above the harbor, air which now could begin the march through autumn, summer gone. Oh Christ, gone.

But he had won, and he was exhausted with joy. He let out a breath, and felt that every muscle had left his body and that that was fine. He looked into the crowd before him, the clapping, whistling, laughing crowd now finally able to grab up their stuff from the hillside to go, and he did not care about the applause, though it washed over his exhaustion like a river that would sustain and carry him. He looked for his family. He sought out his girls and Win. He looked for his tender, ruined mother to silently promise that he would get her home always. He cast through all the faces of friends in the audience to meet his father's eyes and tell his father that everything had turned out and that his love was what had made the difference.

VICTOR

Three and a half years ago now? Yes.

Impossible as it would have been to predict, the horror began only a year and a half after Barnaby ran out of the Old Ladies Bank to make his extraordinary, mind-bogglingly successful play on the collapse of oil. And then once it began, for the subsequent year and a half the horror mounted and mounted, and the prospect of jail became more real and more real and nearly damn certain, until Barnaby's life took on a cast of ashes and plague, and the wide waiting gates of jail became for him and him alone (whom could he tell? Win and the girls?) the concrete incarnation of death. This for someone who treasured life.

The good thing about it was that the need to focus on avoiding jail became a distraction from all the rest.

A year and a half after Barnaby had won everything he had ever wanted in his oil bonanza, everything was as good as gone in the snap of Peterpotter's fingers. Peterpotter. And Barnaby was so diminished by the loss that sometimes he could not even summon his fury. He ached night and day. There were moments he would not look down for fear of seeing that he'd lost the very arms and legs that his mother had given and admired on him when he was a baby.

Not that Barnaby hadn't lost, or come close to losing, everything before. Not that Barnaby was anything but a past master in the fraudulence of good clothes and empty pockets. Not that in the other matter anyone, Barnaby least of all, could possibly have been surprised at Win finally cashing out. But, Win aside, Barnaby had never before possessed anything approaching such a vast everything as his Old Ladies windfall. And to lose it all. To have achieved sufficient size that everyone knew, everyone noticed, everyone watched and waited with the understanding that Barnaby Griswold had had his highest tide and it was all out to sea now. Barnaby Griswold had become something so hypnotically in the process of final dismemberment that people actually gathered in crowds to look. If it had not been for the pressing issue of prison, Barnaby would have felt compelled to look with them, and might not have been able to stop looking.

Was his father's death two years ago, right when a penal sentence seemed most imminent, also a part of what distracted him? No. His father was more than prepared to die, and secretly Barnaby was even grateful to lose his father's variety of witness. Not that Barnaby rejoiced, but one hardly would pray to be examined in a moment of ultimate weakness by the ultimate judge of what an only son's life had come to.

No, prison was the real distraction. There was first and foremost the issue of prison.

And Barnaby moved his camp to the Point house to focus on that issue.

Which was to say there was eventually nowhere else for Barnaby to live. And so he went to the Point, and from there, where in winter he would be invisible and where even in July and August he would be only one of the many wounded and peculiar in unquestioned retreat at the shore, from there he managed his campaign for freedom. And to manage that campaign in the best possible fashion, he quit the booze, and really, after quitting smoking, the booze was not as hard as he'd expected. Furthermore, he began working out. Yes, in testament to how the fear of jail could transform a man, he signed in at the town gym with the cops and firemen, with the third and fourth and eighth generation of Massachusetts North Shore Portuguese and Italians, and he sat on the stationary bicycles with his big feet folding over the pedals and with his knees waving drunkenly and with his elbows wide, and he went as if his life depended on it.

He pedaled like the warden was chasing him in his dreams. He pedaled with his thighs so heavy and hurting that his suctions and explosions of breath turned to moans. Sometimes he went so slowly and with such difficulty in these agonies of purification that his head was drawn down right to the red digital readouts on the aimless handlebars, and he pulled on those handlebars with all the strength in his flabby arms and grasping, uncalloused hands until his arms and his fingers ached as much as his skinny, pitiable legs. Sometimes he went so slowly that only he could have known the pedals were still turning. But he went. The pedals did turn. He turned as red as sunburned poison ivy, and he sweated. Barnaby was a man naturally inclined to sweat, and now he sweated to fulfill a potential he had never dreamed for himself. He dripped and streamed and splashed. He soaked his shirt front and back; he soaked his jock and his short pants; he soaked anything he touched or leaned over or blasted his breath at. But he never stopped. The warden never caught him.

And every time he wanted booze, he came back and did it again.

It was a use for his father and the Puritan in him. Antidote to the Griswold diet. It put him to sleep from exhaustion. It gave him the strength to look away from his own wreckage, to make the calls and the concessions he had to make. He began using the machines with weights on them, woofing in great grunts of effort.

And the cops and the firemen watched him and circled him as if he were a barely visible scum. Not because he was running from the warden (they couldn't have known that), but because of course he was scum. He was a rich guy, a Griswold, a snob. Oh, more than he had ever had to do before, Barnaby understood the blessings of class. Class hatred was as eternally reassuring as the sun coming up, so much more agreeable than the slithery lines of anathema drawn around him at all his old places in New York, even La Cote, anathema not because he'd done anything wrong, which he hadn't, at all, but just because he'd lost so colossally

much. Well, he couldn't afford those places anyway, if he was
going to last out his suspension once the judgment was paid and
Win was paid and the lawyers were paid.

He nodded and smiled at the cops and the firemen while he
flailed on his bike like a boiling lobster, and he didn't mind that
they hated him. He loved them and he loved their hatred. He
was making a comeback. He was a monk, and he was getting
healthy. He did not yet feel like a secret weapon (he'd only just
started, really), but he could imagine becoming one, an unrecog-
nized athlete in his monk's innocuous robes, slipping up to the
starting line when his suspension was lifted.

Meanwhile he used every contact (by then there were far fewer
contacts than had been the case not so long before) and every
posture of begging he'd ever known (which was a significant ros-
ter of postures) to get the Securities and Exchange Commission
to promise they would take every material asset he possessed
that Win was not already sure to collect, if only he could stay out
of jail.

The threat that Barnaby might mount a high-powered
defense in an expensive trial, the news that an influential fed-
eral agency would get a windfall, Barnaby's windfall, if that trial
were avoided, the certainty that Barnaby could be cast into utter
ruin no matter what—these things were all brought serendipi-
tously together after months and months of arduous conjuring,
and they persuaded the Oklahoma City judge to ask only for a
public apology.

Of course it was also true that the case had been manu-
factured out of Barnaby's honorary, but apparently formalized,
affiliation with Sooner First City, an affiliation celebrated in a
cowboy hat photo. It was an affiliation solid enough to support
a wheelbarrowful of charges by enviously vindictive locals, but it
was also finally a tenuous enough affiliation that the judge didn't
want it at the heart of one of his prominent sentencings. So,
an apology.

Really? Finally? As easy as that?

Because Barnaby had been apologizing all his life.

Well, as easy as that and giving up any claim to all but a few dollars, an amount of dollars that in the good-and-so-very-recent old days would have hardly been maintenance for six months.

But all right. He got on a plane, and he was exuberant.

He'd stayed out of jail, and on the flight to Oklahoma City, a far different flight than the one with Peterpotter and TJ, he sat in coach class and he felt freedom's importance. He felt at one with Eastern European dissidents and with people in undergrounds everywhere. He felt that if he applied himself, if he kept up with the gym he'd started, he could take Dicky Kopus in the Winott Cup, not the next summer maybe but certainly the following year, which would still leave him an autumn of holiday until his suspension was lifted.

He went to his apology with that, with the positive vow to beat Kopus within two summers. He went to his apology and out from under the threat of jail with the powerful understanding that he was Barnaby Griswold and that he was alive with possibilities. He went to his apology already eager to get back to the gym and begin training, really training, for Kopus and the cup and the rest of his life.

It was an early morning apology, so he spent the night at Ada's condominium, and in the morning, for appearance sake and to coax himself into what he assumed was the appropriate mood of sack clothed remorse, he drove the cheapest rental car he could find. He parked on one of Oklahoma City's many downtown streets without people and went into a half-empty, no-longer-new office tower and found his way to the designated place for saying you were sorry, whether you were or not. And that place turned out, much to his surprise, to be an actual courtroom.

Barnaby had never been in a courtroom before, and as plain as it was, it confused him. On the one hand, with its ominously bland officialness, it was a proof of jail, of lives shunted away almost before they could make a smell, proof of all that Barnaby and his own precious life had escaped and preserved, and in that way it was a cause for measured jubilation. On the other hand, it was viscerally not a comfortable place. It was a place of judgment, and Barnaby had never favored judgment where he himself was concerned.

And as soon as the door had swung closed behind him, he became aware of two or three dozen people all turned in their seats and looking at him. It was a smallish room, so certainly he had been aware as he came in the door that he was among people, but they had felt like an audience in a theater where the object of attention was all out ahead the other way, on stage, and he himself could slip into a back pew and watch things anonymously if he wanted. Ordinarily, in fact, he might have coughed or struck his heels to bring people's attention to himself; it wasn't like Barnaby to not want to be noticed at all. But as soon as everyone in this fluorescently windowless courtroom looked at him, he knew that anonymity was what he did want.

At least the separated territory where the jury would have been was empty. Barnaby tried to let that comfort him.

"Thank you for joining us, Mr. Griswold. Why don't you come up here and stand in the witness box."

The judge said this. Barnaby assumed it was the judge who sat without robes, just in a sport coat and tie, behind the raised desk at the front of the room, under the flags.

Barnaby knew what a witness box was from television, and so he walked down the aisle through the middle of all the spectators, and it was a much different aisle and procession from the sort he usually imagined. There was no choir for one thing. The choir would have gone where the jury belonged. And everyone who looked at him, all of them, hated him. And this was a much different hatred from the other guys in the gym who thought Barnaby was just any one of the assholes who'd been born on the top of the shitpile. These people here hated exactly Barnaby Griswold, nobody but Barnaby Griswold. Barnaby didn't look at them, but he knew. He could feel it, and there was no sense that he was the one on top of the shitpile anymore.

He glanced around for someone to swear him in or process him, but there was no one like that in evidence, and so when he was past everybody but the judge, he went and stepped to the witness chair beside the judge and began to sit.

"Stand up, Griswold," the judge snapped too loudly for someone sitting as close as he was now to Barnaby. "And remain standing until we're through with you."

Barnaby didn't like the judge's tone of voice, but he stood up as straight as he knew how to do, which was straight indeed, and he looked out over the heads of the audience facing him and pretended that this was all a play, a dour legal bit of theater in which he was deservedly the star. It was not so different from something he might have staged during a prolonged moment of inspiration in a saloon or for that matter in a pitch during business hours. Though in both cases, he would have tried to insert a bit of humor and good cheer into the proceedings. He stood straight and tall in a good suit (but not a flashy suit) and he wondered if he might not be able to lighten these proceedings too.

Out in the audience, the only soul he was able to recognize without actually studying the faces was Peterpotter.

Of course Peterpotter would have come.

And just like that, Barnaby could taste his own bile, could smell already coming off of himself the murky, electrical fury that he had never known in his life until eighteen months before.

Because Peterpotter had somehow been able to drive a dagger right up to the hilt in Barnaby's back. Peter fucking Potter. When Barnaby could have known, should have known. Had known.

The fury now twisted itself so gnawingly in Barnaby's stomach, that Barnaby began to perspire as if he were afraid.

From beside, still too loud, the judge said, "You've disgraced yourself, haven't you, Mr. Griswold?"

Barnaby took a breath. He knew enough to do that.

He forced the fury back under.

This was another play entirely. An apology was contrition, and Barnaby summoned that and thought about making things easier and more entertaining for everyone. That was Barnaby's true nature and most persuasive gift. He turned to the judge with a wan, contrite smile. He turned out to the room again and let his eyes skim over the audience once more. He actually took in the faces, and he was surprised to see that he didn't recognize any of them except for his assassin Peterpotter. But who else had he known in Oklahoma City besides the real crooks, the go-go guru and his lieutenants? Those assholes would be keeping a low profile if they were still in town. A few of them, quite rightly, had had to take their profiles in fact to jail, though not for the length of sentence they deserved.

But contrition and charm. Those were the notes to be struck. Barnaby shrugged for his audience and said, as to his having disgraced himself, "Well…"

"Shut up," the judge shouted from beside him, and Barnaby was so startled he almost fell back into his witness chair, which he well knew would have been a mistake. If it hadn't been for the strength and agility recently gained in the gym, he would have fallen, like it or not. He righted himself and tried to think of his happy times on the stationary bicycle. He stood straight and tall and he turned to the judge.

And despite his best efforts, the fury, for Peterpotter and for everything else, twisted up out of him. He would not shut up. He would not be spoken to in that sort of language or in that tone of voice.

But before Barnaby could make those things clear, the judge said loudly, "We're going to begin again, Griswold." And the judge went on too loudly and too quickly for Barnaby to interrupt. "This is an unusual and informal process here, which means that everyone in this room except for you can do damn near as they please. You will do exactly as I say. The court has been pressed into accepting an apology from you instead of putting you in prison where you belong, but the court is going to see to it that your apology is the real thing. I'm going to see to it. You are either going to leave this room as humbled and as shamed as any man can be, or we are going to go ahead with your trial, because nothing has been signed yet that says you're free. Is that clear?"

It was not clear, because Barnaby had absolutely understood that really it was all signed and sealed, but he wasn't going to question anything now. He'd had the long moment of the judge's delivery to cool down. Common sense would prevail. He said, "Yes, sir."

"Address me as Your Honor. From now on, I'm going to expect you to respond to every statement made in this room as though you are personally responsible for ruining the lives of everyone here. I expect to see you mortified. Because you are responsible, aren't you? You ruined these lives, didn't you?"

Fine, then. If that was the way it was going to be. Barnaby bowed his head in what he supposed to be a posture of penitence, and he said, "Yes, Your Honor."

"Griswold," the shout again. "Tell it to these people before you. And show them the respect they deserve. Look them in the eye when you speak to them."

Barnaby looked out into the faces and let them look into his face. Was he actually frightened in this tasteless, yellow, little room that should never have had anything to do with his life? He said, "Yes."

"Yes, what?" came the shout.

It was shame Barnaby felt. He was ashamed to be shouted at like this in front of these people who watched him as if all they'd ever wanted was to see Barnaby Griswold yelled at. He said to them, "I ruined your lives."

"And?" came the shout.

"And I'm sorry," Barnaby said to them, and his voice sounded to himself oddly as if he meant it.

"Louder."

"I'm sorry," Barnaby said to them more loudly and just as oddly.

"You disgust me, Griswold," the judge said, and Barnaby kept looking at the people who'd come to witness him. And they witnessed. They watched his shame. "As a man of the law, I find your carpetbagging, flimflam hustling to be repugnant. But as a human being, my feelings are much more powerful. You are sickening, Griswold. Before you are dentists, doctors, musicians, a high school principal, representatives of a wheat growers cooperative, one automobile dealer and the children of another automobile dealer, a men's clothier, a tanning-salon operator, a breeder of quarter horses, and any number of restaurateurs and attorneys. All of these people are respectable members of the community and most of them have families, and you robbed them all of all they had. And not everyone is here. We couldn't fit everyone in here if we wanted to. You have been a foul rot in Oklahoma City, Griswold. A disease. Do you understand that?"

Barnaby nodded and said, "Yes," out to his audience.

Thank God his father was dead. Thank God it was Oklahoma City, so he could not even imagine his father's ghost in the audience. Jesus. Was he going to weep?

Out in the audience, Peterpotter stood up, and Barnaby's rightful fury was nowhere.

"Your Honor," Peterpotter said.

"All right," the judge said. "Go ahead, Potter."

And Peterpotter raised his arm and pointed his finger at Barnaby. "You," Peterpotter said, and instead of vibrating with outrage, Barnaby shied as if in fear, as if Peterpotter were aiming a gun instead of a finger. "You," Peterpotter shouted, "killed TJ Baker. God damn you."

"No need to swear, Potter," the judge said.

"Did you know TJ was dead?" Peterpotter shouted.

Actually, Barnaby had heard that. A heart attack, naturally.

"Well he is," Peterpotter shouted, "and you killed him."

Barnaby felt this at least could be responded to, and he said with shameful mildness, "Actually,…"

"Griswold," the judge shouted. "Shut up."

And with that Barnaby was in fact crying. Not because of TJ or anything Peterpotter could say, but because Barnaby Griswold didn't like to be shouted at. He whispered through his tears, to himself, not to them, "I didn't."

And the judge shouted, "What?"

"I'm sorry," Barnaby said out loud to Peterpotter.

"Sorry isn't good enough," Peterpotter shouted. "You came down here from New York like you were so much better than the rest of us, and you let us think you were a friend, and then you ran away with everybody's money. And TJ was older than the rest of us. He couldn't take it. You pretended you were such a big shot in your restaurant up there, and then you stole everything he and his family ever made, as if you just naturally deserved to end up with it, and he looked at what you'd done and he couldn't go on. He died. These are his sons, right here." Peterpotter finally brought back his arm and his pointing finger so he could put his hand out over the heads of two very large young men seated next to where he stood. "Tell these boys that you're sorry, and see if that makes them feel any better. See if they care about your Yankee tone of voice and all your eastern friends who don't give any more of a damn about Oklahoma than you do."

Barnaby stood and looked at the large young men and looked at Peterpotter and looked at everyone else. He could not even be amazed at always having thought he was liked. He only was sorry. He didn't believe he was sorry enough to weep, but he did weep, and all of them watched him, his father too, dressed in a suit for work, and everyone was glad about the weeping.

Barnaby Griswold had won his big match, and there was no one to see. No one who cared.

No friends. No daughters. Certainly not Win.

Not his mother even in any condition.

Not even the ghost of his father.

The applause died, and people were on their feet and starting off to get ready for the last party of the summer, and none of the faces, some of whom he'd known all his life, were more than acquaintances. A child ran back up the lawn with Barnaby's racket and met a family going down the lawn the other way and tossed the racket toward the court and went away. Barnaby turned around to search the shadows beyond the far corner of the court, through his rope fence and under the smaller of the copper beeches, to where he prayed his beautiful girl waited with forgiveness of his appalling nature.

She was not there. He spun to search all around the court, and she was not anywhere. He had cheated and lost her.

"Congratulations, asshole," Kopus said grudgingly but earnestly, and Barnaby looked at Kopus. It was Kopus who was Barnaby's friend. Barnaby shook his damp, furry hand.

As Winott Cup champion, Barnaby Griswold walked home along the Point lanes by himself.

He had dedicated himself to his cup with such obsessive commitment that he had come to know the very sun would shine if he won. Yet suddenly it was late in the day and the sun was going down. And just as suddenly, he remembered apologizing two years ago.

From the moment he had left that courtroom, he had meant to forget about his apology, and he'd succeeded. Two years, after all. Of course he'd forgotten.

Why should he feel sorry?

With his championship racket under his arm, he walked into the barny, ramshackle house that had been the Griswold summer place since Barnaby's grandfather and great-grandfather had floated it across the harbor from town at the end of the last century. It was going to seed like every summer place, sloughing dampness and salt through the most recent wallpaper that Barnaby himself had helped to paste up as a teenager.

But now it was both more and less than a summerhouse for Barnaby; it was his only house, and it was that only for another few days. One day. Labor Day.

That he got to stay as long as that was Win's one great bow to compassion, to the tournament, to history, to every Griswold whose summer ghost still trod the Point during the warm weather months.

Was it possible that Barnaby had managed not to confront his deadline until the day before it fell? There had been the tournament, and that focus had had to be maintained, but was tomorrow actually the last day? Even for a procrastinator of Barnaby's ilk, such a thing was astonishing. Twenty-four hours left with a roof over his head.

He went upstairs and looked at the pile of his real life on what had been Win's shore bureau. There were transfer papers on the house, going through Win to the girls so that it would stay in Griswold history. There were final papers on the divorce, and with them the number for the cellular phone that Win had thrown off Duane's boat when she ended their last conversation. (And, no mistaking it: the final papers said, Out after Labor Day.) Lastly, of course, there was official notice, now the judgment was paid in full, that Barnaby's suspension from the securities business would conclude on the first of the year.

So the bureau did hold some promise. The chance of gainful employment was not far off, for one thing.

And the girls would retain membership in the Winott Point Tennis Association; that came with the house. They might not care right now about ever being in the house again, much less playing in the tournament or going to an annual meeting in the old Winott boat hut, but with time they would see the value of all that. Eventually they would know to keep the house and the membership for their own children, even if their father never saw Winott Point again.

Well, not never. Not never ever.

Certainly not never ever if he made a bundle as soon as his suspension was up, right after the first of the year. Who cared that he'd already been away almost four years? That he was forty-six and starting over? What did it matter that instead of keeping up his connections and his presence, that instead of making as many calls as was legal as often as was legal, he had made no calls whatever for years?

It didn't matter a bit, because instead of making calls, he had made himself into a championship tennis player. Barnaby's livelihood was all about confidence, and he shuddered to think how much confidence a championship under his belt would give him when he went back out on the street. If anybody imagined they could forget about Barnaby Griswold, they were going to be surprised in four months' time.

Barnaby himself was still surprised that Win could want to be on a boat, seasick presumably, for several months. With someone named Duane, no less. There was surprise too that she could go out of touch from the girls for that long. Though now, the girls had a trustee to dole out tuition and they attacked anyone with more advice than money anyhow. They attacked Barnaby if he even thought of coming near.

It should have been more surprising, just when her mother's long sequence of small strokes had begun to pick up frequency, that Win could leave the world until the first of the year. But of course Win was hoping for Ada to have the big stroke while Win herself was gone and beyond reach. Which was how Ada would prefer it too, no doubt. Was there even a safety net anywhere, besides himself, the ex-son-in-law? Was there something auspicious in Win returning to dry land and Barnaby returning to the securities business on the same day? Barnaby believed that good news lived even more in coincidence than in most other places. But no. He tried to wish Win and Duane well on whatever was their course.

Meanwhile, he rooted through the closet for the pair of red trousers that he'd wear to drink from the Winott Cup, his championship trousers. So what if he only had twenty-four hours? He had to muster a little enthusiasm for Christ sake.

And muster it he did. What a pleasure it was to dress for royal occasions when one was the center of the occasion. A champion. He'd always known that about himself, and he had been right to earn the title.

Yet when he pulled them free of their hanger and brought them out of the closet, Barnaby had no heart for championship trousers.

Now he'd won and he didn't care, and if he didn't care, who did? Or rather he did care, but what was he going to do now?

No. That was not the way a champion thought. Who cared about how broke he was when it was only until the first of the year? The ball would drop in Times Square, somebody would kiss him (somebody, surely), and he would walk downtown and be himself as he always had been—"Remember Barnaby Griswold?"—and the money would come back in as fast as it had gone out. If you lived at the shore and understood tides, this was perfectly clear.

Barnaby had no worries about the first of the year.

The priority was what to do tomorrow.

After the party tonight, if he slept late tomorrow, he would have one afternoon in which to do his laundry and pack something. He'd end up leaving home in the dark. God Almighty. Homeless and no kidding. Barnaby Griswold.

Out the bedroom window on the harbor side of the house, the wormy fruit in the old apple tree waited to fall.

Inside, Barnaby stood in his jockstrap with his sweat-salted shirt dried to a board around his new, more or less muscled chest, and looked at his red pants. Was he going to put them on without taking a shower for Christ sake? Was he going to go to the party and try making a pass at one of the available thrice-divorced of his own generation when they knew he'd flushed his life down the toilet?

The hell with the God damned pants.

He walked down the hall to his youngest daughter's room and went to the window, his own window as a boy, and stared beyond the brackish little pond toward the cove and the great rock and the twilight ocean. He looked down to where he had set up the croquet wickets on the back lawn in the beginning of summer. He had never played and never put the wickets away.

He closed his eyes and was even sorry that he had not, with or without a shower, put on his red linen pants. They would have cheered him. He kept his eyes closed and smelled, even in summer and with the windows open, the mold of the house, the old horsehair plaster under the wallpaper holding the shore damp and giving allergies to soulless people like Win who didn't belong in the house anyhow. He could also smell the breath of low tide, of rot at the edge of the sea, coming in the window. Lovely low tide. He hoped someday when he was done and gone, when the maggots had finished with him and his own stink had run its course, that he could come back as part of low tide.

He opened his eyes and turned to the room's stained little mirror. He was not actually weeping, and of course he couldn't weep while he watched himself (could he? no), but there was no denying that he was red in the face. Was this what he had looked like at the apology? He contorted his face into a mask of anguish to go with all his redness. Good God. No wonder they'd stared.

But that was then. He'd moved on since then. He'd hurled himself with his astonishing, monkish discipline into the quest for the Winott Cup, and he'd won.

If he gave a damn about redemption and expiation (if he even knew the difference), if he were actually guilty of anything (which he wasn't; selling short was no crime), he would have assumed as a matter of course that winning the cup wiped clean any and all slates to do with those things, the spiritual slates he supposed you would call them.

Was there something about the apology he had neglected? Was it possible more was being asked of him than he had already gone through?

More was being asked, and it had to be spiritual more if there were such a sense all over again of remorse and guilt and shame and fear, such a wish for expiation and redemption, whatever they meant. If there were such a spasm of clenching in his stomach. Was this what his mother's stomach had felt like for the last thirty years of her life?

He turned back to the window and looked down at his croquet set. Win's and the girls' croquet set now. He looked out over the pond to the cove and the rock, and beyond to the great horizon of the ocean. He breathed in the riches of low tide, also Win's and the girls' now, emphatically not his own, and he was weeping for real.

No need for a mirror. He could feel the tears.

He was finally crying. It burned, and it felt good.

He was going to weep himself away. He would puddle and then leak through to the living room. He had to leave his house and his Point and his family's tennis association, and this was the way he was going to do it. In tears. This was the end. Absolutely, and it was not happy at all.

Only it was not the end. It was only the beginning, and he knew it. How could he have not kept in touch? How could he have made no calls at all when all of his life had always been lived in his deals? How could he ever have thought that tennis…

If Win were here, he would kneel and hold her bony ankles and weep onto her big, dry feet. He would tell her again that he had tried to change himself. He would tell her not to forget to put suntan lotion on her feet. And not to let Duane do it. If the girls were here and tiny again, he would make them laugh again, just so that when he got to this stage in his own life they would keep him from harm.

It was too late for any of that, however; there was no one here or anywhere to keep him from harm, and there was nothing at all for Barnaby himself to do. Somewhere, yes, were good deeds to be done, but Barnaby could never do them. He had no resources left.

There would be no more deals. There would be no making it all back.

He put his head out the window and regretted that his house was only two stories. He threw off his shirt from the tennis match and leaned his whole naked torso out the window and stared down at the rusted, iron bloom of the old drying rack that stood up out of the edge of the flower bed. It was a massive umbrella of clotheslines, and he wondered if he threw himself down on it whether he would be able to drive his forehead hard enough against the center post. He thought he would; he was an athlete now.

He put one of his own big bare feet up on the windowsill, but then, before he could quite decide, he heard the phone ring out with its bang of possibility.

And he ran to that noise with the release of a puppy let off the leash. He galloped in his jockstrap down the hall to the upstairs phone where there would be the voice of someone who wanted to talk to him.

Oh, let it be someone with something for Barnaby to do and somewhere to go for the next four months. Somewhere inexpensive it would have to be. Starting tomorrow.

"Hello?"

Oh, if only he had somewhere to go. He would promise to make his calls. He could still be ready when his suspension was up. He was ready right now. He was even ready to do good, if that was called for.

"Hello?"

PILGRIM

Like the veteran caregiver he had become, Barnaby wheeled Ada into the doorway to her bedroom and helped her out of the jacket of her sweat suit. He helped her to stand in the doorway in her sweatpants and an undershirt, and he took hold of the flesh that hung congealed and forgotten but not yet quite withered behind her upper arm.

"Here we are again," she said. "Almost in the bedroom with me half undressed." She tried to say it with her old, coy humor, and then added with undisguised revulsion at herself, "Don't pretend you don't hate to touch me."

The back of her arm, even the wrinkling, was smooth as marble and soft as silt and moist from being in the jacket, and Barnaby touched it almost every time he came, two and three times a day, every day for months now.

And once he had taken that dampness in his fingers, once he was inside the apartment and the door was closed and he had taken again his first deep breaths of the condominium's liquid pungency of death, then he was all right, a vessel purely of goodwill.

"One," he said. "Two," guiding Ada's arm out to the door frame and back for her, timing his pilgrimage onward with the rhythm of her exercises.

Ada swayed for balance and farted a long clapper, and, "More gas here than in all Russell County," she said. If it had been the old Ada, Barnaby would have laughed, but her voice had only disgust for herself.

So, "Five," Barnaby said with as much compassion as he could give a number that wasn't a quote.

And if she didn't die before his suspension was up? What did that mean? Without the rules of pilgrimage written down anywhere, it was difficult to speak about details, but Barnaby knew as well as anyone that he had been explicit about the first of the year.

Ada lifted her arm out, six, and with her activated disgust and the increasing repetitions came the pain.

"Shit God damn," she screamed. "Shit God damn. Shit God damn."

And from away in the condominium's kitchen came the voice of Happiness calling with ominous severity, "Don't take the Lord's name. Do not take the Lord's name. We've talked about that, and I'm sure it doesn't hurt so much. You're stretching, is what the Rehabilitation said. Besides, Mr. Griswold is there with you, and you don't want him to hear such talk. Any more than you want the Lord to hear, because the Lord is right in that very doorway too. And the Lord is helping you. The Lord wants to help you heal your arm, and He can if you let Him."

Barnaby let Ada rest, and then in a moment guided Ada's arm out once more, and she went along with the exercises quietly again, conjuring a response to Happiness.

Barnaby wondered briefly whether screaming warranted a drink. He thought that it might, and thought a drink would taste good besides, but no; monks, especially superstars of the cloister, as he had come to understand himself, did not fall back into the booze.

Early on, when he had gotten through the business of activating the support system, of interviewing the companions with the agency and getting a sense for the flow of dollars to everybody, when Ada had finally cleared from the truly big stroke that had summoned Barnaby on Labor Day and when he had actually brought Ada home and begun what he rightly supposed would be his pilgrimage, then Barnaby had had to confront the renewed temptations of thirst. And he had confronted, and persevered. He had learned to sense immediately when the ship seemed to be sinking, and at those times instead of watching the water rise and begin to look like gin, he simply thought of something else, and if what he thought of was a drink, then he thought of something else again.

The bad news was that Happiness, this latest of Ada's companions in the nine weeks since Ada had been home from the hospital, would be leaving forever at the end of her shift. Happiness was a companion who could manage Ada's fury without batting an eye and who could speak if not the king's English at least a language Barnaby understood. Alas, she was also (as Barnaby had been thoroughly instructed) a child of the Lord who would not abide unholy profanity.

Barnaby was not of an order whose members refused profanity, and he preferred not to think of having to find yet another companion, and so he tried to think about matters of the heart. He tried to think about love, or even just sex for that matter. Because he couldn't, after all, survive forever on the memory of his beautiful girl from the Winott Cup.

Yes? And his order's position on sex? That wasn't entirely clear, but Barnaby had to suspect there were restrictions. Which meant he had pilgrim's work to do in his own front yard, special circumstances or not. His yearnings for women had gone largely unsatisfied for as long as he could remember, and that had lead to a lifetime of yearning for deals, where satisfaction always came more easily. But now, with deals long in abeyance, with tennis done, with monastic proscriptions the ruling imperative, now out of the blue, fleshly appetite seemed eager to have its day.

So he did try to think of finding a new companion for Ada, through "the Rehabilitation" as Happiness called the agency. That would be an occupying chore, and Barnaby needed occupying.

Then he wondered whether he could summon the nerve to buy a *Playboy* in a drugstore at some distance from his neighborhood. He knew he didn't have the nerve, in any neighborhood, to root around in the racks of magazines next to upstanding hot-rodders and computer geeks for something as raunchy as a *Penthouse*. Even with the *Playboy* and its purported articles, everyone in the store would know Barnaby for what he was, a liar least of all.

"Ow. Ow. Shit God damn. Fuck. There I said it." Ada dropped her arm back to her side and turned so her speech would carry toward the kitchen. "I finally said it. Fuck. Now before I die I can go to parties with people in the malls. Fuck, fuck, fuck. Stay away, Happiness. I finally said it."

Happiness's briskly angry steps came squishing from the kitchen, and Barnaby gave away control of Ada's upper arms and retreated to the living room where he turned off the early-afternoon editions of the household's favorite television evangelist.

He took from the bookshelves one of the late Doctor Briley's opera books, the one with a singer's cleavage on the cover. He didn't bother to look at the pages; he'd done that before and knew the cover was the book's only good picture. He sat on the sofa and put a hand over the cleavage, partly to touch it and partly to keep himself from it. He did not listen to the furious moans and hissings that emanated from the bedroom. He sprawled out of the sofa like a fifteen-year-old and wished, as if he'd ever been able to make a spiral, that he had someone to throw a football with.

Then here came the rolling infusion of Happiness bringing Ada back into the living room.

Barnaby turned his book facedown and sat up like a human being as Happiness parked Ada at the corner of the couch and hurried with unlikely decorum back to the kitchen. Ada cradled the sore arm in her lap and stared at Barnaby.

Barnaby smiled with what he believed was a pilgrim's joy.

And Ada said, "You're going to die too."

Laughter was the only response that came to him, so Barnaby laughed.

And, "You won't think it's so funny," Ada said, "when your time comes."

So he stopped laughing and Ada called over her shoulder to Happiness in the kitchen, "Well, I made him laugh," as if confessing to a sorry chore done without pleasure.

"You see?" came Happiness's voice from the kitchen.

Ada shouted over her shoulder now in the voice of someone who could hire and fire, "Well, how much longer are you going to be in there?"

"Just. One. More. Sec. Ond," Happiness shouted back in the singsong perkiness of a day that Jesus might have favored even more than most days.

Ada swiveled her attention and leaned toward Barnaby from her wheelchair. With a loathing beyond expression, she said, "Are you listening?"

"I didn't mean," Barnaby said with the martyred sorrow of a fifteen-year-old car wrecker, "to laugh about death." In fact he had never felt so obscenely alive, but it was life at the grave's edge of the universe, and so he was surprised to hear his fifteen-year-old voice.

"She's like that all the time. Sec. Ond. She can go a week without making a whole word at once, much less a sentence. And she's as pleased about it as if her education were the Lord's work." In the center of her face, Ada's mouth puckered with its own separate fury.

In now the limpest approximation of a pilgrim's holiness, Barnaby said again, "I'm sorry I laughed at death."

And Ada said, "I heard you the first time. Why are you sorry? What else are we supposed to do? Laugh. Go ahead and laugh. We should all laugh." She stared at him with her mouth still pouched down by the taste of hatred. "Let's laugh right now. Together."

It was such a great delivery that Barnaby did laugh.

He stopped not because Ada didn't laugh along but because she stared at him with so outraged an amazement that he feared she was into another stroke.

"You laughed," she said.

He nodded.

And she said, "Ha, ha, ha," half in sarcasm but also half in an earnest attempt. "How's that?" she said.

"Well," he said. "Not great."

"Not great," she said honestly, and she reached a hand out to touch his knee. "You try with me."

He shook his head and said, "We need something funny."

"Ha, ha, ha," she said, louder than before, not exactly angry again but not far from it.

So he joined her, "Ha, ha," and in another moment they were quiet, and he said, "Pathetic."

He looked at her disappointment and laughed more or less a real laugh. Surely there was something laughable here.

She looked at him as if he were ridiculous, which he was, and laughed herself, more or less a real laugh.

Of course he was ridiculous; it had been the buoying comfort of his life, and here it was serving him again. The pilgrims who survived used what resources God gave them. He laughed out a great, exuberant laugh of foolishness, and Ada came with him unfettered. He raised his hands for a touchdown, and she laughed with pride in her own abandon to ridiculousness. He thought ever so briefly about putting his own hand over hers on his knee, but he didn't want to encourage that sort of thing.

At which point Happiness turned out the light in the kitchen, and then the hall light, and then scurried past the living room window to pull its curtain and scurry away again.

Ada and Barnaby ceased their laughter.

Oklahoma City's desolate daylight still washed over the wall and through her unwashed plants to Ada's patio door. But this was a week after Thanksgiving, the very end of November and late afternoon.

It was plenty dark enough to see the candles as Happiness now padded with a cake, ever so slowly for processional effect and to keep the candles lit, toward the coffee table from the kitchen.

Everything about the furtive triumph in Happiness's face said that the cake was a surprise. But whose surprise? Something in the aim of Happiness's peculiarity did not say Ada. Could it be Happiness's own birthday? Happiness was not too peculiar for that kind of thing. A real surprise. Barnaby liked the idea.

Happiness began singing, and Ada sang along right away as if she were in on the surprise. Barnaby smiled back at the giggling delight in Happiness's face and joined himself to the second cry of "Happy Birthday to you," singing it out exactly to Happiness. But, while giggling and singing and precariously handling the lighted cake, Happiness shook her head at Barnaby as if she were not in fact surprising herself, and so Barnaby very quickly—he'd always been agile in these things, the legacy of so much booze and bullshit—shifted his delivery of song toward Ada. He'd never known her birthday, though his secretary had of course, along with Win's and the girls' birthdays, in the days he'd had a secretary.

"Happy Birthday, dear..."

But Ada was singing at him, which he could have dismissed except that she appeared so very sure. Had the pilgrimage moved as it often did onto the dry land of terra truly incognita? Christ, how he wished for rules on some days.

Unconsciously he brought the fingers of both hands to his chest and looked inquisitively back to Happiness whose delight transcended itself to the point that she nodded like one of those spring-necked Ted Williams dolls he'd always wanted to put on the shelf behind the back seat of the car as a kid.

"Happy Birthday, dear..." Happiness's spring bounced with rapture.

"...dear Barnaby."

By God, it was a surprise, and Barnaby shouted out his name just as loudly as Ada and Happiness did. He'd always before had birthdays in the summer, but Ada and Happiness had changed that.

And now Happiness, Ada's potent angel, was waiting for Barnaby to make his wish and blow out the candles. She knelt down on the carpet beside the table and held the fingers of her wings, her hands—gad, Barnaby—to her chest in expectation. Barnaby looked at his own fingers on his own chest, and brought his hands down solidly onto his thighs where they belonged and leaned over the heat of the candles and made his wish. If there were enough candles to generate so much heat, perhaps he was old enough to die today. Was that what Ada was saying? Regardless, his paramount desire was for Happiness to stay on as Ada's companion. He wished for that. Truthfully he did not want to work with the Rehabilitation to replace Happiness; he did not want to smell that sequence of lives and their menus. No. He wanted Happiness to stay. This world, with its new birthdays and its early darknesses, had become all of his life for the time being, and he didn't want any more disruption than necessary.

Would he have been better off wishing for something else? It was the end of November; one more month and he was back in business. Shouldn't he have wished that he had business to go back to? Shouldn't he have wished that at least he'd used his time to…What? Learn a paying trade? Come off it, Barnaby. To make some calls then? Ah, yes, that was something he could have been doing. Except that he was here because he was needed, and what was needed of him was that he immerse himself in the doing of good, for months. This was the real thing, and it asked real commitment, and Barnaby's embracing nature told him that the commitment was appropriate. If you gave yourself to your pilgrimage, everything else fell into place. On the other side waited Barnaby's good life, restored. He was a pilgrim, and he was winning his way home, and calls were beside the point.

He lay down for another night in the camp bed he'd taken from Winott Point. Monastic sensibility and the terms of the divorce had persuaded him that there would be no use for a larger or more comfortable bed, and so he lay on his back with his arms at his sides in a straight but sagging line and felt not too differently than he'd felt in his alcove in boarding school during the long, monastery nights of first form year—cramped and lonely, but grateful for the dark relief from everything in the assigned world, from classes and sports and homework and other children.

Tonight, he closed his eyes and relaxed his pilgrim's robes and savored relief at the fact that Happiness was staying on after all.

And so, yes. Tonight, rather than in his boyhood's institutional wilderness of bricks and lawn, he lay in a leased bungalow with thin walls and a postage lawn and one stunted tree on a street with other bungalows and other achingly small trees, a street in Oklahoma City called Wimbledon of all things, one block past Westminster at the fraying edge of the best suburb that was Driscoll Hills.

And he had not been left here by his parents as at boarding school. He had come largely of his own accord.

All right, he'd had nowhere else to go, but he had recognized that phone call on the day of the championship as a higher call, and he had answered it. He had recognized a pilgrimage, and he had made himself ready to care-give. He'd come, and he'd stayed.

Would he have stayed if Livermore had offered the spare room in his good Park Avenue apartment instead of a formal caution under the Crenshaw letterhead that Barnaby was contagious? Who would have thought that when Barnaby needed somewhere to stay in the last months before he came out of suspension, Livermore would write, dictate to his secretary, a letter saying, "Dear Mr. Griswold, don't come anywhere near me until after Christmas at the earliest, very best regards."

The fact was that he had stayed, here in Oklahoma City, and he would continue to stay, and he was glad.

Even so, he remembered how, as his father had said good-bye in a voice that meant good-bye, his mother had looked awfully sad to leave Barnaby at boarding school that first year, and if in tonight's darkness, if on a pilgrimage that was tiring even on days without pornography, if tonight he did not cry out, "Mother," it was because he'd learned once and for all from the world of boarding-school alcoves that that cry did not make life easier. Would the other guys and their families on Wimbledon, hear the cry and call him Barnababy? Of course they would.

He lay without moving and felt his swollen weight fill the little bed. He had been swollen as a first former too, always swollen until now, and now it was too late, no matter how fit, to change his mirrored self in the blindness of bedtime. He'd never been actually fat, but close. He should have been saved because he was tall, but his long legs had always been too flopping, his feet too big, one arm or another in the wrong place and slow to catch up. It was his father's length and his mother's flesh before the flesh left her.

Tonight, he could feel sweat in the crack of his ass and in the creases between his ass and the tops of his legs. He wasn't Crisco anymore by a long shot, but there was still some fat in the can. A grown man with no lard in his ass was either out of work or a gigolo, not to be trusted in any case. Barnaby was out of work and not to be trusted, and he wouldn't have minded making a connection as a gigolo.

He was also scared to death that in a month he was supposed to go back to real work.

No, he didn't want to say scared.

He lifted his covers and let them fall in order to smell what was there. It was him. Without the booze and cigarette smoke, but him. His own hairs and feet and armpits. His own large heat in this little bed. A satisfactory smell, it still seemed, regardless of his true weight.

For years before the Old Ladies Bank deal, actually, there hadn't been any schoolhouse teasing about his weight. He was no longer a pear in those days; he was a businessman porpoise, and he could afford to wear well-made clothes. Also he had learned to move at a measured pace so that if an arm or a foot fell out of sync, there was time to bring it back where it belonged. Those were the days of the Griswold diet, which said all that really needed to be said about body and soul both.

And after the Old Ladies paid off? After that, the clothes were splendidly tailored and the pace was like a king coming down the aisle for coronation when he could remember to keep it that slow. The Griswold diet went into high gear, and the tigers gamboled in the wallpaper from morning to night.

When the Old Ladies paid, it was let the good times roll.

The price of oil fell off a cliff, and Barnaby Griswold was the one who had sold short and made the money on the change, and the money was unimaginable even to Barnaby who had eaten imaginary fortunes for breakfast every day of his life. It was close to a library at one point, and Barnaby could hear the cathedral children singing his anthem as he stepped ever so slowly from his coach and down the aisle between tables at La Cote for lunch. He had Michel decant his clarets at eleven every morning, and it went onto Barnaby's account whether Barnaby came for lunch that day or not. Somewhere was a vision of Michel's three crooked cousins drinking Barnaby's wine a couple times a week as they drove truckloads of stolen computers back out to the island. And why not? Absolutely. Those three Frog hoodlums passing thermoses of Barnaby's hundred dollar bottles back and forth in the front seat.

More important on the generosity scale in those days, Barnaby Griswold had made fortunes for several of the market's very influential people who had in turn made their investors happy for life. Tom Livermore for a while was St. Tom over at Crenshaw. Which had elevated Barnaby to very senior sainthood as well (though with a far different sort of holiness than what was aspired to here in Oklahoma). True, Tom and the others had believed in Barnaby sufficiently to lend him a bit, so he could leverage his own accounts further, but when the returns came in, that was small potatoes. Barnaby was a figure on the Street. A power? Friends? And more power and more friends lay ahead because Barnaby had suddenly acquired the personal funds and the institutional leverage to do the deals he'd seen go by and never imagined he would be able to take for himself. Barnaby had to hold some of the friends at bay, which was not in his nature, but there was only so much time. He had to hold a few women at bay, which was not in his nature either and had never been a remotely pressing problem before.

And then Peterpotter pulled the plug.

Pulled and pulled and pulled.

Who would have thought Peterpotter could or would? Who would have thought Peterpotter anything but fodder for fun. Barnaby from a distance, in days before the long, plug-pulling approach to apology, had lacquered Peterpotter in jovial myth: Peterpotter, guide to Sooner happiness; Peterpotter Dodge, purveyor of high-return vehicles; Peterpotter cigars cigarettes and sundries.

Who would have thought there was a plug?

Barnaby lay all by himself in his first form alcove cot and chose to dwell on other things. He thought through the dark to some drunken memory—he assumed it was a memory—of a woman whose face he could not see but whose breasts were near. He wanted a face; he wanted real affection more than he'd ever wanted it in his life; he still wanted his beautiful red-headed blond from the finals of the Winott Cup, but in a pinch the face-less breasts looked good.

Why? Because he didn't know if he wanted to make his for-tune back again, and who was he if he didn't want that? Was that why he couldn't make his calls? What would become of him if he didn't care whether or not he ever went below Canal Street again? Would he be a fucking pilgrim forever?

It was his own smell in the little bed and in the little night room around him, but Barnaby thought about the flesh of some woman's body. Not Ada. Christ Almighty. A girl. A young woman. From beside the tennis court? It wouldn't be the first time. He slid his hand down to encourage his limp dick, and it did encourage.

He thought about the young woman rigorously.

In the morning on the way to Ada's, in the middle of the best part of Driscoll Hills, the part with real trees, Barnaby felt better. For a man who had once regularly busied himself with late evenings, Barnaby maintained an unlikely affection for morning. If he had no idea how things would turn out, in the morning anything was possible. If he was lacking all company and purpose outside of his struggle with Ada and Happiness and pilgrimage, in the morning he remembered that at least he was not in jail, at least he had not run into anyone from the scene of his apology. If no one at the gas station or in the produce aisle had yet seemed to have any idea who he was, in the morning he remembered what a good thing that was.

And just like that, he saw Peterpotter driving a gang mower down the slope beside the Methodist Church where TJ had been senior something when he lost his car lots and had his heart attack.

Barnaby knew it was Peterpotter instantly, and right away felt a shine of pleasure because it looked as if Peterpotter belonged on the mower, as if Peterpotter had found his right self and his place in life. Everybody likes to see those kinds of harmony. Barnaby stopped the car, rolled open the window, glad to have a window that did roll open, and stared up the broad slope down which Peterpotter's seven-wide, linked, tractor-towed brace of cutters came in their John Deere—green guise of farmness with a slow, reassuring rush of clatter, with the splendid smell of cut grass for wake.

Barnaby did love a lawn. He wondered much more than casually if lawn work might be the best course for himself.

Was that the morning's glorious possibility, a whole new career choice? That and Peterpotter? That, by God, and the fruition of much of his pilgrimage. Because here it was: he saw Peterpotter, and he felt only generous feelings. Here was a day with suddenly (or not so suddenly—three months, after all) the fruition of things vibrating in the very dew.

Was it possible that Barnaby had in fact completed the equation of his penance? Forget lawn work. If Barnaby could smile at the notion of Peterpotter, at the fact of Peterpotter, then Barnaby might nearly have won the chance to go home. Which meant that somewhere, everywhere, but basically in New York, his deals and all the real parts of his life were waiting for him with the open, welcoming arms he hadn't known he would ever see again.

Then he remembered that Peterpotter had ruined his life.

Barnaby's life. Barnaby felt the outrage come up in him like a roar. He had been marinating in venom, and now the venom boiled.

No. Holiness stand forward.

Outrage flamed up in him.

Quench it. Put it out. For a soul such as Barnaby, this had to be made an opportunity.

It all boiled into the base of his throat.

Let it go. Let it all go. This was the test. Be a pilgrim.

He got out and swung the door shut behind him and was surprised to hear it latch properly closed. He looked back at the old station wagon, and the door was in fact closed, and Barnaby felt a bubble of affection. It was not a door that closed all the way very often. It was a station wagon that anyone would have thought destined to rust into its oblivion on Winott Point, but it had made the drive all the way here to Oklahoma, to the prestigious heart of Driscoll Hills this morning, and this very morning the driver's side door had just closed like the door of a new car. Barnaby appreciated effort and good faith in all God's creatures but especially in individuals of a foreign tribe, and automobiles were the tribe most foreign to Barnaby.

It was a sign. God's will was loose. The sky was blue. The smell of new grass was rich enough to make a bishop drunk. In other directions from the clean, shapeless bulk of the church were ranks of deep-lawn houses, a number of them on sale at fifty cents to the dollar but still surrounded by tended yards and by full-sized trees. Yes, many of the houses had doors that were peculiarly enormous; where there had been oil, doors were always enormous. Barnaby allowed the doors. He was more pleased than he could have said that he'd seen Peterpotter and that he'd stopped, that he was ready to forgive, that he could add such a powerful goodness to the care-giving that was his primary errand of goodness. No, the caregiving was not something he did just because there was nowhere else on earth he was needed. Tolerated. It was not something he did because Ada insisted he buy his groceries on her tab at the Center Market. It was not even something he did because of his horror at neglecting his own mother.

No, those reasons and a lifetime of others were there, but Barnaby had finally made himself beyond reason into a genuine pilgrim, and this was a morning for all things right, and he walked across the lane toward Peterpotter's broad, green, Christian pasture. Peterpotter had seen him and stopped in his course down the hill, but the tractor still idled, the mowers all still shook and clicked at a distance. Barnaby stepped over the curb onto the grass. The enveloping, new-mown fragrance of life, a fragrance that Peterpotter of all people was orchestrating, lifted Barnaby and carried him up toward the tractor. In the exhilaration of it, he wished by God that instead of khakis and a plaid shirt he had real robes to wear. The robes of forgiving transcendence which he might very well wear when he went back downtown. He extended his right hand to shake the hand of his enemy. He knew as soon as he saw his hand before him that it was unusual because he still had a ways to walk to the tractor and then would have to negotiate around and inside the mowers to get that hand to Peterpotter, but so what. He kept his hand out and felt medieval or Shakespearean, or both if you could be both. The feeling had vividly to do with carrying a flag of good intentions across a battlefield littered with carnage, a flag that offered, that cried out for, that commanded with the gods and the children and the mothers, peace, peace and good fellowship now and evermore.

Maybe Peterpotter had in fact been enough distressed by TJ's death to lose his bearings. Maybe TJ had not, as Barnaby thought, been camouflage for Peterpotter's obsessive recrimination simply because Peterpotter blew his own car lots through bad investments. Maybe Peterpotter really believed that Barnaby had wronged him, and if so, then maybe the apology had been good. As this was good. Both of them had lost everything (though Peterpotter did apparently have a fine mower), and so the apology, painful as it was, had been prelude to this blessing.

He held his hand ahead and went up the hill slowly. Not as slowly as a king (regardless of Shakespeare, those days were gone; besides, his rank was of a different sort now), only slowly enough so that he could keep from falling down when his feet caught in the pitch of the slope.

Peterpotter sat on the tractor and waited for him, exactly as Barnaby would have had it. And it was a different Peterpotter, which was also as Barnaby would have had it. It was Peterpotter in a sweatshirt with the arms torn off, a return to the roots that Barnaby had always imagined for Peterpotter. But it was also Peterpotter in blue jeans and very expensive, very worn out loafers with no socks. From the waist down, which was determining territory in some respects, Peterpotter looked like an eastern gentleman on his fake, weekend farm. Barnaby's father had had precise and fixed definitions for such things, but for Barnaby, if someone looked remotely like a gentleman, that was usually enough. Barnaby hoped that he himself appeared as much a gentleman to Peterpotter. He reached the tractor with his hand still extended and thought that he did.

It was meet and right. That echoed from one liturgy or another and sounded just the note Barnaby intended. He wondered if he should say it aloud. He wondered if, along with forgiveness, he needed to offer another, real apology. He felt as if he could.

He stepped past the small, but not that small, front tire, and looked up over his hand into Peterpotter's tanned face. Peterpotter had aged and lost a good deal of weight. Good. Good.

Barnaby suffused his own face with gravitas and spoke just one word at first to Peterpotter. He said, loudly enough to sound out with truth above the reverberating clatter of the idling tractor, an old and rusting tractor as it turned out, he said, "Peace."

Peterpotter shouted back two words. Much louder than the tractor. Far louder than Barnaby.

"Fuck you."

Barnaby was taken aback, but he had so much momentum that he could not quite stop playing the event into which he thought he'd brought them both.

He addressed Peterpotter and was surprised to hear anger in his voice and surprised not to hear more anger.

He said carefully, "It is meet and right," and right away he wondered what the hell it meant.

"Fuck you," Peterpotter shouted back. "You ruined my life, you piece of shit."

Along with outrage in a voltage that made him shake from his ankles to the top of his head, Barnaby felt some surprise that Peterpotter's Oklahoma cadences had taken on the nasty urbanity of one coast or the other. Peterpotter had been watching too much television. Dry spit was at the corner of Peterpotter's mouth. Peterpotter also had stolen Barnaby's line, and that Barnaby would not stand for.

"You ruined *my* life," Barnaby said, shouted, and only now thought to bring his hand of peace back to his side.

Inside him, his father's voice said icily that this was a guy you had to hit. A Peterpotter was somebody you punched, and not just one swing.

But Peterpotter, without taking his eyes from Barnaby, slammed his own fists at whatever were the gears around his knees and his crotch, and the tractor lifted itself in a roar that drowned even the sound of outrage from inside Barnaby's ears.

The mowers joined their noise with the tractor. There was nothing pastoral in that when you were close to it. It was loud like the end of the world.

As he tried to think how to reach Peterpotter with his first punch, Barnaby shouted again, in vain against the noise, "*My* life."

But that wasn't the issue. Or it was.

The tractor was in motion.

Peterpotter was making a long, silent bellow of attack from inside his machinery's horror of grating, clanking, ever-faster churning, and the mowers were upon Barnaby.

Sure, Barnaby was a New Yorker, or he had been. Also a big shot in La Cote, those were the days. So what? Had Barnaby and his supposed eastern friends taken advantage, as Peterpotter had implied at the apology? Had Barnaby wheedled information with what Peterpotter had called his Yankee accent? Had he gotten any information at all? With which Peterpotter had been betrayed? Barnaby had positively enjoyed coming to Oklahoma for that brief idyll in the days when Ada was Ada, and he had only seen what everybody else in town saw, and then gotten his tip from Ada and from his dead father. And as to Peterpotter's contention at the apology that Barnaby thought he deserved too much, had Peterpotter thought he deserved four desserts and an airplane? Not to mention a newsstand? Had that kind of behavior been healthy for TJ?

No, Peterpotter had done it to himself, and any baseball-card-trading altar boy could have told him so. Peterpotter had put up all his cards to buy a lemonade stand in November because that's what everybody else was doing. So it snowed, and the price of oil collapsed.

Barnaby had happened to be passing through and had seen what was up. Then he'd made a bet with bookies who handled that kind of action for fun. Sold short, nothing wrong there; he'd had a hunch and gone home and bet that oil would lose, and it lost. Barnaby was completely outside the solar system of Peterpotter's misery. The old ladies who got punched in the nose and lost their cafeteria jewels, well, Barnaby felt for them. Still, Barnaby had made a good bet was all, a terrific bet, and all of a sudden got lots and lots of baseball cards, and free lemonade too, exactly as Peterpotter was saying good-bye to all he ever had and all his in-laws and dependents had ever counted on. Put like that, Barnaby could see where Peterpotter might have some envy. But this was life. You didn't crucify your fortunate neighbor. You pulled up your own God damned socks, as Cain said to Abel.

No, no. That was just businessman's vernacular.

But in the spirit of that vernacular, had it been a mistake for Barnaby to have come back to Oklahoma City in a four-thousand-dollar suit and let everyone know he was hoping to pick up a private plane cheap?

Perhaps so.

Had it been today's mistake not to throw rocks?

Fuck. That was how he might have had a chance to get at Peterpotter when there was still time. How had he never thought, on such a biblical errand, to keep a bunch of rocks ready in his pocket? Barnaby Griswold was a fighter; the tigers in La Cote would vouch for that. Neither Barnaby nor the tigers had any idea where Driscoll Hills kept its rocks, but Barnaby wished for all he was worth that he had them in his hands to let fly right now.

Though, as it happened, he didn't have pockets at the moment, and his hands were not free. Wearing gym shorts and an old whale-watchers T-shirt, Barnaby pedaled his stationary cycle in the second row of cycles at the good, modern Driscoll Hills Y and stared at his RPM readout and breathed in rhythm with his pumping legs. And even at this distance of time from the wreck that had marked his life, the word that had for so long during the wreck been his mantra in anything rhythmic, in booze, in cigarettes, in quitting them both, that word crept back into the rhythm of his cycler's breathing. Shit. Goaded by the recent encounter with Peterpotter, it sprang to size and volume, repeating and repeating. Shit. Shit. Shit. Shit.

Barnaby had dived head first out away from the blades and been so amazed that Peterpotter really would have killed him, so

equally amazed at his own agility in evading mortal peril, that he
had simply sat on the grass until it became clear Peterpotter was
turning and coming back for him. Then, because the tractor was
a clumsy weapon when deprived of surprise, he had thought he
could walk away with an air of dignified loathing. Finally, as the
tractor and its mowers and still inaudibly bellowing Peterpotter
closed in on him once more, Barnaby had had to run for his life
back to the station wagon like the chicken he had always been,
no matter what he told the tigers at La Cote. After which he'd
had to knock on Ada's door in the Picadilly Manor for the official morning session of the pilgrimage.

"Hah."

Barnaby shouted out loud to clear away the shits.

He looked around himself. He hadn't really shouted, but
he had made a noise and a couple of guys looked at him. Only
a couple. Hah was a burst of breath, which was fine in a gym.
He had not, thank Christ, been saying shit out loud again and
again. He didn't want things to have come to that, especially not
now when he was so long past the worst of it. And he was past
the worst. Sure, life was hard—strange was a better word—but
Barnaby Griswold always landed on his feet. He had this pilgrimage to play out with Ada before he went back to work, but
he would play it out and win it. He would bring Ada to sus-
tainable contentment, which seemed at bottom to be what the
pilgrimage wanted, and that would be that. A month. He held
his fingers to his throat and looked at the big, school clock on
the wall. His pulse was fine.

And, yes, all right, Barnaby had made a very avoidable mistake.

He had rubbed it in.

He'd genuinely hoped to buy an airplane cheap, but he had
known he was rubbing it in. A cardinal rule for God sake.

He'd looked up Peterpotter before he knew that Peterpotter
had lost his entire wad, and he'd asked if Peterpotter knew of any
nice planes coming available since the boom was over. Had he

asked specifically about Peterpotter's plane? Peterpotter's pilot? Oh, Barnaby. Oh, hubris.

Oh, Peter fucking Potter unleashed. People who'd lost bundles in Oklahoma, people Barnaby'd never heard of, suddenly knew who Barnaby was. Peterpotter taught them who he was, and taught them to hate him, and they did hate him. They came after Barnaby because they didn't know anybody else to go after. Peterpotter made up apocryphal conspiracies around Barnaby, and even sensible people believed him, and Barnaby's feet were held to the flames. It went into the legalities and far beyond legalities. In Oklahoma City, people needed a foreign enemy; they needed a Slime From Away who'd ended up with the town treasure. The lives of an astonishing number of people seemed to depend on collaring that poor Slime and ripping his arms out of the sockets, and Peterpotter made them know that Slime was Barnaby.

"Barnaby, Barnaby, Barnaby," went the punching of his legs on the bicycle. "Barnaby, Barnaby, Barnaby," went his mother's voice as she rocked him in her lap when he was much too big for it. He was fourteen, and no friends had wanted him during a boarding-school vacation, so his mother, impulsive with her afternoon cooking whiskey, had secretly held him and bounced his large head and spoken aloud his name.

"Barnaby, Barnaby, Barnaby."

Oh God, what a comfort mothers were.

He wiped first one side of his face and then the other on the already wet shoulders of his T-shirt.

Thank Christ he sweated like a pig, because you didn't want the other guys at the gym to know you were weeping any more than you wanted them to hear you calling out, Shit shit shit.

Not that it was real weeping.

Not that any of this was appropriate preparation for the battles that lay ahead on this evening's miles of pilgrimage.

So buck up for God sake.

What was fortunate was that while he had been riding his stationary bike, Barnaby had also been surreptitiously keeping track of a girl who was a regular at this time in the early afternoon and whom he kept surreptitious track of every day. She was a girl about whom he had even begun to feel a proprietary interest, which he was at liberty to feel because she was always alone and because she wasn't pretty in the way that rang bells in Oklahoma. Her hair was more rusty than blond, kinky instead of straight or bouncy, and tied back in a coarse, brushy ponytail instead of loose. Also she had just about no tits. With her cheekbones and her high forehead and something intelligent about her lips, she looked like an off-the-range girl from a good family in the east. She looked like a girl he had learned to understand as pretty back somewhere in the provincial, earliest beginnings of his own history. Awfully pretty, really. Which was odd in its way because Barnaby, just like the Oklahoma boys, was somebody who usually preferred fake blonds with big tits. It had always, he thought, in fact been tits that had set off his alarms, and yet what this girl had were great legs and a terrific ass.

So, good. Buck up, one way or another. And if what bucked you up was outside the strictures of your order, well, there you were. Life was no game. The parable of the wheat.

Barnaby swiped at each shoulder once more to get the God damned weeping out of his eyes, and he looked over at her. No more surreptitious. She was standing there next to her mat, and she was stretching one elbow and then the other up beside her head. Barnaby recognized it as the last sequence of her stretches before she went outside for her run. Stretching like that and no tits at all. Barnaby was amazed he found her so attractive. He stared at her legs. He made his face into a leer. Who said he was a mama's boy? Who said he was crying? Barnaby Griswold never cried in his life. He was a guy on the stationary bike at the gym and he was ogling a woman. He was thinking about getting laid. He was a man. Was there any question? He looked her dead in the eye and leered. Some of the guys around him would notice even if most of them were on their way out or already gone in their short-sleeved shirts back to real Oklahoma jobs.

Shit. She was looking at him.

Oh shit. He was staring at her with a face he could not imagine, and she stared right back at him.

Worse. Jesus. All the years he'd prided himself on not being a crybaby, and she knew he'd been crying. She was across the room and her face was the practiced mask of pedigreed girls he'd never dated in beach summers thirty years ago. But she absolutely knew he'd been crying.

All right, then. She knew, and he was grateful. At least she wouldn't believe the leer. She would only know that he was an old man, almost old, who cried when he thought about his mother and about what had become of himself, a man who wanted an old woman's guiltless safety of dying.

She let down her other elbow. God, but she was pretty. He couldn't look away. What did it matter now?

She looked away as though she had never seen him in the first place.

She walked out for her run. Gone.

Barnaby was almost alone among the nine bikes. He was alone. The person on the last bike in the corner was actually something on the wall, one of the colored posters of body parts and muscle diagrams.

Did Barnaby yearn for the tigers in the wallpaper at La Cote? He did. He missed the smell of low tide and he wanted tigers and he wondered if the pretty girl knew he was afraid of Peterpotter. He wondered if she knew he had stained his khakis running from a lawn mower.

Was it possible that she was the one? A real chance, a last chance after his beauty from the Winott Cup? Could she have been looking to him with destiny in her heart and seen him, just as he'd been seen in the tennis match, at the one horribly wrong moment that told the truth about him?

And now she was gone. Lunch hour was over. A single crazy person in a muscle shirt lifted free weights before the mirror in the weird, far lifters' corner of the room, getting ready to shoot all the people who had ever been rude to him. And why not? Beyond, in the glass room with the machines, an ancient man in short pants and cheap wing tips wandered from machine to machine, sitting and touching the handles. In an hour, kids from a phys ed class at the private school next door would come in, and if Barnaby were still around, he would be no more noticeable to them than mulch.

Would his pretty girl ever notice him again? If anybody believed in second chances, it was Barnaby. But after this?

He thought of her standing across the room by her mat, standing up straight as a post and at the same time supple as willow, with tights on for her run, with a gray T-shirt that almost lifted high enough to show her stomach when she lifted one elbow and then the other, with her kinky, rusted hair dull in the gym light but pretty to him, with her eyes dull on purpose but with high fine cheekbones which made him imagine her eyes would shine when she smiled. With her chest like a boy's except that the nipple of first one breast and then the other pressed out hard against her T-shirt. Did they press out? And she looked right back at him and knew he was undressing her.

Shit. He was getting an erection. He'd finished his time on the bike, and now he'd have to stay on for another couple minutes. He leaned forward.

Just as well to go back to Wimbledon, today, to take his shower.

And in his bungalow on Wimbledon, after his despicably ardent but refreshing shower, he ate his carrot, cottage cheese, applesauce, and dry cinnamon-raisin English muffin. Well and good. Sometimes in every cloister, during sieges, when the dark forces were prowling, when everything was coming due, there had to be a letting off of steam. And then the business of the cloister could resume, as it resumed now on Wimbledon.

As he ate, Barnaby, in the great tradition of cloisters everywhere, summoned history and culture.

He surrounded himself with knowledge of Aristotle and Bismarck and Abigail Adams. He robed himself in Alexander the Great and Catherine the Great and Cotton Mather. He cast his lot, today and every day as he ate his lunch, with London and Spain and Virginia, with the tidal stench of the Atlantic and with dear Winott Point, however far. In this fashion he held at bay the lesser and more dispiriting history of Oklahoma such as he knew it; he pressed his crosses and garlics of knowledge resolutely out against the vampire encroachments of Ada's condominium in Picadilly Manor and his own sanctuary here on Wimbledon, against courtroom apologies and every Peterpotter.

He sat sideways at the gouged dining room table that had somehow survived the damp in the garage on Winott Point—a table too sorry even to have had a public life in a summer house. He looked across the no-longer-red back of the sofa, bleached like sand from its winters and summers of retirement on the sun porch of the Point house. He looked past the sofa to the built-in bookshelves filled with World Books stolen from the Point house living room.

When he'd flown back after Ada cleared, to get the station wagon (allowed him by the settlement on the condition he get it off the property) and whatever other provisions might sustain a pilgrimage, he'd been earnest and honest about the divorce settlement to the last inch. Except for the World Books which were forbidden him. He'd known they wouldn't be missed, and his reason for taking them was that he himself would use them; he would read in them every day and get himself a surer sense of that grid of things a scholarly pilgrim was supposed to know, a grid he had let slip by him from the very earliest grades of elementary school.

He looked across at the World Books, and he could hear Win instructing the girls to rack their brains for anything else they wanted specified, and something in the drama of domestic gore, the final shucking off of Daddy, must have driven the girls to think with possessive tenderness of the twenty-two aging but barely used blue volumes. Surely it had been their subconscious gesture of affection for Barnaby. Win from the first had disparaged the whole notion of World Books, and the girls had pretty much taken Win's part, had become real students and gotten themselves real educations. By the time they might have used the books, the girls were already into better source material in the library. It was only Barnaby in the family who had a brick-layer's ignorant fondness for the idea of knowledge. So Barnaby chose to think that the girls had had him tenderly in mind when they told Win's shearer of sheep that the World Books were most essential to childhood's ravaged memories and must must must be sheared from the beast who was already so nearly naked that it couldn't matter anyhow.

Must must must and the beast nearly naked. That was how Barnaby used to talk happily to the girls about life's distractions, about the shearings of people not named Griswold, and the girls had loved him whether he deserved it or not, he knew that they had. He wondered now (now that they had the money themselves) whether the girls ever thought of him as other than the beast of the stories they told to their friends. He wondered if they could possibly care that he had given them one last thing in the Winott Point Tennis Association. He hoped they would learn to care, and not just because it was the last thing he could ever give. The association mattered to Barnaby, and one day he was sure it would matter to them. Even though their membership should have been ensured by their eventual ownership of the Point house, a membership like that could slip away if you didn't pay attention. He hoped they told the shearing of the beast entertainingly. He hoped they were fine and their friends laughed.

But the World Books were the point right now, because the books had become a beacon and a staff for Barnaby as he wrestled to comfort Ada's broken rigging and to comfort Happiness too, and now comfort even Peterpotter it seemed.

For that sort of work you needed the help of books.

Good books made perspective possible, and resolve followed perspective, and rededication to goals rightly followed perspective. And the goal here, never forget, was not pilgriming on forever, but returning to New York where you could work in the securities business and make back enough money to live happily ever after and take your children for drinks at the St. Regis. Just like the old days.

And indeed, once Barnaby had made his camp in his bungalow on Wimbledon, he had begun to read the World Books, and to improve for the effort. He read up on his colleagues the Pilgrims and dabbled with satisfied familiarity in Puritans. He remembered cutouts of hats on grade school windows which were either pilgrim hats or witches' hats, and he remembered the smell of paste and how its congealing gum rolled on his fingers. To read and remember and eat lunch (which was the best time for study) and keep the glossy pages clean was not easy, especially during the handheld dessert that he often allowed himself, so he began to sit sideways at the table, as he did right now, through the whole of lunch, and simply look from a distance across the back of the sofa at the World Books over there in their shelf. He looked at all the volumes at once. He smelled the paste of elementary school days and let all the knowledge come to him by osmosis.

Today, during his nap after lunch, he daydreamed about a personal library of his own in a penthouse cloister, with an honest chaise for book-drugged naps and with French doors to the Central Park reservoir.

How sad to wake, but by the time he'd gotten up and swept a bit in the backyard, which was iron beneath its sparse implant of grass, by then actually he felt rejuvenated, and it was time for Ada and their Friday dinner out. That Barnaby found himself looking forward to the dinner told how very tonic knowledge and a nap were in combination. He put on fresh, pressed khakis and a clean shirt and an old sport coat and stepped back into the big sneakers that had been new for his match with Kopus. To wear sneakers all the time was another improvement in life, right along with knowledge. Barnaby bounced in his sneakers. A night out. Two in a row, by God. It would be dark by the time dinner was done, which would make it seem like a night. And Ada was buying.

On the way to Ada's he drove past the morning's battlefield, half imagining that Peterpotter could still be there and that now, in evening calm, a generous, forgiving truce would blossom after all. In less than twenty-four hours Ada and Happiness had even given him a new birthday, and he had faced in person again Peterpotter's loathing, and he had revealed his weeping, lecherous everything to a beautiful girl. That kind of twenty-four hours could suggest anything was possible in the secret world of pilgrims and catastrophe. But the hillside was mown and stilled, and there was only a curious something that looked magnetically familiar in the loose cuttings where the mower had come away off the curb.

Barnaby got out and looked, and it was one of the baseball hats with wings that the go-go president of the Old Ladies Bank had worn. It was in good shape. It still even had its squeeze bulb and the wire to the wings. As he tested for flappability, he felt he was holding the archeology of his own life, and that his life was ancient.

Then he felt a surge of tenderness for the fact that Peterpotter carried the hat around on his tractor. Did he wear it when he was out of sight of everyone? And why? No, Barnaby didn't want to know why. He would find Peterpotter and give the thing back to him. It was too painful to contemplate.

In the meantime, he put it on. Maroon with white wings. Good colors for Barnaby.

And then when he stood beside Ada's door in the silent, airless hall of the Picadilly Manor at four-thirty, regardless of his hat and his knowledge and his nap and his sneakers, regardless of the balm he felt from his cathartic run-ins with Peterpotter and the beautiful girl, regardless of the fact that all was well and soon he would have pilgrimed his goodly way home to the perfumes of low tide and money, Barnaby did not want to knock.

He thought of his father shrinking down inside his flannel suits and sitting stoically upright until he managed to die when no one was near except the asshole from the mortuary who put him in a bag and cremated him before anyone else on earth had any idea there'd been a death. It was a death Barnaby said he admired at the time, but now he thought it was a hateful death and not just because he'd been left with the fluffmeister line for last words.

Before that, he had gone too late on purpose to see his mother in the hospital for what he knew would be the last time. He had hurried unseen past the nurses' station and knocked and knocked and knocked. The door had been open only enough to see the end of the bed, and yet the end of the bed was more than just empty; it was made up for its next patient and there was no evidence of his mother ever having been there, no sign even of the most recent flowers that he'd sent, because he meant to be late. He'd meant to leave her alone, and then when it was too late, he had knocked and knocked, waiting for her to call from where she was hidden, tucked up at the head of the bed, call, "Barnaby? Is that my pumpkin?"

He knocked. On Ada's door, to which Happiness had taped a half-page, full-color turkey cut from the newspaper on the day after Thanksgiving.

He knocked loudly.

He knocked with a sudden enthusiasm that transcended any knocking he'd ever done before. It was Friday night, and it was an auspicious Friday night. Yesterday he'd been given a new birthday and whatever new soul came with that. Today he'd been given, one right after another, Peterpotter and beauty. It was a

Friday night to make things happen, a night when he knew that he had to gallop blindly ahead and bring the pilgrimage to fruition no matter what.

On the other side of that fowl, which had survived Thanksgiving but was doomed for Christmas, at the instant of Barnaby's knock, Ada bleated her courting surprise.

"Oh!"

Barnaby didn't wait for Happiness who locked with the same rigor she decorated.

He threw open the door, and he burst into the apartment in a hat with wings instead of a cape.

"Ada!" he hailed, and he was so loud and large that he did surprise her.

And she made an "Oh" for real. She straightened up in her chair at the hall desk where she always kept herself in expectation whenever Barnaby was expected, and to her credit she looked as pleased as any actress should who has imagined a scene and brought it to life.

"Did I surprise you?" Barnaby called, louder still.

"You surprised me," she said with pride. Then she saw his hat and called, "Happiness, go get one of my hats down from the top of my closet, the one that ties under my chin." Happiness passed by on a course for the bedroom, and Ada said to Barnaby, "I always looked well in hats."

Barnaby pointed at her desk and shouted, "Checking out the mail?"

He shouted it loudly enough to be heard in the parking lot where the day maids were loading the afternoon silver stolen from other widows into large, battered Oldsmobiles.

"Yes," Ada said, loud herself, more delighted by the moment at the drama of Barnaby's enthusiasm, holding up the handful of bills and new circulars that the mailman delivered every day in place of the royalty statements that once had been common.

"Did we make any money?"

"No. I was expecting a lot of oil checks, but not a thing. Are you going to leave me?"

"I'm going to have to leave you, Ada. I need a rich woman."

"I knew it," she said, and she laughed with her head back like a debutante in a convertible as he took the grips of her chair and turned her for the living room. She waved one hand behind her head just like the pretty girl at the Y stretching an elbow to the ceiling. God but she had been pretty, the Y girl.

Ada's stretching tightened the folds of her sweat suit (pink, Happiness had her in this evening), and that stretching and tightening flushed air out of the sweat suit so that Barnaby was bathed by condensation in which was distilled the smell of death that described the apartment.

Fine. And instead of withdrawing from the long fingers so slackly covered by parchment slick that once was skin, he let Ada's knuckles strum his belt buckle. Then he took that hand in one of his own hands and steered the couple of yards to the coffee table with his free hand and with nudges of his hip. Ada's fingertips pried a hold into his wrist while she tried to think of something to string out their banter.

At the coffee table she let go and brought her head upright as Happiness arrived with a soft, tan, turbany hat that reached down as though with ear flaps into ties that went under the chin. It was an expensive hat once, with a mannered elegance that suited Ada, and Barnaby nodded powerful appreciation.

"Oh. I know what I was upset about," Ada said, and her tone went to enthusiastic seriousness, and Barnaby sat down into expansive readiness on the sofa. Really, Barnaby was at the top of his game, pilgriming like a house afire. "Happiness?" Ada called over her shoulder. "What was it this afternoon? The

Declaration of Independence? That your television minister was talking about."

Happiness made the ties into a bow among Ada's dewlaps and then stepped around on the good gray carpeting of the living room to face Ada over the issue of the Declaration of Independence and over the coffee table. She wore her white, synthetic pants and her pink synthetic shirt with its brave, unwrinkleable ruffles. She also wore the pale, doughy, infuriatingly kind face of intelligence never received and never missed, the face of every soul who knows they will fail and tries hard just the same and never thinks to hold it against the people who do well without trying at all. For just a second Barnaby wondered whether Happiness might not be a role model for some new reality when his suspension ran out. Because her sorts of people did always seem to enjoy themselves. And Barnaby was already pale; he was ordinarily kind; it would be fun to become doughy again.

"The Declaration of Independence?" Happiness said. "Or the Constitution? I think that he was saying the Constitution."

"Really?" Ada said, in a rejoinder of absolute and earnest collaboration. "Perhaps it was. Yes, I think so. The Constitution. It's the same man every afternoon, and this afternoon he was right."

No, Barnaby thought to himself when he heard this.

He had more than one responsibility on this pilgrimage. He had World Books back at the cloister, and he could not let Happiness and Ada wander into wrongheaded discourse on the Founding Fathers. He held up his hand to stop them in their tracks, to prevent civilization from sinking another notch.

"Did I tell you," he said, to bring things at least back into the relevant sphere of Happiness's afternoon television evangelist, to avoid himself, Barnaby, having to lecture sternly on profound American documents, "did I tell you that I looked up Nebuchadnezzar? In fact the whole Fertile Crescent has become a hobby for me."

The Fertile Crescent?

Nebuchadnezzar certainly was one of the names invoked by the evangelist to puzzle Ada and Happiness, and Barnaby did not completely lie; it was very much on his biblical mind to pull out the N volume and to look up Nineveh as well. He'd also promised to do the Assyrians and Babylon. The thought of research always appealed to him. The research itself, alas, drove him away, a weakness of his in the securities business too, though not a crippling one.

But the Fertile Crescent.

This was a good, resonant phrase that had not come from the television preacher. Had it come out of his daughters' homework? Out of his very own classwork in fourth grade at the Hoyt School? Barnaby remembered right this minute that the Fertile Crescent was the place where things began. Was it possible that the grid of essential understanding really was in place inside of Barnaby despite everything, that the truths of Western civilization were only waiting to be dusted off now that he needed them to finish out his pilgrimage and get himself home? A scholar of the fucking Holy Land. In a month's time, who knew; if the investment business did not beckon after all, he might be ready to teach.

"You should come over and watch with us," Happiness said.

"I beg your pardon?" Barnaby said.

"Our afternoon program," Happiness said, joyously alert to a weakened victim (as she supposed) whom she might snag and reel into that world of hers where she had God to share. As if Barnaby didn't have a piece of that world himself. Though Ada was certainly in Happiness's corner of it now. Did the fact of Ada joining up only after the big stroke say something about a ruthless side to Happiness? Dim, relentless Happiness? Given a workforce of a dozen Happinesses, Barnaby might make his fortune back with a boiler room telephone sales operation. What would he sell? Penny stocks? Religious aphorisms? There might be a little seed money from Ada who would love the sleazy risk of jail. But no, Ada didn't have anything to spare. And even in the abstract, Barnaby didn't feel the smallest spark of ambition to make any kind of fortune. Really? Gad. That was a discouraging thing to think, also quite false.

"Yes," Ada said about something else, and Barnaby snapped himself back into the focus that pilgrims had to maintain if they hoped to reach, tonight, by God, the end of the trail.

Happiness continued to nod to the notion of him coming every afternoon and watching the Bible channel with them.

But Barnaby shook his head at Happiness and mouthed a soundless "Gym." Then he flared his shins to bend his knees, because invoking the gym on a good evening made him feel like an athlete.

"Yes," Ada said again. "And what the preacher said was that this country was founded on religion. The Constitution demands religion. But now the enlightened liberals, the humanists, the seculars, have gotten around that and forbidden it. You can't even say a prayer in school. Where else would you learn? The Founding Fathers knew. And now it's everywhere on television, and you only have to look at the newspapers to see here in Oklahoma City. All those vans kidnapping shoppers from the parking lots of the malls. I never would have believed Oklahoma City could get worse, but it has. And the Constitution forbids it."

"No," Barnaby said. "Demands religion? That's not true."

He couldn't be sure quite how it was not true, because what came to him in the way of academic ammunition for the moment were Tigris and Euphrates. What were they? Rivers in the Fertile Crescent. Suddenly he knew that, and he felt a flush of pride and reassurance like discovering a bearer bond for a million bucks in the back of the closet; the grid was there. Barnaby Griswold had his wings and he was flying. He would have to find Peterpotter and thank him.

And of course it was in the ways of Peterpotter's world (once his own world, and soon to be his world again) that Barnaby saw through Ada's television huckster. Here was a guy who preached about Nebuchadnezzar and Nineveh, accurately as far as anyone would know, and then started using a fraudulent Constitution as his sharp stick at people's pockets. Barnaby had been around long enough to recognize used cars and desert land schemes behind that. It was not a technique Barnaby had tried very often, but there had been occasions.

Ada, meanwhile, was adamant. "It is true. He said so this afternoon. Happiness heard him. And it's written in the Constitution: there must be religion. Tell him, Happiness."

It was a real conversation about vital issues, and Barnaby was racking up goodnesses. How many conversations like this had there been? Not many. Just as Barnaby was almost back, Ada was back, recovered in mind if not body, available to real and continuing pleasures. Barnaby had done what he'd come to do, and here was the brow of the very last hill. Redemption and expiation were at hand.

Happiness nodded happily, and Barnaby shook his head, waiting confidently for the grid to provide him with something of a more appropriate tenor than desert land and the Tigris and Euphrates.

The Federalist Papers? Did they have anything to do with religion and the Constitution?

"Oh, God," Ada said, and gripped the sides of her wheelchair in a way that demanded Barnaby and Happiness look at her with a different order of attention.

"What time is it?" Ada said more loudly, and Barnaby and Happiness looked to one another for a moment as though caught unprepared in their class on quantum mechanics.

"The restaurant opens at five," Ada groaned to herself, and Happiness rushed to bend over her, thrusting a forearm and its wrist-watch into Ada's lap, a Bugs Bunny watch.

Could you trust emergency blood pressure to such a second hand?

But Ada was in a fury past watches.

"Late," she cried, very loud again, and now she gripped and shook the sides of her wheelchair so hard that her fingers looked like steel, only white, pure bone, and Happiness and her Bugs Bunny watch were frightened back, and the elegant hat slid to one side like a loose saddle.

Barnaby squeezed his own hat into flight, hoping to contain things.

But, "Don't anybody come near me," Ada shouted, and then, still gripping the armrests of her chair, she leaned at Barnaby and put her voice into a hiss. "Are you still going to have dinner with me? You don't want to. I know that." Then she threw herself back and shouted, "Happiness, am I dressed? God damn it all to hell. Listen to that. Foul. But, we have to go. She has to be fed. She has to be everything'd. So get it over with. Wheel me out. I hate myself. Late. I hate myself."

The First Amendment; that was where religion and the Constitution met.

But for the moment, he had other things to manage.

He pulled open the door of Picadilly Manor, turned to grip the handles of the wheelchair, set a foot to hold the door, swiveled the chair and pushed its front wheels out over the threshold, caught the closing door again with his hip on that side, and then drove the rest of the way out and felt the door whoosh shut behind them.

Ada went "Oh" in a faint voice of fear and helplessness as Death in the large and heavy shape of the manor door tried to take her.

The diagramming on Barnaby's exit move was simple but not simplistic, and Barnaby managed it both gracefully and dramatically. He admired the practiced illusion of being an athlete, and if torturing Ada was a spin-off, so be it.

Because he had not been a bit intimidated by Ada inside just now. Ada was a power of the first water and had an arsenal of difficult gifts, but the judges, no matter who they were and how they chose to manipulate their card, knew that Barnaby was still pilgriming on, paying everything off and winning his way home. The judges and Barnaby both knew that he was soaring.

Also, of course, Ada wasn't really afraid of the manor door. She made her death-peep to warm up for her Buick which Barnaby had parked in its ready position against the curb with the front passenger door open.

Now he parked the wheelchair alongside the Buick and locked the wheels.

"Oh," Ada said more loudly.

Barnaby stepped around in front of her and said, "Are you ready?"

"Take me back."

He squatted to move her white, geriatric, nurses shoes off of the footrests.

"No," she said. "Please."

He stood over her and pulled her hands up around his neck. She held them there but only barely as he reached to grab under the armpits of the extra pink sweat jacket Happiness had put over her. When he had a good grip on her weight, he said, "One. Two. Three."

Ada said, "Oh, oh, oh," and balanced up almost to standing as Barnaby pulled.

"Help out," Barnaby said serenely.

"One two three," she said. "One two three," and humid air from all the seams and surfaces of her body flushed up out of her clothes.

Barnaby hugged her against him as he turned to the open door of the Buick.

She farted and said over Barnaby's shoulder, "More gas than in Russell County," and let her legs go slack entirely.

Ada was not small, and when she let her legs go slack she handled like a great, loose bag of sand. Barnaby held that bag like her life depended on it (as it did) and backed her against the opening to the Buick.

"I can't," she said with volume, as he tipped her blindly into the doorway toward the seat.

"I can't see where I'm going," she said in nearly a shout, and now her wrists bit into his neck as everything else of her continued to sag limp and his hat tipped forward over one of his eyes. Fitness. Always be fit for the big effort at the end of things. Ask your Friar Tucks and your St. Georges. Ask your Sebastian.

"Duck your head," he said.

"*Oh.*" This was a shriek, and she shrieked it again so that it vibrated over Barnaby's shoulder and off the high, pilastered, fake-door facade of Picadilly Manor. "*Oh?*"

He fed her weight down and in, and then, just before she'd quite reached her seat, he had to let go. The weight was too much to support when he was bending over, and besides, he needed to get a hand up and be sure her head, even protected by its turban tonight, did get under the Buick's roof.

It was with only inches between her and the seat that he let her go, but as she released into free fall, Ada's eyes went wide and she made, very faintly again, much more delicately than before, one last, "Oh," a sound so childlike and so surprisedly polite that she might truly have been looking at Death instead of Barnaby.

Then she was on the seat and it was done, and he straightened his bill and squatted down to collect her sweatpanted pencils of legs and lift those with their nurse's shoes into the car.

As he hugged her again where the weight sat in the middle of her body, to align her in her seat and to get the seat belt around her, she said, "I don't know how you did it. You're a wonderful man, Barnaby Griswold. I'm going to kiss your cheek. There. My only and favorite ex-son-in-law. Take me to dinner. I'll take you to dinner."

Barnaby stood out of her embrace, out of her seat and out of her breath, which was a wallow of unhealthy mold beneath the antiseptic shine of toothpaste Happiness had rubbed in her mouth. He closed her door and took the pad from the seat of the wheelchair and folded the wheelchair and hoisted and slid the chair into the trunk. He reminded himself not to count his chickens as they mounted beyond counting, but there was no need to remind. He was so good at this, so smooth, that it was just plain fun. He was enjoying Ada as he never had done before. He'd passed a threshold, and he was enjoying his pilgrimage. Heavenly.

It was no more than several hundred yards from the walled parking lot of the manor up past the shops around the Center Market and the pharmacy and then across Sussex Avenue to the other half of Driscoll Hills' little merchant village. Near the Center Market and the pharmacy there were usually cars, but not since the boom had anyone had to watch for traffic in the meandering enclosure of expensive strip mall and parking lot that made up the village. Even at five o'clock rush hour and less than a month before Christmas, there were hardly a dozen cars to steer past during a drive to the Dinner Box.

The collapse of her weight in the plush double seat, however, no matter how Barnaby tried to balance up her head, left Ada in a wad, a hatted wad tonight, beneath the level at which she could see effectively what was going on outside the car. So she stared at the glove compartment as if that had become the accident of her death hurtling toward her. She made gasping intakes of air to be ready, and she strangled the seat belt with both hands beneath the bow at her chin.

Barnaby kept the First Amendment in mind, but the drive was no more an occasion to broach serious discussion than leaving the manor had been.

Nor was getting out of the car a moment for talk. Ada did relax her death watch when they stopped, but Barnaby had the physical mechanics to manage, and he wanted to manage those mechanics with the style they deserved.

He parked up the little pitch from the Dinner Box, and Ada said with the fire of someone ready suddenly to begin her night on the town, "Here we are."

Barnaby set up the wheelchair and revolved Ada's bulk and pulled her feet out the door of the Buick, and now when he reached under her arms, she took a practical hold on his neck, careful of the body of his hat as well as its wings and wire, and when he lifted, she engaged what muscles she had and actually stood.

As he hugged her and swiveled her to the chair, she hugged him back and made an effort at shuffling her feet.

When he dropped her down into the chair and said, "Feet," she said, "Feet," and shuffled her feet again in a gesture of helping to arrange the footrests.

Then she said, "Let's go."

They were a team.

Barnaby stood behind the chair, unlocked the wheels, pulled into the clear, checked the nonexistent traffic and aimed downhill.

He held both handles, locked his elbows, leaned over the sparse, gray perm of Ada's head, way over, so that his shirt brushed the brittle curls supported by the perm, and so that also when she put her head back finally in terror at the speed, her skull would press right into his belly.

And he let go.

He gave his weight onto the handles, and with Ada's weight in the front of the chair, they could roll.

They did roll, with Barnaby's big sneakers spread like fins and dragging behind for steering and for a brake on the speed.

But not much of a brake.

"Go," Ada said.

It was an electric ten or twelve yards.

Then, "Stop, stop, stop," and her bony skull was against his stomach.

"I can't," Barnaby said, and went an extra yard past the restaurant to get an extra howl from Ada before he dragged down hard on the left sneaker for a rudder and put out his other foot and stood and paced the wheelchair, in easy and perfect stride, to the door of the Dinner Box. Perfect stride. He was an athlete, and it gave him pleasure. And as they reached the door, the disappointed young woman who worked as waitress was just opening the restaurant for the night, so she could hold the door for them and they could push right in.

"Good evening," Ada said to the waitress firmly. "I see we have it to ourselves. Good. We'd like a corner table. There by the window. That's the best. It's just Mr. Griswold and myself."

Then she leaned her head gaily back to speak up at Barnaby as they navigated the few feet to the table. "We weren't late after all. I made a fuss for nothing, as usual. Oh, well. Can you forgive me? Should I sit at the table in a regular chair tonight?"

"You'll sit in the chair you came in, and like it."

She laughed, and waited while he put on her brakes to see if he had anything else interesting to say.

Which he did. You didn't spend your afternoons in the cloister library for nothing. "The First Amendment," he said when he'd sat down himself, and she heard the authority in his voice and leaned forward over the gingham tablecloth.

She was too low in her chair to get her elbows up on the table, and her fists hooked over the table edge might have been vestigial limbs raised in a scrabbling gesture of cartoon supplication, but her attention was there. Barnaby could see in her eyes that this was not just one of her good hours. This was better than any hour she'd yet had. The adrenaline from rolling down the hill was not a drink exactly, but it did always get both of them going. And tonight they both were going faster and better than ever before since the stroke. The hats were a help too; certainly Ada looked fine beneath her turban. But Barnaby knew this was more than hats and rolling. Ada was back, and Barnaby had brought her back. He had answered his call.

"The First Amendment of the Constitution?" she said.

"Yes, the Constitution," he said with the ebullient anger of a triumph which was both righteous and American. "It specifies in so many words the separation of church and state. Your television preacher forgot about that this afternoon when he said the Constitution demands religion."

"Barnaby, you're absolutely right," Ada said, and now she leaned an elbow on one of the arms of her wheelchair, giving herself a pose of considered intelligence but also catching the lace curtain beside her in the sleeve of her sweatshirt.

Gingham cloths, white lace curtains, pastel pink walls, and portraits by the reigning society photographer of precious children posing insipidly beside dogwoods in spring. Christ Almighty, what a restaurant. What would Michel say? What would the tigers?

Barnaby reached to free the curtain and said, "I am right. Thank you for saying so." He felt generous beyond bounds. He was glad to have brought elevated discourse into such a dining room. He was glad also that Ada's having asked about freedom of the press several weeks ago had caught his attention and driven him to actually open the World Books. Who would have known that freedom of the press and separation of church and state needed to be in the same amendment? Had the preacher, Barnaby wondered, been deceitful on freedom of the press questions also? He was a very busy fraud, the preacher.

"Frankly," Ada said, "I'm not surprised he forgot. In fact, I'd be surprised if he ever read the Constitution at all. The man is a fool. But Happiness loves him and I can't very well tell her not to watch." As she spoke, Ada herself realized she was having much more than just a good hour, and her voice took on a tone not unlike Barnaby's, satisfied indeed to be talking capably of something as meaningful as an Amendment.

Any audience would by now have forgotten his pilgrimage to simply marvel at the happy dance of souls which Barnaby had wrought. But this really was the fulfillment of the pilgrimage; Ada was as nearly Ada as she was going to be, and along with that, because of that, the old Barnaby Griswold, the real Barnaby, was back as well. Who but Barnaby would have known a pilgrimage could come to its spiritual reward in the Dinner Box? And in a month, maybe two if he was going to be frugal at the start of things, he would be back in La Cote for his other rewards.

He nodded soberly about amendments for Ada, and watched three elderly couples, an audience of sorts, all in pastels and country faces, come in the room and sit at two tables, the men exhausted and the women already making it clear that they would put food they didn't want on the men's plates. As he nodded and watched, Barnaby also turned over in his mind Ada's calling the preacher a fool. She was right of course: preaching was a distinct possibility as a line of work for Barnaby, should he ever need work; he filed it away.

"Good for you, Barnaby, for knowing your Constitution."

"Well," Barnaby said. "After all."

"There was," Ada said loudly for the benefit of three more new members of the audience passing by, two old women and an older, addled gent, "there was a time when everyone knew their Constitution."

And with that, they were off discussing earlier, better times, discussing with feeling, stirred by their own attention to it, the very beginning of the country. Barnaby tried once more to place *The Federalist Papers* and then let it go to concur in Ada's outrage at any American president who could compare squads of hired Nicaraguan murderers with Washington and Jefferson and Adams and Madison. Scandalous.

Then, as Barnaby reached his knife and fork to cut Ada's scabrous fillet of sole for her, there seemed to be reason to talk of the arts. Which brought Ada, and Barnaby too, into heydays of personal history. Barnaby could nod well enough at the names of painters and operas he'd once or twice (or more often) been dragged past. He could easily invoke the names of fine restaurants near New York galleries that Ada had admired.

Both he and Ada remained aware of rapt attention from the audience as those folks raked their way through their own soles and corn breads. It was not a dining room in which there could often have been conversation of any caliber. Barnaby recalled briefly and happily his friends the tigers and then made the mistake of perceiving once again the lace and pastel and, most dispiriting, the large, cloying photographs of hideous children.

And it was just then that Ada's hour was up. He looked across the table to see her strike her pecan pie an irritated slap with the bottom of her fork because she could not pry a bite loose.

Barnaby beat his wings once to get her attention and said largely and blithely, "Enough? Shall we move on to the rest of the evening?"

"Yes. Let's go. Let's go home and talk some more."

And he shouted, "Check," like an asshole in the old days, and as they made their exit, Ada recovered herself just long enough to remember the good Sloans at Mrs. Krashauer's gallery, and so they could negotiate around the cheap audience tables in a parade of refined and cosmopolitan momentum. It was dark outside, and the heartbroken young waitress held the door again so that they could disappear into the night with heads and hats flung back but still rightly attached. He got Ada up the hill and into the Buick, and she turned to mush.

She moaned in a whisper, "I'm so tired, I'm so tired, I'm so tired," for all the very few minutes they drove.

She shrieked horribly once as he hauled the limp sack of her out from the Buick and into her wheelchair again.

"Happiness," she moaned as they came in the condominium, and she began picking with both hands at the bow under her chin, but the bow did not come untied, and the hat slid slowly down around the side of her head.

"Here I am," Happiness said. "Right here. Did you have fun? I bet you did have fun. And the Lord brought you safely home."

"Take me," Ada said. "In there. I have to. And then put me in bed. Put me to sleep. That's what I need. Put me to sleep like a dog."

"You're tired. Praise the Lord and pass the pajamas." Happiness took the wheelchair from Barnaby, but instead of heading away with it, she turned it around to face Barnaby. "But first, did you say good night to Mr. Griswold?"

Ada looked up at Barnaby with her hat now all the way down under her chin like a feed bag, with the bow intact on top of her head, and she said in a firm and matter-of-fact voice, "We're dying. This is what it's like."

Barnaby beat his wings.

"Don't be silly," he said.

"Get me pills, Barnaby. I don't want to live. If you love me, get me lots of pills, so I can go when I want. Tomorrow. It's time for me to go, and I want to go like a human being."

Her eyes lost their attention once more, and Happiness turned her around and started off for the bedrooms. "Here we go," Happiness said. "A wonderful time. Good night, good night."

And without looking back, in a slurred whisper but loud enough for Barnaby to hear, Ada called as she disappeared, "I don't want to go alone, Barnaby. You go with me. You're dying anyway."

Barnaby drove the station wagon home to Friday night Wimbledon but did not get out. It was dark and he was all by himself and he could not go in that desolate little house again.

Could absolutely not.

Why?

Because Ada was right. He was dying. Peterpotter and the girl at the gym told him so clearly enough. Ada told him as clearly as possible. There was nothing more; he would never make it beyond his suspension no matter when it ended. He would never make it back to his life. And he knew it. He should have known for years. He had known.

He opened the door of the station wagon and thought of crawling down onto his tiny driveway and curling up in a fat ball in his broken hat and crying like a baby. He was a crybaby and always had been, and he was aware that unless he curled under the car, he would extend off the driveway and onto the loveless tentacles of Bermuda grass which made a tacky, threadbare, wall-to-wall carpet across his supposed lawn. And nobody cared. Was this what it had been like for the go-go president on the way to prison? Had he worn his hat through the prison gates? Barnaby could feel the strength in his legs evaporating just like Ada's.

He stuck a foot out to the asphalt to test whether or not he could stand and walk to his front door if he chose.

Absolutely fucking not. He brought his foot back and shut the car door. Before he spent another night alone in that cot, he'd drink himself to death like his own mother. As quickly as he could. Why wait around? If today weren't the first of December, it would be light for hours more. Would it be better if it were light? No. He wanted it to be dark. He didn't want anybody to see him sobbing on his lawn. He was dying, for Christ sake, with Ada in Oklahoma. Of course he was. He would get pills for both of them, and they could curl away under her covers together.

That was the thought that brought him decisively to his course.

He really would get drunk. His own mother's poison. He had let her drink herself to death and never cared to stop her; for years when he was a boozer himself he had never even dropped by to keep her company. He'd been busy with deals, and there were no more deals. He turned the key in the ignition and frightened himself with the grating howl the engine made because it was already running. The station wagon would die here too. His only friend. Maybe he'd wreck it tonight. He put it in reverse and backed out onto Wimbledon without looking, knowing that it was too early and the wrong street for a real wreck, but hoping nonetheless.

He drove across Driscoll Hills and through the village again to a place his radar had picked up, a restaurant that would have a bar. He'd seen too many cars in the parking lot at happy hour for there not to be a good bar. Expensive cars and not so expensive cars. Barnaby could still recognize a serviceable place to get drunk. Called Doug's, but who the fuck was Barnaby to quibble about the name of the next place he'd throw up in? Would he have to throw up? He'd often thrown up when he went off the wagon halfway through Lent, and now he had been years on the wagon. What had he been thinking, not to drink for years?

He parked and said good-bye to the station wagon and went in.

Perfect. Well-to-do-ish young families eating expensive, fake spaghetti on cheap steel tables in back. Swinging, highbrow secretaries doing motor-skill dip nibbling with bread and olive oil in the dimness near the bar. And along the bar itself were all the honest happy hourers doing the right duty and ordering full-price drinks now that happy hour was past. Good souls. A safe and congenial place to drink unnoticed until he threw up, there, in a large pot of greenery that Doug kept out of the way just for the purpose. It felt like a recognizable challenge. It felt like the old days when he had something sensible that needed doing. He would drink himself to death without even a good club to do it in. True, he had had a twinge when he'd let all his memberships go, but the days of a club carrying you until your liver killed you, those days had ceased with improvements in medicine; the fabled reprobate corner in the common room and the dingy sots' bedrooms all the way upstairs, those were long since history. And just as well, Barnaby thought. Democracy. *The Federalist Papers.*

Beaten, he thought.

You're dying anyway.

You tried your heart out, and then, suddenly, it was over. The point, the match, the career, your whole fucking life. The cloister was in ashes, and the other pilgrims had been asked to work for Disney somewhere, and you were naked in the town square. And glad of it. Tried. Could always say that. But lost it all, and glad of it. The point of the pilgrimage had never been doing good or sneaking back to the lark of easy money, or even passing time. The point had always been to make it clear that Barnaby Griswold really and truly was finished. Dying, dying, dead.

He began his plunge at the bar, and the pretty girl from the gym walked right by him carrying dinner orders out to a table of the young well-to-do-ish somewhere beyond the pale. She walked so close to him that he could have pursed his lips and blown from her left eye the kinky, curly strand of hair that had gotten loose from the rest of her hair which was pulled back tight. Was it golden hair in this light? He'd thought it was red. She was gone before he could be sure. Certainly though she was that girl from the gym who stretched before she ran. Who had seen right into Barnaby's septic tank. Whom Barnaby (was he crazy?) had almost determined to speak to on Monday. A waitress. And more than a waitress—weren't they all? He tried to watch her, and some new guy, a big fat guy like Barnaby used to be, got in the way. God damn him. Maybe Barnaby would get in a fight tonight. He smelled her, imagined he could smell her. Not sex for Christ sake. She smelled like falling in love in the summer by the ocean. Barnaby had never been able to quite do that, when it was the time to do it, as he imagined it should be done, but he knew what it was like. It was just like that pretty girl. And he knew perfectly well that all he could really smell was the garlic and oregano in bad sauces, that and the sweet mash coming off the booze around the bar.

The hell with the booze.

He would wait for her to come back. He would speak to her.

And if she were too busy?

He would wait all night for her.

He would?

She would look at him—Barnaby fucking Griswold, for Christ sake, aiming toward fifty and broke, an almost ex-con wishing he could die with Ada back in the Picadilly Manor— she would look at him and tell him to go fuck himself. Just like she would have done if he'd been twenty years younger. She was that pretty, would always have been too pretty for Barnaby. Only before he had always thought that tomorrow was going to be his day.

And some days truly had been.

No more. No more days, period. He wouldn't speak to his pretty waitress. He wouldn't wait for her. Ada was whom Barnaby charmed today, and there would be no tomorrow.

She came back by him, just as pretty, just as close and without all the food this time, and he watched her pass like an express subway train going the wrong way on an unreachable track.

He stepped to the bar rail and knew that this was the kind of place where, as a stranger, he'd have to spread out and speak up, and he didn't feel he was as large as might be necessary. Yet, lo and behold (friendly Oklahoma), the barkeep stopped before him and made the half smile of every barkeep's eternal question.

Barnaby could see himself through the bottles in the mirror behind the bar. And among those bottles, Barnaby Griswold shook his head at the barkeep.

He didn't order.

He couldn't so much as order a drink, and the barkeep was gone. Barnaby fucking Griswold and he couldn't even drink himself to death. Flunked. Just like caregiving. There was nothing left of him. Right here, surrounded by a lifetime of colleagues, he was done. The muscles in his legs did let go, just like Ada and for real this time, and as he began to go down, as he fell, he began to weep more of the real tears that had become his only specialty. By the time he hit the floor, he'd be making the wet noise of a blubberer. He would try to tell Doug that he'd meant only to throw up in the greenery.

All that, the falling and the tears, was glitteringly full of motion downward, but it stopped.

Men grabbed him under his arms from both sides, and they held him up.

Barnaby had long been a believer in the milk of human kindness that occasionally flowed in the very lousiest saloons. This time, however, he didn't want it. He wanted to lie down and cry on the floor among all the careless feet of strangers.

But they held him up.

"You okay, good buddy? You don't look so good."

It was Peterpotter.

Peterpotter stood in front of Barnaby, smiling, wearing fancy sneakers instead of the alligator loafers he used when he drove his mowers.

"Peterpotter?"

"You got it. Real life. Sorry I missed you this morning."

"No," Barnaby said with the last of what strength he had left, with even some residue from the discarded righteousness of his asinine pilgrimage. "No, I'm sorry. Maybe it really was all my fault somehow. I shouldn't have asked you about your plane. But can we talk about it another time?"

Peterpotter smiled more widely and said, "I don't think you understand," and he stepped up close to Barnaby with his smile.

And Barnaby remembered that he was wearing the hat. He confessed. Finally a genuine confession. He said, "I found your hat, forgive me."

But then Peterpotter shrugged hard, and although Barnaby didn't see it, Peterpotter punched Barnaby in the stomach.

At first Barnaby thought it was only the surprise he felt, and then it hurt. Peterpotter stood in front of him smiling. It hurt, and Barnaby didn't know what to do, but before he had a chance to figure it out, Peterpotter started backing away, and Barnaby was following him. The young men on either side were carrying him. They were large young men, one of them the guy who'd blocked his view of the pretty girl however long ago that was. They could have been TJ's sons from the apology. Wouldn't that have been something? Did Barnaby need to be afraid? He saw the greenery at the end of the bar and thought again about throwing up.

"No, you don't look good at all, buddy. Let's get you some air."

Barnaby didn't say a word. He didn't think a thought except that he'd never been slugged as an adult when he wasn't drunk, and so he didn't know what it would feel like. Only he did know. His stomach hurt. Was he drunk? He felt like he was.

He was outside and around the corner with them, and he could not understand why Peterpotter was running away. But then Peterpotter turned around and ran back, ran right at Barnaby, and Barnaby watched him and wondered without a thought. Peterpotter ran and jumped, jumped at Barnaby from close in, and swung a flying punch into Barnaby's mouth, and then Barnaby's mouth was full and he was falling down like he'd wanted to do before, so there was nothing he could say anyhow. This was probably why some timid souls refused to leave their cloister, but Barnaby didn't care. He wanted the truth.

He curled into the ball you make when you're giving up on everything, and a voice in him said, "Hooray for sneakers," as all of them kicked at him.

He knew he could get up. He knew the hat was lost somewhere, and still he thought he could get up. And then if he made a great roar and charged at them, he might have a chance.

But he didn't want to get up. He didn't want to make any sound. This was what he wanted and what he deserved. He cried silently, and they kicked the shit out of him.

LOVER

His father's time for nature and that sort of thing was the summer, when they were all at the shore, and what his father wanted was for Barnaby to learn about shore life. So there was a book about tide-pool creatures, and on Saturdays for the whole summer he was ten, after Barnaby had spent the weekdays in sailing and tennis lessons and his father had spent that time in town at the office, Barnaby and his father walked along the shore.

There weren't quizzes, though Barnaby knew that the reason there weren't was because his mother forbade it. After a couple of weeks, there were hardly even lectures and pointings out. Still, his father carried the book. His father learned about anemones, while Barnaby stood and wondered why kids that summer thought he himself looked like an anteater. Before the middle of the summer, since it was uncomfortable trying to spend a lot of time at any one tide pool, Barnaby and his father began walking around the end of the Point every Saturday, from the pond and the cove all the way down to the lighthouse, along the boulders and the ledge on the ocean side. After the first few times, his father had found the several pools he wanted to keep track of, and Barnaby had found near those pools the supplies of rocks with which he could practice throwing.

Because if Barnaby practiced a thing, he could do it eventually, and throwing rocks, really throwing them, was something nobody would ever think of him being able to do. If he practiced again and again, which he did while his father checked on other lives in the tide pools, then Barnaby could pick out one split granite boulder a good ways away and hit it; sometimes he could even hit ones when the tide was in and a boulder was surrounded by water. He imagined bringing kids out on the walk, though he wouldn't call it a walk, and saying, "Hey, can you hit that?" and then throwing at a boulder, or at a tree if they were close enough, and hitting it as if it was nothing. Or else he wouldn't say a thing, just throw when he was sure they were looking. Then they would know. Pretty soon everybody would know.

Afterward, if they met people on the road back, Barnaby and his father both said that Barnaby was learning about tide pools.

The next summer was supposed to be the pond summer, the first of several pond summers because there was so much life around a shore pond and there would be individuals of species to follow from year to year. Except that before they had even begun, Barnaby's father accepted the job of managing partner at his firm, which meant him staying in Boston to work on Saturdays all through the summer. Which meant Barnaby could wear long pants to sail in on Saturdays. Which meant, really, that Barnaby's father could not bear to spend another summer of Saturdays with Barnaby.

Barnaby's father, after all, didn't want to be managing partner. Barnaby's father didn't want to manage at all. He wanted to do good law, period; everyone had heard him say that. In the summer he wanted to be at the shore when he could. He wanted to study the pond, especially after having read all the books about pond life over the winter, all the books Barnaby did not read.

The problem was Barnaby.

Barnaby's father could not bear the thought of capturing turtles, of learning where the night heron slept, of recording dates when the swan babies appeared, of mapping the marsh on graph paper—with his son. Not when there was little walking or when there were no rocks to occupy Barnaby for whatever in God's name reason. Not when Barnaby would end up simply standing there like a thumb with his hands in the pockets of his long pants on even the warmest days. Not with Barnaby, for Christ sake, trying to crawl through the swamp edge of the pond and under the lowest thatch of the swamp maples to get near the swan nest, still with his God damned hands in his pockets. Barnaby's father knew that if they spent a summer around the pond together, he would not be able to keep from saying something awful to his son. He knew that the better thing to do was to undertake the abhorrent chores of the firm's management, and to do so on Saturdays particularly, and in that way maintain for himself and everyone else the illusion of love for his son.

Barnaby's father knew these things, and knew that Barnaby knew them too. Barnaby and his father knew them together.

Barnaby wandered through his father's disgust with his hands in his pockets, focused on finding perfect targets to throw at. Which was somewhat the way Barnaby's mother focused on her cooking whiskey, because of course when Barnaby's father wasn't having to spend time with Barnaby, Barnaby's father had to spend time with Barnaby's mother.

So it was arranged that on one Saturday afternoon of what was supposed to be the pond summer, Barnaby and his father would go to the zoo.

That came to be the summer event for Barnaby and his father in the summer after tide pools.

On the given day, Barnaby took the train into Boston by himself for the first time. The conductor knew Barnaby's father and was expecting Barnaby and kept an eye on him, and the near-empty train rattling through bright salt marsh and into the slag of the city made Barnaby feel like this was a special day for tigers and that he, Barnaby, was especially ready to meet them.

The conductor held him by the hand on the platform, and his father was right there, and they walked back to his father's office to drop off something. The downtown was quiet, and his father's office was mostly empty except for the young associates who wanted so seriously and respectfully to please his father that Barnaby could imagine his father as their idea of a tiger. Certainly Barnaby knew from watching the associates that seriously and respectfully was how you wanted to approach tigers.

It was a sidelight during those minutes in his father's office that Barnaby realized he himself wanted the trappings of respectability but did not want a real job. He was only eleven, but he knew.

Then they took a taxi.

Ordinarily his father disapproved of taxis. Legs were intended for walking. So a taxi meant that again this was a day gloriously designed for tigers. Barnaby vowed to himself that he would always take taxis and that he would make an effort to talk agreeably to the driver as his father did. And he vowed in whatever were the words of his heart to always revere tigers, because a train and an office and a taxi to the tigers made the tigers more magical than even Barnaby had understood. To go to tigers was a pilgrimage, and Barnaby no longer regretted that he didn't have on his sneakers. The associates at his father's law firm wore shoes with laces, and so did people at church in his mother's universe. Which was not at all to say that once you'd been respectful you couldn't be friends. Barnaby wanted to hurry for just that reason, so that he and the tigers would have all the time they needed to become friends.

Barnaby's father felt, though, when they first entered the zoo, that it might be good to stop and see the seals.

After the seals, though he knew tigers were what Barnaby wanted to see, Barnaby's father followed the map to the jungle birds, and after that to the monkeys. In order that Barnaby would get the benefit of more in the zoo than just one thing.

Barnaby said, "Can't we go to the tigers?" but he only said it once and he didn't whine. Whining never helped with Barnaby's father, and it occurred to Barnaby that tigers might not care for whining either, so he made himself listen to the birds and he made himself look at the monkeys. In the snake house he pretended to look at the snakes, and back in the bright sunlight he was dizzy, but he made himself strong enough for that too.

All he said was, "No, thank you," when his father asked if he wanted a hot dog before the tigers, and so his father took that extra time to walk by the elephants.

But then.

There they were, and Barnaby was a better person for having had to look at everything else before he got to them. Much more now than an ordinary person ever could, he deserved to know them, which they would recognize. He realized he was tired, because when he saw them the tiredness fell away. He left his father and stood up straight and walked firmly along the path that approached.

Tigers.

They didn't see him yet. They paced.

And Barnaby's father caught up with Barnaby and walked with Barnaby right to the edge of their world. Didn't his father understand?

"Did you study tigers in school?"

His father said that as if tigers, or Barnaby either, could have anything to do with school.

"Were they homework for everyone, or did you do a project of your own? What caught your interest?"

Barnaby ignored his father and hoped the tigers had not heard. He put his hands on the rail and looked through the bars to the tigers, and both of them stopped pacing and turned their heads to look at Barnaby. Only at Barnaby. They were magnificent tigers. They were real tigers. They were orange and black, and their eyes were yellow and as big as baseballs. Barnaby let them know without speaking that here he was. He wanted to smile and to be friends with them right away, but he understood that respect came first and so he slid one of his feet to where they could see that he wore dress shoes.

"What can you tell me about them?" his father said. "Are they Bengals?"

The tigers stared at Barnaby, and Barnaby looked back at them and urged them to pay no attention to his father.

"Let's see what it says."

Barnaby's father went to the board that told about the tigers and began reading silently.

Barnaby looked at his father and then looked back to the tigers and shrugged. The tigers did not make any sign to Barnaby at all, although he wished that they would. He smiled, and the tigers stared at him, and he stopped smiling. He tried to make clear to them that if he were wearing his sneakers he could climb through the bars, but the tigers did not seem impressed. So he let them know that he could probably even throw a rock through the bars and hit whatever he wanted. Wouldn't that be something.

Barnaby held to the rail in front of the bars while down the way his father read.

And the tigers stared at Barnaby as if, despite everything, they knew Barnaby was no more than an eleven-year-old kid out of school for the summer and too big for his age.

He couldn't even say why he was interested in tigers, because he didn't know anything at all about them. He didn't even know if they were Bengals. He was supposed to be visiting; he was supposed to be a friend, and he didn't know what Bengals meant.

He had as good as pretended that he was a tiger himself, and the tigers stared at him, and he was ashamed.

More than anything in the world, Barnaby wanted the tigers not to be disappointed in him, and they were. They stared at him and were as disappointed as could be.

He let go the rail and turned away. He turned his back to the bars so that the tigers couldn't see him.

When his father looked up and saw Barnaby with his back to the rail, Barnaby expected his father to tell him all about Bengals and insist that Barnaby look and then be angry because Barnaby didn't care anymore.

But his father only took his hand and brought him away.

His father led him without a word to the rhinos and the giraffes and the ostriches, and Barnaby ate four hot dogs which he didn't want and threw up out the window of the taxi on the way back to North Station. His father quietly, almost even gently, wiped Barnaby's mouth with his handkerchief, and after that let Barnaby pretend to sleep on the train.

The next summer Barnaby went to camp, and then to boarding school. He became devoted to short pants, and he went to college, and he never so much as imagined another tiger until he ran into those most personable and cosmopolitan of tigers in the afternoon wallpaper at La Cote.

Those were not the same tigers as the ones at the zoo years before, but they had heard about Barnaby; tigers all knew one another apparently, and the La Cote bunch were quick to say that there had never been any ill will toward Barnaby. And just like that Barnaby found himself telling them in their marvelous wallpaper forest, telling them over his right shoulder after he had completed the preliminary subscription on a so-so deal, telling them without any shyness whatever, that for the end of that day at the zoo when he was eleven, for not saying a word when Barnaby had turned away from the railing on the tigers, Barnaby loved his father.

Barnaby told this loudly to the tigers in La Cote, and the tigers could not have understood more completely. They nodded and murmured with every sympathetic appreciation.

And it was with just such an understanding that he opened his eyes in the grimy shrubbery behind Doug's.

He lay on his back, and he was surprised to feel that his legs were straight out. He remembered Peterpotter, naturally, and he thought he'd had the sense to curl into a ball as everyone in a decent city is eventually advised by their pessimistic friends to do in violent circumstances.

He looked up and saw a part of the pale green neon palm tree that overhung the script of DOUG's. He could make no sense of Doug and a palm tree and Italian food in Oklahoma City—he was perfectly aware that the municipality within which he lay on his back was Oklahoma City—but it was mostly of tigers that he thought. He looked at the palm tree and thought, with no basis in research, that tigers could live anywhere.

He raised himself halfway from prone, and he sat.

Inspired, he shifted himself onto his hands and knees. Beneath him was a carpeting of small, porous bits of volcanic decoration which Barnaby had once before (when, he couldn't say) met in the dark. So be it. He didn't bother to look for his hat. The hat was gone. Carefully, sensibly, he got to his feet. Once he was to his feet, he straightened himself with decorous caution until he was erect. This was the sort of procedure he had learned when he was a drunk, and now it stood him in good stead, and he was grateful.

Barnaby was by nature a grateful soul; tigers alone were cause for gratitude.

Because tigers did things. Tigers attacked. It wasn't a question of waiting to die by himself behind Doug's. Nor was it a matter of waiting to be kicked to death by Peterpotter (should he return), much as Barnaby honored Peterpotter's distress. It was not a matter of waiting somewhere else to be drowned in Ada's death, much as he owed Ada and much as he loved her. Did he love her? Of course he did.

The point was, Barnaby had to more than wait.

And he had to more than simply refuse to die.

He had to more than fucking care-give.

Barnaby had to act, and he had to act with passion; he had to act like who he was. Not some simpering pilgrim for Christ sake. This was Barnaby Griswold. Had he been out of his mind?

He didn't yet know what, but Barnaby Griswold was going to do something.

He took a step without thinking and very nearly fell down. If he had really been drunk, he would never have taken such a careless step. He felt as if he were drunk, and was surprised that he was not. He walked with stately care out of the knee-high trailings of black leaves and around the dim, stucco corner for the door. He did not try to figure out from the glinting shadows of the few automobiles left in the parking lot what time it was. The first priority had to be getting back inside to avoid more kicks and punches. Then he could sit down and decide what to do. He could make lists of possibilities. Other people might have made lists at earlier times in life, certainly at some earlier point in a suspension, but for Barnaby this was the necessary moment.

One possibility was to begin cheating on his suspension right away. Or he could begin almost but not quite cheating. He could at least begin making the calls he should have begun making ages ago. Not to Livermore looking for a place to stay, but real calls, to Livermore and all the rest of them, to get his name in the pot again and to learn in what swamp the strangest deals were fermenting (because he knew he was going to have to start back with the strangest of the strange). Yes, because the wrong calls during a suspension would be illegal, but now he would just be priming the pump; now, with just a month left, anything short of moving real money would be legal. "Hello? Remember Barnaby Griswold?" Face it; these were actually calls he could and should have been making twice a month for years now, and some of the people might be nice to talk to besides. Of course he didn't want to refuse evangelism out of hand. Nor lawn work, even if he couldn't count on overflow recommendations from Peterpotter to prime that pump. He wondered if his financial magazines were still in the Dumpster behind the Center Market.

At the door of Doug's, before he went in, he brushed himself off as best he could to be ready for making his lists. You didn't want to look like a bum when you were laying out your future.

But inside Doug's, before Barnaby even got to a chair, was another cause for gratitude. The door bumped shut behind him, and ahead in saloon illumination no brighter than the parking lot, long before he'd found pencil and paper to list anything, was exactly what Barnaby wanted to do.

The pretty girl.

She was stopped in her tracks, by Barnaby apparently. She held her tray at her side, with the darkened, near-empty dining area behind her, and she stared at him.

There had been moments in his life when Barnaby understood that he achieved a presence, rather a prolonged moment just after the Old Ladies Bank deal, but those moments were hardly the rule, and even less frequently, if ever, did they involve girls. Never pretty girls. Still, this prettiest waitress from the gym stared at Barnaby, and Barnaby was resolved to action.

He knew what was called for.

He stepped directly to her. He held out his hand and said, "How do you do? My name is Barnaby Griswold, and I think you are perfectly beautiful."

She looked at him as if she couldn't understand a word, and he turned toward the bar and caught the eye of that good-hearted Oklahoma barkeep and called, "Where are all the tigers?"

Which he knew was a peculiar thing to say, particularly in a place with no wallpaper, but he was overflowing suddenly with new horizons. He was as happy as a clam to be in Doug's. With the hand that the girl had been too shy to shake, he reached for a chair that one of the secretaries must have abandoned. There were in fact numbers of chairs and very few secretaries, so, yes, time must have passed since he was last in the area.

Sitting into his chair he felt vividly for an instant as Ada must have felt when she was falling with blind terror back into the Buick.

But he made it down.

He gestured to another chair nearby, and he smiled at the pretty girl.

She did not register the gesture, which he could understand; she was still on the clock after all. She did register his smile, which was the important thing, and as if in a panic of shyness, she ran from the smile. What long legs she had. She ran in black sneakers and in long, black pants. Above the pants she wore a white shirt that was winningly too big for her; it billowed, a man's oxford cloth shirt with the sleeves rolled up. And before he could list all those ingredients of her dress, she had disappeared through the crowd of other people. Just one long stride, and she was gone, and Barnaby was sorry she was gone. He was also sorry for tigers because it occurred to him in a new light that their quarry too would always run away.

The other people stood around and stared at him, people he'd never seen before in his life. He nodded to them. The first lunge of his attack had missed, but Barnaby was not daunted. He didn't want to use the word *stalk* in the current tabloid climate, but he could understand that there might be a need for patience. Right now, among these strangers who gaped at him, he would be patient in his chair where he was comfortable. No wonder the judge had not let him sit at his apology.

Immediately, his patience was rewarded.

The pretty girl came elbowing her way back through the crowd.

Had he been on television, Barnaby would have spoken about the virtues of patience to his congregation. Had he the time and more quickness in his lips than he felt at the moment, he might have given a little homily to the very strangers before him.

As it was, he steadied himself to watch her go on past with a load of desserts or something. Patience. She had work to do. She was not coming to Barnaby yet.

Except, she was. And carrying only a stainless bowl and a bar cloth, she kneeled down before him.

Who needed to stalk? No, that wasn't what he felt. What he felt was that if he didn't hurt all over he would have gotten up and run away.

She kneeled, and she stared into his face. Since when was Barnaby Griswold afraid of a pretty girl? Since always, for Christ sake, but he didn't feel able to run away, and so he smiled at her with as much delight as before. He pretended it was a pitch.

Along with all the late Friday night bar strangers surrounding them, she gaped at him in a kind of horror again, but this time she didn't leave. Nor did Barnaby leave. That was a real beginning for someone as worried as Barnaby had always been about his aptitude for love.

With a pitch, with deals, he had never worried, and from the very first plunge he had known he was where he belonged. With his marriage, of course, it had been Win who plunged, an Oklahoma only child determined to have an eastern quarry and not sure or not caring about the markings. Barnaby had just kept quiet and pretended it was meant to be, though if he had been someone who bet on the downside in those days, if he'd had the sense to think of marriage in corporate terms, if he hadn't been persuaded (by his mother and father? Gad) that a proper life of love was a necessary undertaking and that it went (true enough) through a part of the forest for which he possessed no maps… But that was all water under the bridge. Right now, he wanted to do something else. He wanted to court this lovely girl for real, but he was a fat boy; the few times he had gotten pretty girls to listen to him before, years ago, he had never had anything to say to them, and he had nothing to say now. He sat now with one arm on the top of the tiny, round, wobbly, steel table, and he could feel whatever the secretaries had spilled coming all the way through the sleeve of his tweed sport coat. He could feel himself failing in a singles bar when he should have known better. He didn't belong in singles bars. Real bars, yes, of course. He was a drunk. But he drank in saloons, in places grown men in good suits ruined their lives and pissed on their shoes. Never in singles bars.

Yet here she was, deliriously pretty and kneeling in front of him. No wonder he was scared.

Was it a singles bar? He didn't think so, actually. He was sore enough that he could hardly remember a thing.

And what was she doing? She was wringing water from her bar cloth into the bowl she held in her other hand.

Now she looked at his face as if his face were a messy spreadsheet upon which she had to concentrate if there was going to be any hope, and she raised the cloth toward his mouth. Was he still smiling? He didn't think so, but it looked as if she meant, considerately, to wipe any smile off of his face. There. That was something he could have said. That would have been funny. He was often funny when he was pitching. Barnaby Griswold, after all. Just now, however, he was not using his mouth and so could not speak even to be amusing.

Instead, he smelled the warm wet of the cloth which she seemed reluctant to go ahead and apply.

Much more than warm water, he smelled her work. He smelled a night's worth of food on her hand and her wrist and on the sleeve of her shirt which came almost all the way down her forearm even though the cuff of the sleeve was rolled back. He glanced at the collar. As he thought, it was a Brooks Brothers shirt. She was from another life than here at Doug's. She might be from his life. Now she might.

He could smell oil and butter which had begun to turn rancid with the length of the evening and with the heat of the place, with her own heat. And mingled in that, he could smell her sweat. It was bitter, and it was hers, and he wished it was his. Was that what he tasted? Yet she only studied his mouth, against which she could not bring herself to press the wet cloth that she held.

A fleeting current of self-preservation passed through him, and he scanned the crowd for Peterpotter and the big friends. He should have thought to do that before, but outside of himself and his family, he had never had real enemies until Oklahoma.

He leaned forward and pressed his mouth, his lips as he understood it, against this lovely girl's damp bar cloth.

With six or eight Friday night stragglers watching him, Barnaby made a puckering and kissed at the cloth of the prettiest girl he'd ever seen. Gym or no gym, he could feel his stomach slop over his belt when he leaned. He was a fat old drunk, and he waited for the other drunks to laugh and to razz him. But he didn't care. This was a brave thing to do. He kissed.

He felt the cloth, and he stared into this lovely child's face, willing her to look at him rather than at her cloth or at whatever it was about his mouth.

Her hair was still mostly pulled back, but it had been damp and had dried now, and so it was loose. Her forehead was high and smooth beneath the frizz of hair that had fallen forward. Her eyebrows were thin but pronounced and wanted to meet above her nose, and that made her concentration appear fierce like an eagle. Her skin had been slicked and dried with her sweat, and still it was the rose and golden color of all the shore girls Barnaby had ever dreamed. Barnaby imagined he could taste her salt and taste the summer with it. Her nose was not at all a beak, but it was straight and strong and proudly there because she held her chin up. Across her cheekbones she had freckles like pale war paint on an Episcopal savage. Her mouth was wide, but her lips were more thin than full.

Her lips were delicate and very smooth, and now they were pressed close, holding everything inside herself except for a drop of wet in the slight, freckled channel beneath her nose. She had a cold.

He could feel the cloth, but he could not feel it with lips.

He felt it with pain, and there was whimpering. Whimpering? Christ, it was him, Barnaby, out loud. It hurt that much. But out loud? He was appalled; people were watching. He was also appalled that it hurt so much, as if his mouth belonged to a museum of precious breakables.

She took her cloth away because of his whimpering, and there, on her sleeve, was blood.

He looked down the front of himself, down an old Brooks Brothers shirt which should have been just like hers, as if she were wearing something of his the way he'd always hoped any girl would do when he was a teenager. And he was covered with blood. Some of it was damp still, some caked; altogether it was a lot, as much blood as if there'd been a pouring.

His own blood was what he tasted.

Oh, no. Oh, no.

Barnaby was a sissy and he hadn't, even when he'd whimpered, realized how much this hurt. Was he proud? Did he want to stand up so the other drunks could get a good look? No, he was afraid. Because, Christ. How had he managed to do this when he wasn't even drunk?

"No," said the pretty girl, and she put her hand and its cloth back in her small, stainless bowl.

No? Her voice was deep and not quite sure of itself and as full of good things as crystal on a summer evening.

"Somebody has to take him to the emergency room," she said.

The emergency room? Barnaby? He looked anxiously up into the faces for confirmation, and the good-hearted Oklahoma barkeep nodded.

The pretty girl shifted into a crouch. She was going to leave him.

"Don't go," Barnaby said, and even to himself he sounded like oatmeal, but she looked at him and she hesitated long enough for him to reach out for her forearm. It was a thin, strong forearm, and he got it, and as soon as he'd gotten it, he couldn't believe he held it. She didn't seem afraid. He could feel her bone and her veins and her skin and the fine hair.

Did she look at him? Did she see him?

She let go her cloth in the bowl, and her fingers were still wet. The water ran in her palm and over the smoothness of her wrist and touched Barnaby's thumb.

He brought her hand back to his face.

She didn't stop him. He wouldn't have made her.

Her eyes were brown and green, and she was there, the same person inside her eyes who was inside the firm tenderness of her concentrated lips.

Somebody alive was looking right at Barnaby.

She absolutely saw him, and as soon as he understood that, he didn't want her to see after all. He closed his own eyes to hide from her.

Still, he brought her hand to his mouth, and even with his eyes closed, that was more courage than he had ever imagined for himself.

He held her forearm gently back and forth, and her true fingertips touched wet and slowly like windshield wipers across his mouth.

He was glad the other drunks were there. The kind barkeep. He would never have had the courage alone. He would have run away even if his legs were broken.

He felt the muscles and the bones of her wrist roll and swivel ever so slightly, weightlessly, soundlessly, full of the same life she held in her eyes and her mouth. She wiped at the pain that should have been his lips.

With his eyes closed, but out loud nonetheless, he said to the tips of her fingers which he knew were red by now from the mess of his bleeding, "I love you."

"You see?" said a voice that could only have been the kind barkeep running the ship at the end of the night. "It's not so bad after all. A mouth gets smacked, it bleeds."

Barnaby opened his eyes and looked up to see the guys on either side of the barkeep nodding, but they looked like citizens who'd never been punched in the mouth in their lives.

The girl took her fingers away from his lips.

She looked at him and smiled and took her forearm back from him too.

She smiled, and he could see her teeth, and behind her teeth, somewhere on her tongue which he could not see, there she was. He didn't know her name. Her lips thinned for her smile, and the smile was happy and worried but a real smile, and her lips were the tenderest lips on God's green earth. He would have told her that, if he'd thought she could understand it.

He would not have told her again that he loved her, though he loved her only more.

His courage was gone.

Courage wasn't something he was used to, so he didn't mind.

She looked at her fingers which were as red as he'd known they had to be, and she arched her eyebrows and rolled her eyes to say Christ Almighty without a word like only kids could do and really mean it.

She dipped and rubbed her fingers in her water like a finger bowl at a good dinner party, and then she smiled at him again.

She smiled, and a sun shone in Barnaby's chest, and she stood up, tall and thin, almost skinny, a goddess who'd come to Barnaby Griswold.

"Thank you," he called out, and she understood that. She made a little shrug that said, "Oh, okay, no big deal," but that said also that she knew what he thought about her lips on God's green earth—that she knew he'd seen her in her eyes and her smile—that it really was a crazy thing to touch his gory mouth.

Then she wiped the shine of snot from under her nose on her Brooks Brothers shoulder and was gone.

He saw her black sneakers go away beyond other people's legs, and he looked up to the good-hearted barkeep for help in managing the practical things now.

A helping hand out to the station wagon.

Directions maybe to the emergency room after all.

It did hurt.

With a month left on his suspension, Barnaby Griswold was as far from a pilgrim as could be. He was courting.

The next day, Saturday, when except for clean clothes he looked far worse than the night before, he went to Ada's for Saturday afternoon dominoes. He had missed his morning visit, but that had been overlooked in the past. He had called. He was a hundred percent on time for the dominoes, and he was eager.

It wasn't, after all, as if he wanted or could afford to leave town yet. Nor, to be fair to the goodness of his heart, did he mean to throw over caregiving altogether; just caregiving wouldn't be all consuming. Even by his own calculations, he owed Ada through the first of the year, and he meant to honor that debt. But the baton of pilgrimage, thank God, had been passed off somewhere in the night, and Barnaby had much else on his mind.

He was sore, for one thing, though he had pills for that. And actually, between the pills and some confusion with his olfactory operations, he couldn't smell. Which meant that the vapors of death were not such a shroud inside the door to the condominium, not for Barnaby anyhow, and he could concentrate on feeling with his tongue at the stitches reattaching the inside of his lower lip to his chin.

Yes, because the ultimate issue had never been anything other than to resurrect a whole and healthy Barnaby, the Barnaby of old who would issue from suspension (and from Oklahoma as things had turned out) with not just the same old gifts and enthusiasms, but with above all the same size, the same cohering mass of self that magically attracted money. For a while he had thought tennis and fitness would recover that size for him, and they had in part. A championship could never be taken away.

Then, out of awkward, perhaps diminishing, necessity, he had thought someone like himself might actually approach his version of magnetic mass through a pilgrimage into deeds as pure as driven snow.

But now.

Now Barnaby's size, and with it all the good things his gravity would once more attract, now Barnaby's size was building itself back hour by hour, minute by minute. And the agent of all this, the combination which opened the lock that athlete and pilgrim could not crack? It was romance, it was a beautiful woman, it was the age-old vitamin of courtship. It was love.

Would Barnaby the lover have the necessary gravitational mass to launch himself back to his true pole on the first of the year? Would he get himself to New York and to La Cote and to one recognizable version or another of his good life on New Year's Day? Yes. He would. He had always known he would, but now the proof was in any mirror. Barnaby Griswold was a different man this morning than he had been yesterday afternoon, and anyone at all could see it.

The truth was that he couldn't wait to show himself off to Ada. She might or might not be able to see in as far as the stitches, but the outside of his face was plenty to look at. His mouth was so swollen and bruised he could have been someone else entirely, a movie star playing a career boxer who was more sexy than Barnaby had ever hoped to be. His eyes, which he hadn't realized were also a problem during the initial excitement about his mouth, had taken on layers of putridly glistening color while he slept, as if the boxer had decided to masquerade in the sunglasses of a raccoon. His nose, blessedly, had not been broken at all, so why he couldn't smell was a mystery, but a happy one; he was left with the smells that had surrounded his very pretty girl last night. All in all, he looked rakishly amused, overpoweringly masculine, just the kind of man who would profoundly interest that pretty girl at Doug's when he dropped in tonight to thank her for her attentions. This was Barnaby Griswold.

Rather than hesitating at the door of the condominium to chat, he cruised past Happiness with only a cheery hello so that he could observe her without having to suffer her reaction frontally.

She stared, and as best he could tell, she might have been expecting Barnaby to show up looking like this. It didn't feel to Barnaby as if she disapproved, exactly, but clearly Happiness was not pleased. Good. He'd made an impression.

He was wearing an old turtleneck shirt, which was not his usual style unless he was shoveling snow and which had been hell to get on over his face. It might have been the turtleneck that put Happiness off. If so, too bad; boxers wore turtlenecks after a fight. Also the girl at Doug's would see a new side to Barnaby from the Brooks Brothers shirts. And just the same, he was glad he had lost the beret his daughters had given him for whatever was his last loved Christmas. He would have worn it, and it would have been too much.

But Ada wasn't waiting expectantly at her desk as she always liked to do. Where was she? Did she know already that the pilgrimage was over?

No, sometimes Ada thought mail might not be delivered on Saturdays, and then she abandoned her usual post in the hall to avoid appearing confused by whatever was on her desk. So Barnaby cruised on into the living room. Ada's scrutiny would decide official approval of his appearance, but he already knew from Happiness that he cut a splendid figure. Who would have thought last night when Peterpotter led him outside that Barnaby would be grateful for a sock in the mouth and then all that kicking while he was down? But he was grateful. He looked like a new man just as he was undertaking the looks-intensive business of love, and he felt in his every fiber ready and able to preach about gratitude. Perhaps television was nearer in his future than he thought. He would have to attend to his list of priorities some time, and evangelism was moving up the rankings. Should he preach to Happiness? That was fertile ground, if ever there were. Happiness, though, with her relentlessness, might turn into a long session. By the time he finished with Happiness, Barnaby could very well look like himself all over again, which was exactly why people preferred to preach on television where the congregation couldn't get you into a dialogue after the sermon.

But should he worry about that, his face healing? Would he have to ask Peterpotter and the big friends to punch him again in another few weeks if the pretty girl wanted him only as a boxer? Oh, come on. Listen. You worked one scenario at a time, and if the deal didn't close before there was trouble, if your scenario didn't migrate into the truth, then you just had to hope a new and better scenario would present itself as necessary. It was not, after all, as if everyone didn't always live next door to the end of things. The market could crash tomorrow, and if it did, there would be opportunities. This week, if you looked like a boxer, you were a boxer. And this week Barnaby did.

Ada, however, was not in the living room.

She was already around the corner and wheeled up tight to the dining room table. She had the dominoes out of the box and turned down. She had chosen her own dominoes and pulled them over in front of her, but she had not yet turned them up. She stared at her dominoes, waiting for Barnaby.

Barnaby checked his watch. On the dot. Not that in today's mood, now that he was limber enough to have gotten out of bed and taken a shower, he was likely to be late for anything. In fact it was going to take all his resources of will not to be first in line when they opened the door at Doug's this evening.

Though, actually, Doug's door was already open. Doug's served lunch, and just that thought was enough to send Barnaby's pulse into a spike.

He stood beside Ada, and she did not look up, so he sat down in his assigned chair from which he could reach her dominoes and adjust things when she made impossible plays.

He leaned his face over in front of her, and he smiled largely and gruesomely, and he said, "Good afternoon, Ada."

Briefly, with stony indifference, she glanced at him, and then looked back to her unexposed dominoes spread across her nice but no-longer-polished mahogany tabletop.

"You love somebody else," she said.

"What?" He stayed leaning toward her, showing her his face, giving her a second chance.

"You heard me. You love somebody else. Fine. Choose your dominoes. I've already got mine. You don't have to worry. I shuffled them. I didn't cheat."

Out of the blue, this came.

And she meant it. She said it all with the stoic, accusatory conviction of a broken heart.

How did she know?

He marveled at her radar. Did Ada, of all people, understand something about love? Ada was one soul Barnaby would have classified, along with himself until just recently, as a thoroughgoing inept in love. Her life, as best he'd gathered, had been bitterly deprived of romance. Her late, long and admirable marriage of friendship (but for Win) was the proof of her deprivation and the seal on her bitterness. One of her favorite lines of martyrdom was that the important achievement she'd managed in her life was to become the doctor's wife, and on hard days, she admitted that that was what her father had thought too. Otherwise, she never mentioned the doctor. And now for God sake she'd had all these strokes.

How could she possibly know?

He smirked.

He wasn't sure why he did. A light, dismissing laugh was what would have been appropriate, and maybe his mouth turned it into a smirk. If so, his mouth, with its swollen and bruised contortions, should have hidden it too. But Ada was oblivious to all those swellings and bruisings that were the large events on his face; she knew about the smirk instantly.

She hunched lower in her wheelchair and swiped the back of her hand like a flipper across what she could reach of the tabletop, sending a dozen dominoes to the floor.

"Go ahead and smirk. Is she a blond? Of course she is. Happiness, come congratulate Barnaby. He's in love with a blond."

All of a sudden, Barnaby was as furtively giddy as a fat boy could be when teased jealously on the playground, when teased out loud for loving the girl he could hardly dare to imagine.

"Don't be ridiculous," he said.

Now Ada did look at him. "Do you deny it?" she said.

Barnaby wasn't dumb enough to actually answer any more of the teasing, but because she was looking at him and because he was confident (how could he not be?) that his face would distract anybody from anything, he met Ada's look. He smiled back at her. He ran his tongue out over a particularly scabby corner of lip.

She continued to stare at him with her question until he was almost giddy enough to blurt out everything. But now he didn't want to blurt it out; he didn't want to jinx his pretty girl by talking about her. To keep from blurting, he squatted uncomfortably down and picked the dominoes up from the good, gray, soup-crusted carpeting beside Ada's wheels. Two double sixes. He was giddy with love, but two double sixes were interesting just the same. Barnaby would have to decide whether to keep those sixes himself or arrange for them to fall into Ada's hand, in which case he'd have to be sure she played them properly and got her points. Ada did like to win. But she also liked for him to win, particularly with the big numbers. Here, in other words, was a moral quandary right up Barnaby's alley: what to do when you can please people no matter how you fluff.

"Happiness. Come in here and congratulate Barnaby on leaving us."

"I'm not going anywhere," he said smugly, and sat back up with his illicit dominoes.

Happiness came to them out the near, swinging door of the kitchen, and Ada said, "Tell him good-bye."

Happiness said, "You look terrible, Barnaby Griswold."

There, finally: acknowledgment, even if it was stern.

"You poor man," she said.

You poor man, that was better.

"He's leaving us for a blond."

"I'm not going anywhere. Would you tell her that, Happiness?" He heard himself trying to sound irritated because Ada would be looking for irritation as proof. Then he checked his watch. He knew he had hours, but he wanted to be sure how many hours, and he wanted Ada to see him checking.

"He's checking his watch," Ada crowed. "He has a date."

He sat silently and let his silence suggest that she was right. He was properly ashamed of lying, and he was nervous about pretending to something he wanted so much. But a date. If Ada thought so, it could be true.

Happiness took his hand and pressed into it two whole bulbs of garlic.

"I could feel evil near you, Barnaby, and I knew something was going to happen. I should have given you these before. Whenever I am not well, or fear illness, I take extra garlic. You can read about it. Even when the Lord is near and the day is bright, I take a regular amount. When your body gets used to it, it doesn't hurt your breath a bit."

"Is she talking about garlic again? Oh for God sake."

Barnaby was moving (because of the garlic? Barnaby was in a state of mind for almost anything, but garlic?); he was moving anyhow beyond his knee-jerk giddiness. And beyond that giddiness was something serious and calm.

"I'm glad to have garlic," Barnaby said to the insistently hovering presence attached to the bulbs. "Thank you, Happiness."

Love. Barnaby was calm and serious with love.

"Well, I'm not going to eat it," Ada said. "Period. Do you hear me? So don't give me any."

Happiness ignored Ada and bent closer at Barnaby. "You need it," she said. "I can tell."

"Actually, I got beaten up last night. That's why I look like this." He spoke more to Ada than to Happiness, and he watched to see what Ada would make of it, if it changed her sense of portent, but she was now intent only upon setting up and arranging her dominoes.

Happiness squeezed his hand that held the flaking, papery wads of garlic and said, "I was in danger and sick a lot of times before I found out about the Lord and about garlic."

"Let's play," Ada said. "No more talking. Choose your dominoes, Barnaby. And you can go first. I'm going to win today, but I'm going to give you a chance."

Happiness looked at Barnaby with deep significance and backed off into the kitchen, and Barnaby set the garlic down on the table away from their playing area. He put back, facedown into the common pool of dominoes, those pieces he had picked up off the floor, and then he drew the two double sixes, which he played to start. Ada made a wonderful groan of outrage, and he beat her horribly for a while, and then he let her begin to win a little, and then by the end they were close enough that they could each argue the other had won the day because Barnaby's accounting was confusing, as ever, even to him.

Through it all, he was calm.

The afternoon was a success, and Barnaby was calm. In his way, he was serious. How much easier things were when you were courting.

Ada had fun and became tired and ready for dinner and for early to bed. Barnaby had managed to string the afternoon along into early evening, much later than he'd thought he would be able to hold out, but still early enough that there would not yet be lots of diners at Doug's when he went over.

He was calm about that too. He was serious about it. He did look like a boxer, and now there was so much more.

There was more because the real success of the afternoon was Ada's accusing him of being in love. She had said, "Barnaby's in love," and that reverberated outside any boxer's giddiness, outside the teasing of envious children; it reverberated like honest encouragement from the real world of adults.

Ada was supremely an adult, after all. She was old enough to have had strokes.

That was what it was. The strokes had taught Ada about love.

Barnaby was surrounded, maybe for the first time in his life, by love, and Ada couldn't help but notice with her new and marvelous stroke-activated radar.

When he'd finished stacking the dominoes in their box, he stood up to leave and Ada said, "You're off to see your blond. Have a good time."

Now, at the end of the day, Ada spoke without her earlier power. She was tired, and she sounded almost glad Barnaby had somewhere to go so she didn't have to worry about entertaining him herself.

But Barnaby had heard the conviction in Ada's voice earlier, and the conviction was inside of Ada still. It was inside of Barnaby. Love was real, and Barnaby was going to Doug's to court a Brooks Brothers waitress who was more of a redhead than a blond.

Before he got around the corner and through the living room, however, Happiness came out the other kitchen door to intercept him at the door of the condominium. He had left his balls of garlic on the dining room table, and she had them, and she looked at him severely.

"Don't forget these," she said, and pressed them into his hand again.

He took them from her and kept moving.

"You look terrible," she said.

"Thank you," he said, and with profound calm he cruised out of the condominium toward the station wagon and the blossoming of his fate at Doug's.

He did think about glancing at himself in the station wagon's rearview mirror, but that chance of reflection had been a maze of cracks since his daughters' game of mirror mirror on the windshield several summers ago.

In Doug's parking lot, it was only just early evening, but it was already well dark, and a man's voice called out from the darkness, "Barnaby." Barnaby looked over to the lighted main parking lot. He looked on down along the dim stretch behind the kitchen where he'd parked not too far from the battered staff vehicles, one of which he hoped belonged to his waitress. He looked out into the wide, indistinct apron of dirt that lay between Doug's and a secondary freeway access road.

But he could not see anyone.

"Barnaby," came the voice again. It was a familiar voice and yet not a voice that Barnaby recognized right away because to be hailed in the proximity of anything like a saloon made Barnaby expect to discover a colleague from other provinces than Oklahoma.

Finally he did see a silhouette there in the dirt field, coming slowly up along the edge of the staff parking, coming from a good ways away. Barnaby stepped out past the front of the station wagon into the field himself and waved at whomever it was. He waved and tried to think whom he could know.

"How you feeling?" came the voice. "How you feeling today, old buddy?"

It was Peterpotter's voice, and it was Peterpotter walking toward him.

To his credit, Barnaby did not right away register physical fear. Perhaps because he was chilly. This was the first week in December, and Barnaby had not put a jacket on over his turtleneck. He was fit and he had thought he should make that point, but he wanted to make it inside, to the girl.

What's more, he had to piss.

And here he was at the gates of love, and Peterpotter had become a private troll sent not just to take his money and position but also to beat him up and now to keep him out of the last and most important place, the palace of the beautiful princess.

Well, if it really were a fairy tale, Barnaby felt as if he could work things out. Last night, after all, it was Peterpotter's violence which had in fact introduced Barnaby to the princess.

And just like that, in the ripple of confidence and familiarity suggested by fairy tales (how could he ever have imagined religion his provenance?), Barnaby's sense of smell returned.

Suddenly he could smell the ripe exhaust from Doug's kitchen as they cranked up for dinner in there.

The smell of the same exhaust would, in several hours, adhere to the beautiful Brooks Brothers waitress, just as it had during Barnaby's sleep last night while Barnaby dreamed of her touching his lips. In his dreams, she had not been perfumed or freshly bathed. Much as he approved of and encouraged cleanliness, Barnaby had smelled her and savored her as a mixture of half-eaten cooking and her own dried sweat, all a tang of effort and aliveness.

Barnaby shuffled his feet with indecision and could feel loose dirt and a scree of stones under his sneakers as Peterpotter approached from a pickup truck far beyond the staff low riders and Volkswagens. Although he was still at a good distance, Peterpotter's silhouette had already acquired purposeful malevolence, and for some reason he chose to veer further out into the dirt no-man's land, luring Barnaby out with him. In the past, Barnaby had never had a reason to believe in malevolence, but that had changed with bankruptcy and with the fleshy discomfort now inside his mouth.

Barnaby wondered briefly whether Peterpotter might not let him just run inside and say hello to his waitress. At a distance, a young couple was over there pushing a stroller toward Doug's door, and Barnaby thought he might go in with them if he promised to come right out again for his beating.

Did he really think something so shameful?

He wondered briefly whether he ought to call to the young couple and their baby for help; the lighted parking lot over there seemed so hospitable with them around. Even the empty, shadowed, staff parking lot looked friendly now, in December, in the beginning of Advent with the green-and-gold neon glow of Doug's palm tree giving the tops of cars a Christmas aura.

Barnaby, unfortunately, was several yards outside the staff lot and its dim, fronded, desert festivity. He was out in the field with Peterpotter, standing in long-since-bulldozed leavings of dirt and rocks and occasional bottles. Out here, the palm tree light was faint, and the dulled colors of that light had submerged the air into something dangerously other than Christmas. Anybody would recognize this as a place for a beating. Jesus, a place to become a martyr, but Barnaby had quit that game—should he mention that to Peterpotter? Would Peterpotter give a shit? Anybody with any sense would just get away, back past the station wagon and across the main parking lot and into the restaurant. What could be simpler? Peterpotter was still far beyond any chance of intercepting.

"Going to run away? Big chickenshit snot going to run on in the restaurant? Go ahead. I won't come after you. But it's only me tonight. I don't have my big friends with me. You know who they were? TJ Baker's sons. Remember them? But they didn't enjoy themselves last night, wouldn't hardly kick you and didn't want to come back, so it's just me and you. What do you say?"

Barnaby didn't say anything, but he had been a chickenshit all his life when common sense dictated and when people spoke the sort of violent local cadences that Peterpotter had reassumed.

Now, however, common sense did not apply any more than martyrdom. Barnaby was coming to win a princess, so it was love that applied. Though he did have to take a piss, and badly.

Scared to death of shitty little Peterpotter. There. He'd admitted it.

He stood in the dark and watched Peterpotter approach, still at a distance but coming, slightly iridescent with the light from Doug's palm which broadcast its green out over the field like a radioactive shadow.

Barnaby shifted his sneakers on dirt and stones and understood that he too was iridescent. His blood would be green. Was it fair he should be martyred after he'd gone off the pilgrim track forever?

"Go on. Run, you son of a bitch. If you don't, I'm going to beat you again, all by myself. And this time when you go down, I'm going to get down with you and keep hitting you with my fists so I can feel it better."

The two big friends were not here. That should have been an encouragement. Instead it convinced Barnaby all the more of how deeply Peterpotter hated and how crazy the hatred had made him.

That he came alone only made Peterpotter scarier. And it made Barnaby, God forgive him, that much more frightened.

But run inside? Did any knight ever beat at the gate of the princess palace and cry that the dragon was after him?

"You want me to beat the shit out of you, don't you, old buddy."

And now Peterpotter was not all that far away.

Barnaby bent down and grabbed a rock up from between his sneakers and in a spasm of frustration flung it at Peterpotter.

What would his father say about that?

Peterpotter laughed and said, "Throwing rocks?"

Barnaby just could not, oh could not, hide behind the princess he hoped to woo, not now when he'd seen her and she'd touched his lips, when Ada had pronounced that actual love was at stake. On the other side of the coin, he was awfully afraid of Peterpotter. He bent down and scrabbled his hand in the dirt and came up with another good-sized rock for flinging and flung it wildly. Who cared what his father would say?

Peterpotter laughed and kept coming. "You dumb fuck. You think that scares me? You know what I'm going to do? After I beat you to death? I'm going to get my car lots back, and I'm going to get my oil leases back, and then I'm going to go to your fucking restaurant and order a shitload of food and throw it on the floor, and when your faggot Frenchman asks if everything is all right, I'm going to take out my dick and piss on his food and I'm going to tell all your friends, 'This is what the rest of the country thinks of you, and this is what I did to Barnaby fucking Griswold.' Then I'm going to come home and plant kudzu on your grave and I'm going to fertilize it with waste from the toilet in my plane. How's that sound?"

With that, Peterpotter bent down and clawed around his feet like an angry crab. Was that how Barnaby had looked when he was grabbing up his own rocks? And then Peterpotter stood and flung a rock wildly back at Barnaby, and another rock, and then came ahead toward Barnaby again.

"Okay? That enough rocks?" Peterpotter shouted. "Or you want some more?" And Peterpotter grabbed up three more and flung those three more, laughing as he did and shouting. "I can throw rocks. I'll throw rocks with you, you fat, poorfuck cityboy."

But Peterpotter, in fact, could not.

Barnaby saw that Peterpotter could not throw rocks at all.

Barnaby made himself stay where he was, and winced at each of Peterpotter's motions of throwing, and Peterpotter's rocks landed nowhere near him.

Peterpotter didn't have a good throwing motion. Peterpotter was in a frenzy of what he thought was deadly rock throwing, but in fact he threw like a girl.

Once he'd thrown again, Peterpotter advanced again.

But Barnaby's fear had left.

Barnaby had learned to throw, really throw, during the tide pool summer, and he had hardly stopped throwing then. His first and loneliest summer away at camp, the summer after the pond summer, Barnaby had thrown rocks every chance he got for two and a half months. He'd thrown every rock he could find, at trees, into the lake, at other rocks, over the tennis court. He had never thrown at people, but he had definitely learned how it was done. He had learned the motion. He was never any pitcher, but by the end of that first, unhappy, camp summer, whenever he threw at trees, usually he had hit them.

Now, with no fear anymore at all, he took his time and bent down and gathered four good-sized stones and squeezed one of them into his throwing hand.

Peterpotter saw that and stopped advancing and bent down himself for more rocks, laughing as he did.

Barnaby sighted on Peterpotter and took one long stride forward as he reared back with his throwing arm. He kept his sights on Peterpotter, and he let loose.

Barnaby threw like he knew how to throw, and the rock went for Peterpotter on a line. Almost on a line. It went true.

It missed.

Peterpotter was so busy laughing and gathering up more of his own rocks that he didn't notice. He should have noticed.

It missed, but it was a near miss.

Barnaby stood calmly as Peterpotter started flinging his new batch, and some of those rocks Barnaby could see in the dark and in the green glimmer from the neon palm, and some of the rocks he could not see, but with Peterpotter's form there was every assurance of safety.

Barnaby himself took another long stride and brought his throwing arm back deep, and fired. Barnaby threw his rock like a rock was meant to be thrown, and he knew as soon as he let go that he was on target. He couldn't see it fly, but he knew.

He heard it hit, a quick thup, a solid, painful sound even from a distance.

"Ow. Fuck. Fuck me. Fuck, that hurts."

Peterpotter grabbed in the dirt and ran several furious steps forward at Barnaby, flinging handfuls of dirt and stones with both hands.

When he stopped to grab more, Barnaby went calmly into his motion and fired again.

Thup.

And now Peterpotter was close enough that Barnaby could see the stone strike off a shoulder.

"Ow, fuck, fuck. Ow. God. You fucker. You fucking fucker."

It was understandable but not particularly to his credit that now it was Barnaby who began to laugh, and the laugh, unfortunately, put off his aim. His last stone kicked in the dirt just beside Peterpotter.

Without even flinging his last handfuls of dirt and rocks, Peterpotter was running away.

Barnaby picked up another couple of stones, but Peterpotter was moving away fast, despite a limp. Maybe the first hit had been a knee.

So Barnaby called after him, "I was never sorry." He dropped his rocks and shouted, "I take back my apology."

That was it. Barnaby brushed his hands.

Nothing stood between Barnaby and his miraculously sustained quest of love (nor anything between himself and his suddenly far-more-urgent-than-before need to take a piss), but the bright, green-and-gold distance to Doug's door. He walked that distance with grave composure.

And inside the door, inside the restaurant dimness which seemed now darker than the lighted parking lot he'd just crossed, right there, as if she'd timed it all out, the waitress stood exactly before him, in front of her wilderness of tables like forest royalty. She stood tall and thin and supple, one loose hand on her hip, an athlete who had gotten somewhere first for the fun of it.

Had she expected him like Ada had, and like Peterpotter had too apparently? Had she known all about him all along?

She smiled at him with a mischief that suggested there was a something going on and Barnaby might be the last to learn.

Her top lip quivered above her smile with mischief, and mischief was also in her pale, elegant freckles which bunched beneath her eyes when she smiled. She was more beautiful than he remembered, and she was teasing him.

Barnaby liked to be teased. All of the noblest people were teasers.

But he couldn't simply stand and marvel at her, and this was certainly no moment to speak about pissing and to ask for the bathroom. Nor was it time for anything resembling sanctimony. He had driven off the dragon and won his way into the castle, and it was time to stand forward and speak boldly to the chalice of his affections.

"Good evening," he said. "I'm Barnaby Griswold," and he could hear that tonight at least, whatever else might be going on, his voice and his mouth were making real words.

"Yeah. Sure," she said through her smile and her mischief. "I know who you are."

"You do?" Did she really? Had she opened the back door of the kitchen and witnessed the battle?

"Hey. When was the last time you looked in the mirror?"

Oh. That was what she meant. She knew his face.

"Last night was messier," she said. "But all in all, tonight looks worse."

"Really?"

"You look terrible," she said, and Barnaby was aware that people had come in behind him and were waiting to get past. "Anyway," she said, "table for one?"

She was still mischievous, but clearly he was not a glamorous boxer, and just as clearly his time was running out. "I wanted to thank you for last night. For helping. For cleaning me. Seeing I was all right."

Was that what he had fought all the way in here to say? He might as well have done a "Bless this food to our use" for the near tables.

"You're welcome," she said, and her smile did not stop, but she looked to the people behind, two youngish women though not as young as she. They pushed around Barnaby, and one of them looked up at Barnaby's face with a start of something like alarm.

His waitress turned from Barnaby and began to lead the women away among the little steel tables.

If she had not still been smiling, if it had been his usual self at any other time, Barnaby would have gone away too. He would have gone quickly for the bathroom and then just as quickly out to the station wagon. What else could he do? Deals had always come to him like ripe bones falling off a truck in front of a dog, and beautiful women had always run away from him—deals and women had always been very different events for Barnaby Griswold, and he had learned to honor that difference.

But she was smiling when she turned away.

And Barnaby was not himself.

This was love.

He called, "Will you come out with me?"

The two youngish women turned back, and both of them were plainly revolted by the sight Barnaby offered.

His waitress turned around, and said, "Me?"

Barnaby understood what she meant now. She just wanted to know if he was really speaking to her. He could have answered. He could have nodded. But he hesitated, and even as he hesitated, he felt his powers of communication bleeding out of him as they had done last night. He wondered if his shirt was stained again.

The women refused Barnaby's unsettling aspect and scurried on past the waitress, but the waitress continued to look back at Barnaby. "Out?" she said.

She hadn't lost her smile entirely, but she stared at Barnaby as if she were questioning everything he had ever suggested in his life. He brought his hands together like an opened book, and put them up in front of his nose and mouth and the bottoms of his eye sockets. He peeked at her over his fingertips. It was an insane thing to do, but he couldn't help himself.

"With you?" she said.

He hid his pale nose and his purpled mouth and blackened eyes behind his hands. He was aware that he had crossed what, even for someone with his history, was a significant line in the sands of behavior, but he would not have taken his hands down from his face for almost anything.

She started to turn away once more, and he dropped his hands and shouted, "To the zoo."

What a wonderful idea. He smiled at both the idea and at his courage in shouting. He was brave again.

"Okay," she said. "But it has to be tomorrow. And you'll never find my apartment. Pick me up here at noon."

Before he had time to respond, she nodded his response for him and turned to shepherd her youngish women on to their table.

Barnaby turned away himself, and not toward the bathroom. He was too shy to risk another moment in Doug's despite his emergency and his moment of bravery. No, he turned for the door out to the parking lot, and as he turned and began to run off with what he'd won before he could lose it, he glimpsed the young family that had come in the restaurant while he was waiting for Peterpotter to beat him. The father was engaged with linguine, and the mother was stirring a jar of something she'd brought for the baby. The baby, who had been elevated from stroller to high chair, stared at Barnaby with more amazement than Barnaby had ever before inspired. Barnaby hesitated. Was it Barnaby's power of love the baby saw, and recognized with the same purity of vision Ada possessed? Had the waitress seen it too? For an instant only, Barnaby stared back at the baby. And as Barnaby's and the baby's eyes met, the baby began to cry.

Christ Almighty. He was frightening to small children.

But there, beyond the weeping child, was the insignia for the men's room.

And emergency won out.

Leaning precipitously forward, sprinting from the knees down, Barnaby powered toward the weeping baby, and the baby began to scream. Barnaby did not look anymore at the baby, but he had to pass that table, and the baby looked at him, and the screams went to shrieks. Barnaby could feel the parents looking up aghast as he went passionately by.

It was one of the new urinals at shin height and he flooded into it, dampening the bottoms of his pant legs.

It was transcendent.

It was more than relief.

He had a date.

He came home and looked at himself in the long mirror of his own bathroom, and he knew that he couldn't possibly go. He wasn't a boxer. He wasn't even a boxer who'd lost. Happiness was right. The shrieking baby was right. The waitress herself had said it. He looked like a drunk who'd been beaten up in the parking lot.

Even as he studied himself in cheap, three-quarter length on the back of his narrow bathroom door, even as he acknowledged that Happiness, no less, could be more astute than he was about his own God-awful appearance, he did not for a moment believe he was disqualified from the courtship of his beautiful waitress. He'd known too many eminently lovable men who'd suffered beatings in parking lots to believe that.

But to pick her up tomorrow at noon was utterly out of the question. For the next couple of weeks until he looked like a human being again, he would have no choice but to lurk out of sight.

Since a couple of weeks brought him that much closer to the end of his suspension, since the hopeful concerns of love were already clearly augmenting his commercial mass, maybe this would be an opportune time, finally and no kidding, to begin making his calls and putting himself back in the world of investments. "Remember Barnaby Griswold?"

How painful could it be to pick up his old associate the telephone? No more painful than boxing, certainly. Because the thing with Livermore had been about Barnaby wanting to move in, which anybody but Barnaby (in a time of some stress, to be

LOVER

fair) would have understood beforehand was not something the
directors at Crenshaw could ever condone. The president of the
foundation has a securities felon for a roommate. Not a felon,
but close enough.

On the other hand, keeping in touch, dropping a hint here
a hint there, collecting a tidbit here and there, that sort of action
wasn't going to frighten Livermore's directors or anyone else.
Especially some of the anyone elses Barnaby would call after
Livermore. In two weeks, everything would be up to speed again;
word would be out and Barnaby would be having to lose all over
again the crazy (but very successful) asshole who cornered drugs
taken off the market and for ten years had wanted nobody but
Barnaby to do his respectable-making initial public offering.

Remembering that kind of thing for the first time in years
made a future in the world beyond Oklahoma seem finally to be
at hand. It was at hand.

Of course with Ada buying his groceries and with hardly
any expenses beyond his dirt-cheap rent and the gym, he actually
had enough dough to last in Oklahoma quite a good while past
the end of the month, maybe years past.

But why?

It had always been understood that he would be leaving on
the first of the year. The year was up. There were professionals
who were prepared and contracted to step in and watch Ada,
and they would do a far better job than Barnaby. Barnaby was
decoration in the larger picture of Ada's care. Also, Win would
be back. He'd forgotten about Win.

Yes, with love on his side (if held in sensible abeyance for
the moment), Barnaby Griswold was ready at last to roll up his
sleeves and do what he did—dial, to begin with. If he made his
calls and got things going, he could absolutely be ready on the
first of the year, and he'd take his glorious princess of the bus-
ing stand, whatever her name turned out to be, back with him.
Tomorrow was Sunday. So he'd start calling Monday. First thing,
what with the time change. He had put off making any calls

for four years, but procrastination had always been his genius. Now was the last minute, the time when he thrived; now his métier was summoning him back with an urgency that could not be denied. Love had made him large again, and it was all he could do to keep from reaching for the phone right this minute. "Hello? Remember Barnaby Griswold? Of course I know it's Saturday night."

He looked at himself in his thin mirror, surrounded less by love (since he knew he had to wait weeks to see her again) than by the operating-room-green paint of his plywood bathroom. At night, as it was now, and with the light on, the green walls showed all the scalloped shadows of their peeling, and the door to the shower revealed its tracings of rust around the edges of scummed, milk-gray glass. With that as background, he tried to see in his own battered face the tiger who could claw his way back to prominence as sorry Peterpotter would never manage to do. Whatever your size, after all, clawing was necessary. He said aloud to the mirror, "Remember Barnaby Griswold?" and hoped that a real tiger would answer with a list of names in the order he should call them on Monday. He wondered if the tigers had heard about how he whipped Peterpotter. He'd tell them on his date to the zoo in a couple of weeks. By then, hell, by then...

And his father said, Take a look, for God sake, at where you're living.

What was that supposed to mean?

He wasn't entirely surprised to hear from his father, but he would have expected his father to side with the tigers and insist that Barnaby get to work and make calls right now if he had to, and all day Sunday too.

His father said, Somebody's used a flat paint in the bathroom, and it's peeling from every surface but where they splattered the mirror over the sink.

Barnaby looked, and certainly paint (flat paint, ever inappropriate to bathrooms), was there on the corners of the medicine-cabinet mirror. Until now, Barnaby had willed himself not to notice, but there it was. He could scrape it off. He could scrape the walls too and repaint the whole bathroom in a suitable gloss. Christ, the entire damned house needed scraping and painting, but what a thankless task. Especially when he was on his way out of town.

He bent over the sink and stared into that medicine-cabinet mirror. Even with its current disguise, it was his own face in the mirror, and disguised or not it was a face that would benefit from a thankless task. It was a face that looked as if it was itself a thankless task.

"But I'm renting," he said aloud to the face, hoping as he said so to conceal the fact that the rent was only four hundred a month. "I might be leaving any day. I've got calls to make."

You're living in a pigsty, his father said.

It was what his father had also said after Barnaby's freshman year of college when Barnaby's grades, despite his best efforts, found their way home. Barnaby had planned to summer at school and had very nearly lined up an illegal bartending job, but his father arrived unannounced and delivered the pigsty line while standing knee-deep in dirty clothes and beer cans in a room with sheets over the windows and no sheets on the bed. Strangely, it was the report of Barnaby's grades at which his father was looking while he spoke, while Barnaby got dressed in the middle of the afternoon, and so there was the sense that his father was referring to all of Barnaby's life as a pigsty. To be fair, it all was a pigsty. Barnaby had discovered that he liked a pigsty.

His father said, "You're going to get things here cleaned up straight away, but some time you may find yourself in a larger sty for which the remedies are not easy. This summer we will practice a remedy, so when the time comes you'll be equipped."

It was the sort of thing his father could say and sound so cryptically like Moses that Barnaby, and plenty of other people too, would expect all the tents of Israel to turn blue by morning.

The meaning in this case was that Barnaby and his father were going to paint the house on the Point. By themselves. Without pay. Barnaby's labor would be repayment of the tuition fees he had squandered, it being his father's most fervent hope that Barnaby arrive at school again in the fall with no spending money whatever.

As it would turn out in the fall, Barnaby was to get his illegal bartending job the day classes began, and all was to be well. But at the start of the summer, facing two solid months of hard work six days (six days) a week, the world and the future were a dark tunnel with no light in any direction, with only his father beside him, watching him, telling him how to scrape, how to feather a brush, how to cut an edge. When had his father ever painted? But he had. His father never faked it. And his father was taking two months away from the law firm. Admittedly this was before the firm began its consuming decline, but it was still the firm; it was still his father who never did allow himself the three weeks he'd promised Barnaby's mother to take her once more to Florence.

For the briefest interlude on the drive away from his life at school, Barnaby remembered with a skulker's epiphany that the house on the Point had been painted just the autumn before. But it was not the outside of the house that would be addressed.

It was the kitchen, and two coats inside all of the cupboards, oil base. It was steaming and scraping and finally clawing with their fingernails at the layers of wallpaper on the horsehair plaster in the upstairs bedrooms. It was oil base in the bathrooms. It was two coats around every pane of glass in eighty windows each of which had twelve lights. For which, his father said day after day, they could be grateful because an older house might have had twenty-four light windows.

His father loved it.

His mother hated it. She had no hiding places anymore, and fewer moments of secret oblivion. She had to consult on the new wallpaper and the new colors of paint when she didn't want to change a thing.

Then finally she loved it, because Barnaby's father was so happy. Barnaby's father laughed. He wore an undershirt and his old navy khakis cut off at the knee. He swaggered at the end of a day. Maybe they had sex.

Barnaby, not without difficulty, endured.

But he endured as a different man than either of his parents knew, because during his freshman year at college, Barnaby had begun to come into his own.

At college, as his peers had begun to recognize the worth of a fool in a new and ever more celebratory light, so had Barnaby. Freshman year was a laying of foundations for deals to come, for a lifetime of deals. Not from the connections—Barnaby deplored the notion of pursuing and trading in other people for commerce, such a shabby attitude toward human beings and such a waste of a good time. Barnaby believed in friends. Barnaby believed in fun. And in his freshman year he saw his beliefs begin to crystallize in his own capacity to be a sort of maestro of friends. As month to month through the school year Barnaby's nature unfolded into the freedoms and privileges of a good and tolerant university, Barnaby could feel himself growing, transcending himself. He, was, what? How did you put these nuanced ripenings of a man into practical terms? Perhaps it was coming to understand that three times in one week he could throw up and still carry on. Other people saw that and came to count on Barnaby. And by the end of freshman year, he wasn't even throwing up anymore. His legend had been established, and he simply carried on, and was happy to carry on. He was Barnaby Griswold. The deals were out there waiting for him, and to tell the truth, once the deals began, then after each deal for the rest of his life he never did have a clue what the next one would be. He learned to pretend that he had a clue, a plan, another deal waiting down the line, but he never did, and he understood the clueless absence of direction as his compass, his true north. Freshman year for Barnaby was unmitigated joy, and the joy was compounded because he knew it was only the beginning.

Now, Barnaby let himself wonder, as he ordinarily refused to do, what the people had felt like who had finally ended up holding the bag on his various deals when the fluff blew away. They weren't people whom Barnaby knew. They were the market. They were strangers who made a mistake after all the people that Barnaby knew had made lots of money. Those happy money-makers were the people Barnaby liked to think of. His friends. But the other ones, the ones who ended up with less than they'd hoped they might, sometimes quite a lot less, the stupid ones whom he had always blessed in his heart and occasionally extolled aloud over Thanksgiving dinner...

No apology, he still knew, was ever owed on the Old Ladies Bank deal; Barnaby had simply recognized a market disequilibrium and made a bet.

But why dwell on that?

Why, for that matter, wonder about all of the happy friends from all of the years of other deals, friends who had turned out again and again to be parts of the deals rather than parts of Barnaby's life? He could still call Tom Livermore, even if not for a place to stay just yet. He could call Dicky Kopus, if he wanted. Would Kopus qualify as a friend?

The good news was that here, under his own two large feet, above his many-colored face, was a house which needed scraping and painting. Wasn't that good news? Perhaps because of his father's reassuring presence, Barnaby felt that it was. It was a chance to build up his credit again in the balance sheet of bad behavior before he went back to work, and that sort of thing was much more important to a guy like Barnaby than anything as sensible as phone calls.

Those calls had waited this long, and they could wait beyond Monday morning.

They might have to wait a good deal beyond, because this was no one day job.

So. Solid ground from which to leap back into the securities fray, with the coincidental benefit of a shipshape little bungalow in which to present himself to his waitress.

He turned off the bathroom lights, went to the kitchen, and got out cold chicken pieces that he had baked early in the week with a jar of picante sauce. He steamed some broccoli. And then as he ate those things, he made a list, not of options in life or of victims to phone but of what he really needed: brushes, scrapers, spatulas, razor knife, electric sander.

He went to bed right after his frozen yogurt and thought about colors of paint.

He sat up in the middle of the night gripped by the realization that he had not told his beautiful waitress he couldn't meet her.

Or that he would meet her, but just not tomorrow.

That he wanted to go to the zoo very much but that he had to be unseen for some weeks.

Should he go back in and call across her tables that they'd meet same time same place in, say, three weeks to be safe? Had she said that she could only meet tomorrow?

He saw from the luminous dials of his electric clock that it was after three and that Doug's was long closed.

All right. To avoid being seen, it was better to call anyway.

But he couldn't call at three o'clock in the morning.

Could he find her phone number?

He didn't know her name.

"I hope you can forgive my face," he said resolutely but not very hopefully out the window of the station wagon as she came across the parking lot from her Volkswagen convertible with its ragged knife slit in the top. He hadn't seen her at first, but she seemed to know it would be him in the station wagon and jumped out of her Volks and came in long, direct strides. She was wearing corduroys and light hiking boots. Barnaby was wearing corduroys. It was a gray, cold day, an awful day for the zoo. She hurried, though she wasn't very late. Doug's was open for brunch, so Barnaby could have called in the morning. But what would he have asked? For the name and number of the girl with the whatever, like he was a kid hoping for a date, picking her up? As opposed to a forty-six-year-old brawler hoping not to see her until he healed? She was almost to him before he could get out and call, even though she was just across the hood now, call again to get it over with, "I'm sorry about my face." She wore a maroon turtleneck (a turtleneck) and a dark blue, heavyweight flannel shirt, an L.L. Bean flannel shirt if he'd ever seen one. Barnaby had on a lighter flannel shirt and a Shetland sweater and an old tweed sport coat. He'd finally decided to come as who he was, and if it turned out that that was from outer space, then outer space it was. She was stopped and looking at him across the big, poxed hood of the station wagon, and she was smiling in nervous formality, but smiling. She'd come. He'd hoped she wouldn't come. He wasn't from outer space if they both knew L.L.Bean. She was just as beautiful. More beautiful. He wanted to button her inside his shirt. Gad, what a peculiar thought. He wanted to crawl across the weather-blasted hood to her on his knees and beg her. But beg what? She stared at him without a bit of makeup on. With her hair still tied back for speed. Was it more red, more golden? She brought a gray day into glory, into a dream of the zoo on a Sunday. Why on earth had she come?

She said, "What?"

"Forgive me," he whispered.

She said, "Your face looks just as good in daylight," and in her smile there was almost mischief. "Do you have a camera? We should take a picture."

We?

He started to go around the colossal hood to open her door, to shake hands and be a gentleman. To be a date? But she said, "I got it," and opened her door herself, and he bumped into the fender but did not fall and did not flinch. He got back in his own door and pulled it mostly closed and did not try to pull on it a second time. He turned to her, and they were in this tiny space alone together. Christ, it really was a date, and there on the seat between them was the garlic.

"Marian," she said.

It was a name like a chord from all the beautiful musics he had never bothered to learn. It sang inside the station wagon, while out in the gray parking lot people went under Doug's day lit neon palm tree to brunch.

"Marian," he said. Today she smelled like fresh soap and water.

"No," she said. "You're supposed to say, Barnaby Griswold."

He said, "Barnaby Griswold," in his regular voice, and she looked at him as if he might be from outer space after all. He still had not yet smiled himself. He did that. "How do you do."

And she laughed. He saw her teeth. Was she terrified?

She said, "How do you do," in a deep and teasing voice and held out her hand for him to shake. She wasn't terrified. And if she wasn't terrified, then maybe he wasn't.

He shook her hand. He held her hand while she shook his. She shook firmly and straightforwardly, and Barnaby pretended to shake back and felt everything he could feel of her hand, the strength of her grip, the runs of tendon and bone down the back of it, the warming cold of her palm and her fingers, the edges of her nails, the delicacy of it all despite the strength, the smoothness of her skin.

He let go.

He was afraid somebody outside would see what he was doing.

He turned and started the car and gripped the wheel.

Christ Almighty.

He drove off.

Should he have offered her the chance to get out? Too late. Was she appalled?

"Garlic," she said.

Garlic. Jesus. She didn't sound appalled, but she didn't sound like it was the happiest day of her life either.

It was Barnaby who was appalled. Scared to death of a pretty girl. Well, at least sit up straight. Look where you're going.

"The garlic is from Happiness," he said.

She laughed again. Had she laughed before? Barnaby stared ahead out the windshield and over the carrier deck of the station wagon's hood. He said to himself, Thank you, Jesus, for making it Sunday, because driving in traffic would have been too difficult. Thank you, Jesus? Was Happiness worming into his syntax now that he'd thrown over a pilgrim's honest religion?

"I've never been that happy," Marian said. "Does the garlic just, you know, come out your nose when you feel terrific?"

Was it possible that Barnaby Griswold could not find a retort for that?

He could not even look at her.

He said, "Happiness is a person," and his delivery made the incarnation sound like the end of all humor.

"Oh," Marian said.

And they didn't speak again.

Barnaby drove.

He got there. He'd studied the map.

Not another word.

Twenty minutes. Half an hour.

Not one.

He'd never been to the zoo, but it was not difficult to get close to the gate because everyone else had stayed home. It was open. Zoos were open on Sunday regardless of winter and the weather.

He stopped and put the shift into park and, still sitting behind the wheel, turned to her to find out if she wanted to go home. That was all she'd have to say. He wouldn't speak himself.

She had the two bulbs of garlic, and she held one toward him.

"I think we'd better take these," she said.

She wasn't smiling, but she said it like the commander of a spaceship in gravest danger, which could very well have been funny.

He opened his own hand and let her drop the one garlic into his palm. He said, like the co-captain acknowledging every ounce of the danger, "Yes."

They got out of the station wagon, and Barnaby put his garlic in a side pocket of his sport coat. Marian put hers in the breast pocket of her flannel shirt, and inside the pocket's heavy material the bulb made the appearance of one breast because her real breasts were so slight they didn't show. Barnaby saw and, more than he could say, loved that her breasts were small. If there had not been the momentum of all the silence from the drive, he might have said so.

Instead, they got their tickets and a map without a word, and now it was as if silence were the plan. It was a nervous plan, but Barnaby tried to be calm with it. He was not used to silence. He was not used to plans. He opened the map and she stood next to him and together, side by side, they studied it. They could hear the seals barking, and she pointed on the map at the seals, and he nodded, and they went that way and looked at the seals. They didn't look at each other. Barnaby didn't look at her. Barnaby was glad to see the seals, and he thought blindly that she seemed to be glad.

From the seals they went on and toward the hippos. Was it the hippos? When they came to a choice of paths, Barnaby opened the map again, and they stood together again, side by side, her arm against his. But she didn't choose. She waited for him to choose this time, and so he did. He chose, there, toward the birds and the monkeys, and they stood apart and walked on.

It was a handsome zoo. Simple and open, large and planted and clean. It was the best of Oklahoma he had seen, even on so drearily deserted an afternoon.

She chose inside to the snakes, but Barnaby didn't think she liked them.

He chose to the ostriches and the giraffes and the African buffaloes.

At the ostriches, a ranger coming out of the pasture with an egg said, "Would you like to hold it? It's still warm."

And they did, and it was, and nothing more was said. They handed it carefully back, as if it had been a marvel. Which it had, like a weight of God. Marian thought so too; Barnaby glanced at her and could guess that much because she was something from God herself. The colors of flesh in her face, and her eyebrows and eyelashes too, were all pale and at the same time in rosy bloom. She was luminous with life next to the gray expanse of grasses in the ostrich pasture. If Barnaby could have held her face in his hands the way he'd held the egg, her face would have been warm as well. And if she hadn't wanted to be held, her eyebrows would have become instantly fierce like more of a mother than any of the ostriches who were talking nearby about something mundanely other than babies. Barnaby took a moment to sympathize with the ostrich mothers because he himself had always before preferred to talk about anything but children.

Whatever was he thinking?

He looked away when Marian's eyes met his own.

She chose the tigers.

There.

The path went right at the tigers' place, and it was a fine tiger world from a distance.

It was fine up close, even in the darker gray of now late afternoon. There were stone cliffs and running water, and there were distances of meadow and tree available behind. It was a much better place for them to live than Barnaby remembered from Boston when he was a boy. It was, in its way, better than the wallpaper of La Cote.

Only there were no tigers. The tigers were not out. The tigers were somewhere inside their fine, cliff-seeming house because it was a lousy day. Barnaby didn't blame them. Still, he stood at the rail hoping.

After a few minutes, Marian turned to go, but Barnaby waited, not hoping so much after another few minutes as just waiting.

He waited a little longer.

And a little longer still. It occurred to him to mention to no one in particular that he had whipped Peterpotter, but he didn't.

"No tigers today," Marian said. It was the first thing she'd said, the only thing, and she said it gaily. She couldn't know.

But Barnaby sank down to his knees.

He didn't look up at her. He couldn't possibly. He looked under the rail and through the fence into the tigers' fine world. What would become of him now? The walk was damp, and his knees were already wet. He was kneeling down, God help him, Barnaby Griswold, for no reason at all. He was not sad. Maybe he was happy. Done with tigers? He knew Marian looked at him, but he looked only into the tigers' world.

As much without exasperation as he could manage, with as much authority as he thought respectful, he said, "Oh, come on out."

And a tiger came out.

Honest to Christ.

And another came out right behind.

Strolling, both of them.

And a little bit stalking, or prowling. Then stretching. Slow, less than interested, but moving with long, loose, threatful muscles like only tigers could move, like Barnaby had always known tigers would move.

Orange and yellow with white underneath, and with black lightening on top as if somebody'd flipped the lights for Christ sake.

And one of them, the biggest, a massive tiger, had whiskers. Jowls. Fur like Edwardian sideburns. Barnaby had never known of those, but he should have known. Christ, what a tiger.

And that monster of a tiger with sideburns like the headmaster of the world came right at Barnaby. He stared from his elegant, Frank Lloyd Wright porch across the moat at Barnaby. He made a sound, a gurgling in his throat, like a belch after eating a village. He made it at Barnaby.

He knew Barnaby.

He belched in the casual, agreeable acknowledgment that the important sometimes give, and turned away, and Barnaby could either have cried like a baby or sprung up in his own roar of triumph.

He started to spring, and he hit his head on the rail and didn't care. He sprang again and made it up, and he didn't roar, but he turned to his most beautiful waitress on earth, and he looked her in the eye, and he smiled. Her eyes were green and brown and watching and difficult. Her chin was up and her back was straight, and even so she might not have known how regal her cheekbones were.

She said, "Are you okay?"

And he didn't care if she was worried about him hitting his head on the railing or about him kneeling there like a lunatic.

She said, "That tiger knew you."

Exactly.

"If my face were not black and blue," he said, "would you kiss me?"

And she did.

She was not far away, a step, but she took that step to him, and she was almost as tall as he was, and she kissed him as lightly, as gently, as completely on his lips as her fingers had touched him last night in the bar and in his dreams.

She did not close her eyes. She looked at him as she kissed him, and he was too shy to look back. He closed his eyes and felt only in all of the universe her thin, tender lips touching his own lips no matter what.

She stopped and said, "You closed your eyes. You're a romantic."

Then they walked without speaking back to the gate as the afternoon gathered to dusk. Barnaby had to go with his fists in his pockets to keep from reaching out to hold her hand, and there were trees and there were the sounds of creatures. There were other people but not many. There were no cars, no houses really, but there were structures and hills and cages that were inhabited. There were cared-for paths and tidy bridges. It was all a blanket of life. It was almost Central Park.

They got the concession stand's last hot dogs on the way out and ate them on the drive back to Doug's.

The speechlessness in the car now was a preserving bubble of the afternoon. The station wagon, with its large effortful engine and its spent shocks, with the smell of hot dogs and the sound of bites and paper, was an ark of memory for the zoo's reverberating cries of dinner time.

When they were stopped once more in Doug's parking lot, Marian said, "Thank you," and when Barnaby started to get out, she said, "Don't get out. I mean, you can get out if you want, but I'm all right. I had a good time. I'm glad we went to the zoo."

So Barnaby didn't get out. He said, "I had a good time too."

She grinned and said, "Listen, somebody should call you Tiger instead of Barnaby."

Barnaby had forgotten about sitting up straight, but he sat up straighter at the thought of a name like Tiger.

Before he could bring himself to ask her if she meant it, she said, "What did that big tiger tell you?"

"That he'd just eaten a village."

She laughed, and said, "See? We can talk." Then she opened the glove compartment like it was her own car and she knew her way around. It could have been her car; Barnaby would have given it to her in a minute. She rooted for a ballpoint pen and an old registration which she brought out to her lap. "Anyway," she said. "This is my phone number. Though actually I've got a month off now. Tomorrow I'm going home and I'm not supposed to be back until the third of January."

"Oh no," Barnaby said before he could stop himself.

Because they'd just begun. They'd been to the zoo. She'd kissed him, and they'd ridden home in the station wagon.

"Or I mean, I'm sorry," he said. "I mean I'll be sorry you're away such a long time."

"That's why today was the only day I could go. And actually…"

She'd kissed him and said people should call him Tiger. A month. He had to wait a month, when he wanted them to be in love today. He told her, "I'm sorry. Forgive me if I sound too strange after just an afternoon."

"It was a lovely afternoon, but…"

"A month is not so very long. I mean it's a nice long time to be home. But it's not so long between trips to the zoo." If he'd dared, he could have closed his eyes and felt her lips against his own. He said, "Where will you go? I thought you might live here." He wished he could touch the back of her hand again. He thought about reaching out to do that as she was fiddling to get the glove compartment closed again. Gad. "Gad," he said. "I've just met you. You're back on the third of January. Wonderful."

He suddenly remembered they were supposed to be gone by then, home by then. Barnaby's true home. Didn't she know? That was supposed to be the most important thing. New York.

"Actually, the thing is, I don't know if I'll be back at all."

What?

"Oh," he said.

Then this was it.

This was what they told you when they didn't want you. This was what they'd told Barnaby always. Except for Win who'd made an honest mistake.

"At all?" he said.

He couldn't believe it, but it was true. Done.

He said, "Well, that's all right, then. You don't have to give me a number."

"No. Really. Call. I think I'll be back. I might be. This is a strange early escape for Christmas vacation from graduate school. I thought I did live here. I'm only part time as a waitress. Or I'm supposed to be only part time. I seem to be struggling as a physical therapist trainee. The medical center has a great training program, and I came all the way out here to discover maybe I'm more waitress than therapist. But anyway. The career. You're not interested in all of that. Right? I had a good time. I would have given you my number even if I was going to be here forever. And maybe I will. Call me on the third."

So it wasn't done? After all?

Or at least she didn't not want him. She hadn't utterly refused him. Was that right?

Did he believe that?

No.

She opened her door and got out and then leaned back inside holding her bulb of garlic.

"Can I keep it?" she said.

"The garlic?" he said.

"It's good garlic. It worked. We had a good time at the zoo," and she laughed and closed the door.

Barnaby rolled down his window as she strode to her Volks with her joke of garlic in one hand. When she had backed out and turned to go, he waved.

He would never see her again.

She put her own window down and waved back and smiled.
It was a smile of thank Christ I've escaped.

"Good-bye," he called.

"Good-bye, Tiger," she called, and drove out into the street
and off.

Barnaby sat in his old Winott Point station wagon and let himself understand.

Marian didn't like him and didn't want him.

That was plain enough.

But actually the thing was (which was how she'd phrased it about her not coming back: "actually, the thing is"), Barnaby didn't want her.

Not that she wasn't sensible to turn down (kindly, for which Barnaby was grateful) someone old and whatever (he hated to say ugly now that he was so relatively fit, though even in the best of times his face had never been pretty). Not that she wasn't sensible to say no thanks when she herself was young and beautiful. But sensible behavior had nothing to do with Barnaby. He could perfectly well imagine young and beautiful women loving him if he chose. He could imagine several at once waiting around the corner.

Yes, of course he was a fool, and yes, obviously Marian would have been crazy to want him.

But he was not a lover. No more a lover than a pilgrim.

That was the point.

Some people were many things, and God bless them.

But Barnaby was only a fool.

There were surgeons who were great painters and spoke five languages, and those surgeons had been peculiarly receptive to Barnaby's snake oil in the early stages of deals when a local surgeon/ painter/linguist was a useful beacon to have on board. But, secretly, in the occasional low moments that had come even to him, Barnaby had often wished the worst for people with too much confidence in too many fields.

"Do one thing well," was something his father had felt he had to say regularly to Barnaby; it was something that in fact his father had told Barnaby far more regularly than "Don't be a fluffmeister."

Well, in his heart, in his bones, in his purple face, even if he never fluffed again, Barnaby was a fluffmeister, and a good one; that was the professional expression of a fool.

He was not a good lover. It was the less-than-comfortable truth that he was not a lover at all. He had never loved his daughters, for instance. He had provided for them, God knew, but, no, he'd never loved them.

He'd never given them a thought except at official occasions, at holidays and graduations and confirmations, all of which, true to his calling, he had performed superbly. Nobody ever sang Happy Birthday with more gusto than Barnaby Griswold.

Nor, despite his surprise at so liking her long, awkward body, had he ever loved Win. As she would be the first to tell anyone. Perhaps right now she was telling Duane for the umpteenth time, trapped as they were with one another's conversations somewhere out on the isolation of the world's liquid surface.

How could he ever have hoped to be a first rate at what he did and get home for dinner? How could he have passed out in time to get up in the morning, how could he have remembered what promises he'd won from Tom Livermore, if he had had to talk before bed?

Of course it had been Win's happy assumption, and Barnaby's too, a bargain really, that when they married Barnaby would cease at foolishness. And he had tried harder even than he'd tried for his father. Barnaby took his bargains seriously, and he was still young then. But his nature refused. Foolishness was his being and his calling.

Which was something he should have brought to his father's notice in so many words. He should have, when it could have been done, told his father, Here, look at this, look what I'm terrific at. Rather than pretending at respectability, he should have told his father that he had found the one thing he could do, and was doing it for all he was worth, killing himself with doing it.

Who knows, maybe it would have made an impression.

After all, his father had taught him to ignore his mother.

That wouldn't have been a comfortable truth to tell either his father or himself out loud, and so, really, Barnaby would never have brought it up. But the fact was that neither he or his father felt anything but relief when Barnaby's mother died. Barnaby wished he hadn't been late to say good-bye at her death, but it had still only been good-bye. His father had said good-bye years earlier in order to grieve and sweat entirely for his dying law firm.

Just as Barnaby later, in different but no less consuming fashion, grieved and sweated over the toilets at La Cote when the Old Ladies Bank deal was going belly up and the Griswold diet had begun to scour his bowels.

Good-bye, Tiger.

Barnaby might as well have said it himself, said it to her, to Marian, instead of the other way around. Because whether it was a deal going belly up forever, or a saloon shutting down for the night, Good-bye Tiger meant Turn out the lights.

It meant Marian didn't like him, and it meant Barnaby could never have loved her anyhow. Barnaby held the steering wheel of the station wagon as if it were all he had, which it was, and he felt fine.

She was gone.

Where had he been? How had he not expected? Peterpotter, yes, Peterpotter had been a surprise, but Good-bye Tiger with Marian should never have been a surprise.

In his earlier incarnation, in saloons and deals, Good-bye Tiger had always eventually been a cause for excitement, a beginning toward new deals and new saloons, and Barnaby Griswold was somebody who loved beginnings.

So Barnaby, who also enjoyed maple syrup, put his mouth to the plastic of his steering wheel, which had long since come to look like crystallized maple syrup, and tried to imagine beginning.

He felt as if all his victories were ridiculous and his failures were true. It was a way he'd often felt. That was who he was.

Good.

Barnaby scraped and painted and did his best to forget about love. Day after day for weeks. He was a good scraper and a good painter, and since Marian would not be back, he became a good forgetter. It helped the forgetting to finally confess about Marian to Ada and then to hear Ada's own consoling tale about having loved Charles, the senatorial fool in Wichita who turned to a cheap blond. Charles, the wastrel and plunger who married the blond and stayed with her and stayed in Wichita and years later struck oil.

Barnaby also went several times to the zoo, where the large tiger with the furry jowls remembered him and came over to gurgle deep inside a busy stomach and occasionally to sweep a majestic tail. Barnaby gurgled back. Sometimes Barnaby kneeled. Barnaby and the large tiger admired one another across their moat and shared stories about moving on between episodes of fat children and waitresses.

The day before Christmas, the letter arrived from Jerry Childs and the Winott Point Tennis Association.

He would not even have mentioned the letter to Ada unless he had to, but plainly he did have to. He mentioned it directly on Christmas Eve and then discussed it at depth for most of Christmas Day.

He tried to explain it as the weight and motion of history. Martin Luther's theses. The Winott Point Tennis Association covenants. When Ada would have none of that, he tried to invoke the hero in history, Bonaparte, Budge. When that provoked

Happiness to tearful discourse on Jesus and Galilee and problems of degradation around holy sites, then Barnaby invoked at full voice the theory of the asshole in history.

This was a risk on Christmas Day, with Happiness trying to maintain the Lord's joyous moment, with everyone dressed up more or less, with goose fat reeking in the kitchen, with holy music turned on and off to assist Barnaby in focusing on an issue that was both political and genealogic.

But the notion caught Ada's attention.

And of course the asshole in this case was Jerry Childs who had persuaded the very vaguest of ancient Richardson's grandchildren to marry again so that he, Jerry Childs, could become installed in the tennis association. Now installed, even though he was not a tennis player, Jerry had taken the reins of the association's official chariot. It had always been true that assholes had wanted and been encouraged to run the association; several generations in fact of Swifts had had the qualifying gene. But now that the association had been sued as the de facto governing body of the Point's private acreage (which was all the Point except the lighthouse and breakwater), even the most devout of the Swifts balked at further service. Jerry Childs was so desperate to be director of anything with the illusion of inherited propriety, so desperate to belong in the venomous nest of old families and newly arrived Kopuses, that he not only submitted to the vilification attendant upon making up the annual tournament draw, but he also stood tall in the face of fire from the litigious parents of all the drunk off-Point delinquents who cared to murder themselves and their motorcycles against the Point's good stone fences.

Barnaby might once have found Childs interesting, since Childs happened to be one of the newly risen technical stars at Fiduciary Funds in Boston and had much to do with lots and lots of money, even if Childs's digitalized relationship to all that money was not exactly Barnaby's cup of tea. But Childs had arrived on the Point and risen in Fiduciary just as Barnaby was evaporating professionally. And then Barnaby's focus within the Winott Point Tennis Association had gone entirely to hitting the ball, beating Kopus.

And after that of course it had been Oklahoma.

But now, here was a letter from Jerry Childs on Winott Point Tennis Association stationery—he'd had fucking stationery printed up—announcing the annual meeting in the Winott hut on December 26. At the end of the letter—but still part of the letter, sent to everyone—was the casually dictatorial assertion that "since Barnaby Griswold has severed Winott Point connections and his children have never expressed an interest in the Association, if neither Griswold child attends the meeting on the 26th, it will be assumed that the Griswold family is to be removed from membership rolls in the Association."

Phrased in the best tradition of Swift family attorneys. And drawn from the covenants, naturally.

"Everyone must continue to own a house on the Point and must attend the annual meeting to be held in the week between Christmas and New Year's or face expulsion from the sacred privileges and premises of the Association."

Well, fine. Or fine if the letter had come from a Swift. The Swifts had been paying lawyers to try and throw out families and reprobates and spouses and Brittany spaniels for fifty years, though in fact there were no premises, and the only privilege was playing in the tournament on the old Richardson court. The tournament, to be fair, really was a privilege, since there were only very few people in the association who could hold a tennis racket and walk at the same time, giving the Barnaby Griswolds of this world a chance to win at something physical. What was much more, Griswolds had been members always. Always. Which counted with Barnaby. The Winott Point Tennis Association was the last arena left in which Barnaby could do his part to keep Griswold history honorably alive in the world and in his children.

That was probably all Jerry Childs had to understand (and he would have understood it along with everybody else) to decide Barnaby and his kin were not a sufficient credit to the association. The Griswolds' worth, in other words, had been reduced to a playable card for Childs: successfully expunge an old-liner family like the Griswolds from the association, and Childs was established as arbiter of Point behavior, not to say Point genes.

And with Jerry Childs, it didn't matter that the covenants were famously a joke, written when the only people anywhere near the Point during Christmas week were the last retarded generation of ice cutters and the first wave of off-season thieves and private police.

Before her strokes, Ada would have gotten it right away, but on this year's Christmas Day, with Happiness for foil, she interpreted Barnaby's troubles as part of some deception to do with Babylon, and despite Barnaby's pleas for intercession, Happiness nodded and listened and stared with such a crushing weight of mindlessness that Barnaby wondered for a few minutes whether she might herself not be a lost Richardson grandchild, an Anastasia of the Point's idiot royalty.

Nobody but Barnaby seemed to understand, or care, that Jerry Childs was not a Swift.

What had happened to Barnaby's powers of explanation and persuasion?

Was Ada actively refusing to grasp the fact that the Swifts were known assholes? Everyone had swum in the same pond with one Swift or another. But Jerry Childs was a new and unknown asshole. Unknown except that his fervency had been proved twice over by his marrying the Richardson princess and by his seizing directorship of the association. Jerry Childs came to the Winott Point Tennis Association covenants with the fresh, humorless ardor of a shouting Baptist to an Episcopal pulpit. Jerry Childs was not pretending; he really was capable of anything.

"Don't you see?"

"You're leaving. I knew you would leave as soon as you fell in love with your blond. Your Marian. All this about her disappearing. Your painting wherever you paint every day. I'm still enough of a woman that I know when I'm not loved any more. I know when I've been discarded. I don't know why you bothered to pretend anything. Except that Charles pretended right up to the end just the same way."

She tried to bring part of her stack of religious comics across the coffee table to her, and Barnaby grabbed them away.

"I want to read," she said.

"I'm weak," Barnaby said. "Don't you understand even that much, Ada?"

"Oh, Barnaby," Happiness said. "You're not weak. You're a big strong man. You go to the gym."

It was the sort of line she could offer with such deadpan abundance of truth telling that Barnaby, never a violent man, understood, in the flash of time it took to clench a fist, all he'd ever want to know about the nature of violent souls.

"He is, too, weak," Ada said. "He is horribly weak. What's the matter with you? Look at him. He's a spineless betrayer. And I love him. What does that make me? Pray for us, Happiness. Pray for us all."

"Now listen to me, Ada. I'm weak. And Jerry Childs is an asshole, an extreme, fundamentalist asshole whom no one knows but who has gotten hold of power. Should I let him come near me with a sharp knife?"

"What?"

"I'm ruined financially and every other way; I'm defenseless, and Jerry Childs is a crazy asshole with a knife. Do I turn my back on him?"

"No. Don't turn your back on anyone. That's what they say in the mall parking lots."

"Do I ignore him, like I ignored Peterpotter? Remember Peterpotter? And in those days I was far from defenseless."

"Happiness, isn't this what happened to the Assyrian kings?"

"Forget the Assyrian kings, Ada. I'm talking about Jerry Childs, who is really and truly going to try to get Griswolds thrown out of the Winott Point Tennis Association to which Griswolds have always belonged. If the Griswold name comes off that roll of membership, Ada, I will have lost my very last anything and everything. And lost it for my children, for my daughters and their children. Can't you understand? This is what I have left to hand on to my girls."

"When I didn't make Theta at O.U., because of all those women who still hate me, the ones who aren't dead, I went to Arizona and made it there."

"Yes. Absolutely. The Thetas. But there is no chapter of Winott Point in Arizona."

"No, I don't suppose there is."

"Absolutely there is not."

"You really have to go?"

"Yes. I have to. I'll be back in no time, a couple of days, but I have to go. I have to be there in person to protect our membership."

"Then I understand. He has to go, Happiness."

And in that moment, Barnaby deluded himself into thinking he had made everyone happy, and so he was pleased with himself.

He was a tiger of Christmas ease despite Jerry Childs.

It was Christmas afternoon and time to eat the goose of which Happiness (a farm girl, Barnaby'd thought) was afraid.

Barnaby imagined growing sideburns like his friend the immense tiger once the business with Jerry Childs had been wrapped up.

He said to Ada, "May I turn the Christmas music back on?"

"I always hated Christmas," she said to Happiness, spitefully. "Hated it."

"Then this can be the first happy Christmas," Barnaby said. "Happiness, will you carve the goose? Or should I?"

Barnaby stood up from the sofa and stepped around the coffee table and started for the kitchen.

And Happiness said, "You're crying."

"No, I'm not," Barnaby said, surprised she could think so.

Ada was crying.

Barnaby turned back and stood before her wheelchair. He'd thought everything was fine. He said, "What's the matter?"

"You're leaving," Ada said.

"I'm not."

"You are," she sobbed.

"I'm coming back in a couple of days. We're going to spend New Year's Eve together."

"You aren't," she sobbed. "We won't ever. Ever. I'll be dead before I see you again. I'm going to die alone. Or with Win. My daughter who hates me. It's her turn now. Your sentence is up. Why would you come back? It was always the first of the year. I haven't forgotten. Don't let Win come. I want to die alone."

"I have a return ticket, Ada. I don't care about the first of the year anymore. I'm going to stay with you. The hell with the first of the year."

"I know perfectly well that you want an early release from my jail. Well I don't care about the first of the year either. Go ahead. I'm giving you a pardon. You can leave a week early. I don't know why you came in the first place, and I don't know why you stayed so long. Good-bye."

Already she had wet her face with tears, and their gloss on the thin, translucent softness of her wrinkles was like a decoration. It could have been gaiety. Her lips were pulled back from her large teeth and her shrunken gums, and she could have been hilarious in a grin.

"I promise," Barnaby said. "I promise with everything that makes a promise sacred, that I will be back and that we will spend New Year's Eve together. The end of my suspension doesn't mean a thing now. I haven't called a soul, and nobody would know who I was if I did call. I have to finish painting the house here on Wimbledon. The landlord's going to give me free rent. I'm thinking about a job."

"I don't believe you," she said, and suddenly her wetted face grew smaller, and her mouth became nothing but a grimace. She might have been in the real throes of death.

"Ada?" Barnaby bent to her in the earliest tide of panic. "I promise, Ada. Ada? I don't care about the securities business anymore. It's been four years, and I don't want it anymore. That's why I never made any calls. I live here now."

"On the telephone?" she said.

"On the telephone. I never made a single call."

And she threw her arms up at him.

She threw her arms up so suddenly and so surprisingly that Barnaby stood away from her in a start.

But she had him around his neck. She had ahold of him and she held on and she stood up after him, with him.

Against him.

She stood in sweatpants and a silk blouse with a green ribbon pinned to it like St. Patrick's Day, with a hooded gray sweat jacket tied around her shoulders.

Her soaked face was almost up to his.

Her arms held rigid around his neck.

She said, "I don't care about promises. I want you to love me. I don't want anything else."

She let go with one arm and pulled at the sweat jacket in a quick, manic jerking until it fell from her, and then she grabbed at the collar of her blouse and tore at that so three buttons broke loose and the bone white curtain of skin that lay loose across the top of her chest was bared to the tops of her large weights of breast supported in thick cotton brassiere.

Happiness appeared close beside them.

"Get away," Ada shouted, and beat with her free arm to keep Happiness off.

And then put her mouth at Barnaby.

With her mouth open and soaking, Ada kissed onto Barnaby's mouth.

Into his mouth.

She pushed Happiness away again, and said into Barnaby's face, "I'm taking my clothes off for you. I'm taking them all off. I love you. I want to go to bed. You can touch me anywhere."

FOOL

By the time he finally got to Will Rogers World Airport on Christmas night, he was nearly late for his flight, which was the last flight out and his only chance to make the association meeting.

But he wasn't late, and he'd known he wouldn't be. He'd known it even as he was doing his emergency pack while the taxi waited on Wimbledon. Traffic to the airport late on Christmas night was going to be easy.

Along with a certainty he'd make the plane, however, he felt something else. Grabbing suits and shoes and shirts, doing what in the old days he had called his coup d'état pack, he felt something he had not felt for so long that at first he was not certain.

He sat in the cab racing through the already sagging lights of everyone else's holiday along the highway, and knew that a wave was in fact building and that he himself was on the front face of it.

This was what you felt when suddenly you were into a fast-moving deal. And when you felt it, you simply tried to stay in it. If you could stay in the wave, you knew that it would carry you.

Wouldn't you know that as soon as he admitted out loud he was never going to make any calls, he would pick up a wave. But that was the way it had always worked for Barnaby.

Jogging to the plane at the last minute, Barnaby felt as if he were already onto a deal with genuine money, a deal large enough to move the tennis association headlines back to the second section of the newspaper.

The wave that Barnaby and his deal had caught felt as if it might be a tidal wave out of dead calm, a wave only Barnaby knew and only Barnaby rode. The plane took off, and it was an inexpressible thrill to lift into the night with that kind of wave beneath you.

Some people might have advised their friends that this was a manic episode and needed to be contained, but Barnaby, free of friends for the moment and full of his own personal history of manic successes, only wondered where the wave was headed, and really he didn't wonder very much about that.

He had enough on his hands managing the actual geographical destinations. To get a ticket on Christmas Eve for travel on Christmas night was to arrange a tour of the country. Barnaby's itinerary passed through Phoenix and Dallas and Atlanta, where there was a layover until a dawn flight to Pittsburgh and then on to La Guardia in time to catch a shuttle flight to Boston and then the train and a taxi out to the Point.

Was it when he learned he'd be coming into La Guardia that he began to feel the very first stirrings of the wave? Perhaps it was, because La Guardia was so close to town that on the way back Barnaby could stop in for lunch at La Cote and still make his return flight. Since he couldn't afford even a salad at La Cote, here indeed were the first stirrings: financial considerations fell away. They had already fallen away to some extent with the rush back to Winott Point, but that had a goal. There was no goal in La Cote. Yes, somewhere, the foolishness of a deal was opening itself and beckoning to Barnaby.

As Barnaby rode at least partly in answer to that beckoning, as he toured the southern night, his wave built still more. There was nothing else to notice.

Well, there was hunger to notice. The goose in Picadilly Manor had never been carved; there had been no Christmas dinner, and at the time Barnaby had not regretted it. On the flight to Phoenix there were no nuts left, and Barnaby did not too much regret that either. He did regret their absence on the legs to Dallas and Atlanta.

Hungrily, he watched other travelers for the ghost of his own past Christmas travels. There had been one or two very good deals cemented during the cheer of exactly Christmas Day in parts well removed from his hearth. Naturally there had been not-so-good Christmas deals that likewise had claimed his Christmas presence as a firefighter, but it was the good ones he remembered especially on this Christmas night when, just hours after he'd as much as admitted he would never do another deal in his life, he found himself riding an enormous, inexplicable wave of momentum.

And then while he sat for several hours in Atlanta, Barnaby lost the wave.

Barnaby sat in Atlanta and tried by force of will to keep the wave beneath himself, and felt it slide away and leave him.

Gone.

No one but Barnaby would have noticed, but the wave rolled on, and Barnaby was left eddying.

He tried to console himself with the fact that even after the expense of this trip, he did have enough money to live as he was doing for a couple of years. Once he would have considered those years as a limitless time in which a million great things could happen. But now he calculated like an insurance actuary that he might have another forty years to live. Which meant thirty-eight years with no money.

Less than a week until January 1, and it couldn't matter less, regardless of what he'd promised Ada. If another deal ever did come along for him, he couldn't handle it. He couldn't stay on the wave.

He had to hope that Oklahoma was looking for a résumé like his.

A résumé?

A job. He'd told Ada he was thinking of a job, and he had meant it, even if he had only begun thinking about it in the moment he spoke. But now the truth came home. A job. Just the word was a terror to his soul.

The thought that he might have to get one—*would* have to, and no jokes about lawn work—was enough to make him want to climb down off his plastic chair in the Atlanta airport and hold his cheek against the footprints of people who were glad to have jobs and belonged somewhere because of it.

He tried to tell himself, and it was true, that he had gone irredeemably beyond the precipice of financial doom more times than he could count, and those had always been the times when he had soared. Risk and reward were the terms he had used to talk about it with the graduating nephews of friends, kids who imagined he could tell them about the nature of work with investments, but in his heart he had always known that his own dynamic was the buoyancy of foolishness. It was: leap, spread your arms, and think exhilarating thoughts of money. Only now he had lived through every wreck he was entitled to survive. His odds were up. There could be no more leaps, and money would never again be anything but the humiliating measure of its absence.

No, the money was not coming back. And a fool like Barnaby Griswold, after a certain age, which Barnaby had long since passed, needed money for his foolishness. Without money, the fluff blew away. Without money, foolishness like Barnaby's withered, and in the Christmas of Atlanta's airport, Barnaby had to acknowledge that he himself was withered. His nature had dried up. He had pretended for as long as he could, and now it was time for a job. He was afraid of a job, but he would get used to the idea. He would have to. Everybody else did, and Barnaby Griswold was no different now than everybody else. Now he had to hope that he qualified for a job.

Finally, before his flight to Pittsburgh, he went to the can, shaved, bathed as best he could, put on a good suit and saw in the mirror that the suit hung on him as if there were nothing left of all the fat and noise that had made Barnaby Griswold. Which of course was the case. What would become of him without his noisy fat? Would he have to eat and drink and give up the gym to get a job? Oh Christ, a job.

He got on the plane to Pittsburgh with a *Wall Street Journal* and with half a dozen financial magazines so that the other still-going ghosts of himself in years past would imagine he belonged in his suit. He never looked around to see if the wave were alive and might pick him up once more and carry him somewhere. The wave had passed through.

By the time he got to La Guardia he had learned only that the market was continuing up and that trading was erratic but heavy for the holiday season and that there had been no tax sell-off earlier in the month, no selling to lock in year-end profits for decoration. Any ten-year-old watching the evening news could have told him that. So Barnaby had become a slower learner than ever before. Just as he was about to go back into the job market in the suits he couldn't fill. After twenty-five dollars of the moment's financial literature, Barnaby passed through the holiday wasteland of La Guardia without any perspective whatever on a holiday market up and erratic and heavy.

Which made the tennis association a blessing. The association took his attention. The association became again his focus by default. Today, Barnaby Griswold was going to see to something more important, his daughters' birthright. He was tired, and he dozed on the train up from Boston.

By the time he got in the cab at the station for the run out to the Point, he had reclaimed purpose in his life. He instructed the driver to hurry and he threw a twenty into the front seat. He told the driver to blow the God damned horn every inch of the way down the Point Road, and when he got out of the cab he threw another twenty into the front seat and said, "Merry Christmas, Happy New Year, and come back in an hour or so."

For Ada, despite a membership at the Driscoll Hills Country Club, there had never been tennis or even golf.

To the best of Barnaby's knowledge, in the last fifty years Ada had never walked when it was avoidable.

Since the big stroke, she had not moved a muscle for any purpose other than to chew and turn her dominoes and do whatever Happiness helped her with back in the bathroom.

But make no mistake. There was strength now. She was a large woman, which was easy to forget when she was in the wheelchair. She was large, and right now she was passionate. Right now she was a Valkyrie.

She faced Barnaby, and with one arm she held his neck in a brutal headlock.

With the other arm she alternately beat away Happiness and tore at her own buttons and at the cotton brassiere to give Barnaby her antique but still hefty breasts. With her mouth she kissed soakingly into Barnaby's mouth and at the same time cried, "Touch me. I want you to touch me."

Happiness may have been speaking too, but Barnaby didn't hear it. He could make out Happiness's shape beside them only as an indistinct component of the room's furniture, a weaving, witnessing lamp.

Barnaby himself stood with his arms out to the sides and with his neck painfully forward, with the bottom of his face wet and his mouth lost to another nation. He stood with Ada's brassiered sacks of breasts swinging their oddly substantial Cream of Wheat weight into his rigid trunk.

Christ Almighty.

And there was no getting away.

There was instead a squeal of horror from the outside, from Happiness.

From Ada at the same moment came an animal shout of triumph.

One breast was actually loose in the air, loose against Barnaby. God, he could feel its nipple.

"There," she cried. "Touch me."

He made one mighty surge of flight, tried with all he had to get free, and could not do it. She had him. She beat Happiness away and had him.

So he held her.

What else was there to do?

He brought his arms forward and around her, and he stood into her. And he held her. He hugged her.

"Barnaby," she said.

She pressed her hands now against his chest, driving her fingers into him like a lover. He hugged her more tightly, and her hands went around his back and now she hugged too.

"Keep away, Happiness," she shouted. "Keep away or I'll kill us all."

She was up against the length of him now, and her head was onto his shoulder, beside his ear. She stopped shouting at Happiness, and she whispered, "Barnaby?"

Was it possible that Barnaby had the slight, the very very slight, beginnings of an erection?

Oh, he didn't want that.

He hugged Ada as tightly as he could, and she was no dead weight the way she was when she was going into the car. She stood and held herself against him, and he could feel her shaking with the exertion. He could feel the furious beat of her heart in the squeezed pressure of her breasts against him.

"Oh, Barnaby," she whispered. "Do you love me?"

"Of course I love you," he said with great heartiness as he tried to think of something besides that tiny, appalling hint of swollen eagerness below his belt.

"Barnaby," she whispered, her voice a gasp in his ear. "Do you want to get in bed?"

He took a deep breath and said loudly, "Yes. Let's go to bed."

He brought his eyes into focus and found Happiness, and to his amazement, Happiness was watching now with quiet bliss, with a sympathetic, transported joy.

"Happiness," he said. "We're going to go to bed. Will you help us into the bedroom?"

Ada hissed into Barnaby's ear, "Happiness?"

"You don't want to have to go in the wheelchair, do you?"

"No," she said. "Not the chair."

He arrived at the Winott hut after everyone else had arrived. The parked cars, covered with road salt and the other slop of winter driving, looked, on the afternoon after Christmas, like tired ornaments. They were strung around the circled, otherwise empty Winott lane, in eight inches of snow, under black-barked, winter-bare trees and an iron sky. The tracks of boots went at the door of the hut.

But Barnaby didn't think anybody would have begun proceedings yet.

They all had to have heard the horn of the taxi blaring down the length of the Point Road. The Portuguese driver, who hated everyone ever connected with the Point, except now Barnaby, had been more than happy to blare. He had in fact offered to go to a friend's boat and get a couple of air horns to further disrupt the holiday quiet of the rich, but time had not allowed. It was a near thing for Barnaby as it was, with his several flights and then the local train from Boston.

It was a doubly near thing when, before Barnaby reached the door to the hut, his good shoes slipped on ice beneath the snow and he hung suspended on the balance of one fine English heel, his other heel far before him and above waist height, one arm up, one arm back, the velvet collar of his chesterfield prying into his mouth. It couldn't have been more than a second, but it felt like the eternal minute during which an acrobat falls to his death in front of thousands. During that minute, Barnaby balanced on the precipice of final humiliation when he had thought all final humiliations were behind him. There would be no splendid entrance after a sprawl—if he got to make an entrance at all; they might open the door, all of them, and see him go down flailing. He would present himself prone, beside the sagging, snow-thatched wall of pea vine that had taken over the old boat racks in the decades since the last Winotts moved to their ritzier compound down the coast.

He had time to imagine that and to listen for the opening of the door to the hut. He had time to imagine them lifting him, a sopping wreck in a handmade, oversized suit. He imagined acceding to expulsion from the association on grounds of ridiculousness before he was taken by some expendable teenager to the emergency room. Back to the emergency room when he'd only two weeks ago gotten the stitches out of his mouth from a previous ridiculous moment.

And then an organic message reached his core of cerebration and balance, and the message told him to turn around.

So he turned around on one foot with composure but rather rapidly, spun would be more like it, his weight shifting miraculously, athletically, from his heel to his toe while the other foot stayed in the air, while the velvet edge of the overcoat's collar slid back under his chin, while his arms spread wide for flight back toward the taxi. While his taxi driver stared at him, begging him silently not to fall, not to let the rich people win again. The cabdriver could not know about the covenants, but he had to know that Barnaby, no matter how he spoke, no matter what his clothes looked like, was here in the bastion of summer money as an adversary.

"Stand up," the lips of the cabbie said noiselessly through the dirty glass of his window. It was the voice of all the policemen and firemen from the town gym, all the locals who had hated him impersonally forever and in person for the couple of years while he became healthy in their midst. Was there also on the cabbie's face a conviction that Barnaby didn't have it in him to stand, that only a town guy would be able to walk down a path to a door and not fall?

Barnaby stood up.

He brought his other foot down, and his chesterfield fell straight onto his shoulders, and there he was.

The cabbie grinned. Barnaby had pulled it off, and the cabbie showed Barnaby a fist with his thumb pointing up. Two of the cabbie's fingers were missing, Jesus, but his thumb was up; that was the message. The cabbie brought the fist to his cab's horn and blared, and drove around the rest of the dark circle of maples and off. And as the blaring sang back away on the Point, Barnaby managed to hear in it the grudging approval of a whole locker room of civil servants, even the ones who worked with free weights.

Barnaby turned and opened the door of the hut and strode in.

It was one bare little room, generations removed from stored sails and centerboards, but still with its tiny, salt-pitted cleat at the end of the pull string for the light. There was even a feel of summer to the rows of cast-off chairs in which sat many of the people (minus the children and most of the old ladies) who had watched Barnaby triumph in the Winott Cup up the hill on the buried Richardson court.

All twenty or so of them watched at Barnaby again, though their chairs faced across past Barnaby to where youthful Jerry Childs stood dressed in a brand-new everything out of one of the catalogues for people who want to look as if they graduated from boarding school to a life of country-weekend privilege on Winott Point. It was clothing not unlike what Barnaby wore most of the time, but it was so new and so perfect that Barnaby felt ready to subscribe himself to all the prejudices of the townies. Childs even had the stern, fatuous upper lip of the catalog models, and now he aimed that stern lip at Barnaby.

Barnaby tried to see if the sweater under Childs's canvas jacket had a monogram of the association. After all, there was stationery these days.

But the jacket was not open enough for a view, and so Barnaby turned from Childs to greet the rest of the room.

Barnaby said a quiet, inclusive "How do you do" and scanned all of the faces and made what he thought was a gesture of courtly graciousness with his right hand and arm out to the side in the balletic shape of a scythe. He could afford to speak quietly because there was not another sound.

If one had to come back for a visit from beyond the pale of want and ruin, this was the way to do it, the way a tiger would do it, magnificently.

He nodded a special attention to Dicky Kopus, the nod of an assured superior, but not too superior since Kopus was probably the closest thing he had to a friend in the room.

He was surprised there were quite so many of the rest of them, but more and more people retired and winterized and came year-round, and most of the rest came, as Barnaby's family had begun doing, to have Christmas on the Point. Of course there were also a few who'd been downsized and now pretended they had figured out how to consult from the Point, and they were delighted to see someone with Barnaby's magnitude of misfortune. Barnaby sought out all the faces and eyes, and nodded with the nobility of a deposed monarch. He breathed deeply in preparation for his speech to Childs.

He looked to the farthest back corner, and there was Choate Winott, the senior Winott, the banker, the patriarch, not seen here, Barnaby thought, for at least five years. And now he'd come for this meeting in the hut which he lent to the association in perpetuity. What a happy surprise for Jerry Childs in his new country-privilege outfit.

But something of a discomfort for Barnaby.

To have to look old Winott in the eye, despite his palpable authority, was certainly not the same as having to look his own father in the eye. Choate Winott probably didn't recognize Barnaby now, and had never met him in more than passing even in the old days. But Choate Winott had known and respected Barnaby's father, and Barnaby's father had returned the respect. And so Barnaby chose actually not to meet Choate Winott's eyes.

Beside Winott was someone with a silhouette of too much hair, a renegade offspring from the Winott compound who had been pressed into service as the old man's driver and who had decided to survive this trial of youth by turning away from everything and staring out the window at the snow-covered pods of day sailboats pulled from the yacht club anchorage.

As Barnaby looked past the frizz of all that hair and out the window himself, as he prepared to fire on Jerry Childs in the next breath, the sun broke through and for a moment shone weakly off the tipped hulls and the snow, and that shine of light came in through the window and turned the renegade frizz to a transparent copper halo the color of Marian's hair.

It wasn't Marian's hair. It couldn't be Marian. But it was the same color.

It was the color of the girl's hair from the Winott Cup finals. That was who it was: the most recent of the thousand summer girls he had seen and loved and then forgotten about—without their ever knowing, most of them. She must have been Winott's daughter from the not-quite-scandalous second marriage. How nice to be an important banker and to have married a younger woman before the term *trophy wife* came into vogue. And now a pretty young daughter in his old but still rock-solid age. If Barnaby had had a hundred million bucks, he would never have been the man Choate Winott was. Nor would anyone else in the room, which was what they were probably all thinking before Barnaby arrived to distract them, all except Jerry Childs who probably still imagined that that kind of thing rubbed off if you got close enough. As if it weren't already too late for Childs even to be a legendary schoolboy hockey player, not to mention the rest of it.

The sun went away and the hulls dulled, and the girl turned around into the room and looked at Barnaby.

It was Marian.

Marian with her hair undone.

And Barnaby had to speak now or lose any hope of ever speaking.

He felt as if his stomach had fallen out from inside of him. He felt as if the hut's worn, board floor had fallen away from under the reach of his legs and feet. Marian with her hair released into a radiance around her face, Marian looking right at him with an expression of not complete surprise, as if she knew him and even knew him here. She did know him, and she was more beautiful than he had ever understood, and he held his breath. She'd known all along. He held his breath because he needed breath to speak, and he must speak and speak now.

He turned with as simple and elegant and forceful a motion as he could manage in a circumstance when his feet were not in contact with anything, and he said to the asshole Jerry Childs, "How do you do, Jerry."

That took all of Barnaby's breath, but a pause was appropriate to let Childs feel the impact of Barnaby's presence and attention, to let Childs stew in the deserts of his assholeness.

To give him his due, Childs did not flinch before Barnaby's imposing ghost of fortunes past. Childs had fiber. He also had Kopus in the room for proof of at least a little ascendance, and back in the corner he had old Winott for example and aspiration.

"Hello, Mr. Griswold," Childs said.

Mr. Griswold. Christ. "Barnaby is fine, please."

"Merry Christmas to you, Barnaby," Childs said with an invented politesse that almost really did get to Barnaby.

It was all he could do not to shout, Don't Merry Christmas me, you asshole. But he held himself in. He was a cop and a fireman. Truth and justice were on his side. He stared at Childs and waited.

"Barnaby, to get right to the point, I understand that you have turned over what was always the Griswold house to your ex-wife. Unless you have another property on the Point, that would mean you are no longer a member of the tennis association."

"Yes," Barnaby said. "I hope, however, that has not prevented my name from being inscribed on the cup as this past year's winner."

"Your name is on the cup," Childs said with the slightest evidence of relief.

Relief?

Ah. Childs thought it was over. Childs didn't know about the deeding of the house. It was always a surprise when everyone did not know everything about the terms of a divorce, but it was an agreeable surprise in this case.

"Good," Barnaby said, and waited for Childs to finish his business.

"Since you are no longer a member of the association, since your daughters and your ex-wife have never demonstrated any interest in tennis, since the house is now in your wife's name, since your daughters have not come to assert any right to association privileges, I thought it might be best to simply take the Griswold name off the association rolls of membership. In fact I was about to move that we all vote on that as you came in just now. If your daughters were here, of course, they might argue with some reason for continuing membership. But they are not here, despite notification, which is I think fair evidence of disinterest."

Oh Christ, what an asshole. With the Swifts, at least you had always been able to hear the hatreds and perversions that provoked each scheme of expulsion; often you were able to get formal recountings of the specific outrage behind the hatred. The Swifts had been an entertainment, a reason to get out of the house during Christmas week without going back to work.

"If you'd like to sit down, Barnaby, we'll go ahead and take the vote. You won't be able to vote yourself of course, but I'm sure we're all happy to have you here as a visiting friend of the association."

Barnaby did not move to sit.

Now was the moment, but Barnaby paused for effect. You didn't make as many pitches as Barnaby had made without learning something of dramatic presentation.

"Mr. Griswold? Will you sit for the association vote?"

Barnaby drew the papers on the house from his breast pocket and turned to the rest of the room and spoke.

"These papers will show that the Griswold house has been deeded not to my ex-wife, not to Win, but through Win to my daughters. It is still a Griswold house and will remain a Griswold house for some considerable time at the very least. I am here on my daughters' behalf to be sure that as Griswolds they remain members of the Winott Point Tennis Association and retain the right to play in the tournament whenever they choose, regardless of whether they ever show up for these annual meetings, which were originally meant to be honored, as we all know, by every member's absence."

He did not look toward Choate Winott. He certainly didn't look at Marian. He didn't let himself conceive of Marian. But he looked at the rest of them, and they looked back with wonder and delight. He was providing the best show since Asa Swift's wife had tried to throw crazy Asa out, bodily out the door, while he was director. Barnaby smiled at them all. It was too late for a career as an actor, but it was never too late to appreciate one's own gifts.

He turned to Jerry Childs again.

"If you'd like to look at these papers to be sure that I am not lying about control of the house, you are welcome to do so. If you wish to contest my right to speak on my daughters' behalf, I am prepared to step outside with you where we can pursue that contest with our fists. Although I should warn you that I have been working out and that if I punch you in the nose it will hurt."

He held his posture at its loftiest. He tried with all his might to feel the floor so that he could know he wasn't tipping over. He stared at Childs and held the papers on the house out with one hand.

"No," Childs said. "That won't be necessary. If the house belongs to the girls and you want to urge continued membership on their behalf, I'm sure we can all agree to keep the Griswold name on the rolls with the girls as active members."

It was an easy victory, perhaps an automatic victory once he'd made it in the door, but it was a necessary victory just the same. It was a small victory by some lights, but for Barnaby every victory right now, especially this one, was important.

Nor was he finished.

There was a part of him that wanted to really take a swing at Childs, because Childs was not a big man even if he was ten or fifteen years younger than Barnaby.

But that wouldn't do any service for the girls once Barnaby was back in Oklahoma or wherever he was next year or the year after.

No, Barnaby put the papers to the house back in his breast pocket and stepped to Childs and said, "Thank you." He said it sincerely, and he shook Childs's hand.

Childs shook back and said, "You're welcome," but Childs was not happy. Of course he was not happy.

So Barnaby held on to Childs's hand and turned to face everyone else with his own free hand around Childs's shoulders.

"Traditionally," Barnaby said, "the champion takes the Winott Cup home and keeps it from the time it has been engraved until the beginning of the next year's tournament." At this, Barnaby nodded past Childs to where the cheap silver-plate trophy stood polished but battered on a small table which also held Childs's notes for his meeting. "I cannot know what my prospects will be in the next months and years, but circumstances are likely to keep me far away from Winott Point, and my diminished finances may not let me return at will. So instead of taking the cup home with me as is my right, I will ask Jerry Childs please to take custody of the cup in my stead. I can think of no more safe or proper repository for the cup during my unfortunate absence than in Jerry's honorable household."

Why had Barnaby never seriously considered a political career? Because here was a true and viable gift.

There was applause.

Of course there was applause.

They were seeing one of their own who had lost everything go nobly away. What a figure. Ruined, and walking head up, conscious to the last, out into the great, gray sea of unwashed reality, into the broth and under, beneath the surface and lost to view. Barnaby Griswold. He was moved himself.

Beside him, Jerry Childs was close to tears at being in the center of such an event here in the Winott hut, with even Choate Winott watching. Childs held Barnaby's hand and shook it and would not let go. For just a second Barnaby was afraid that Childs might press his perfectly combed head into the shoulder of the chesterfield because of so much emotion.

Barnaby's daughters were now members of the association forever, whether they liked it or not and whether they moved to Sri Lanka in the morning. And if the girls didn't care less about tennis, and if Barnaby's father wouldn't have cared less, and if his mother had always hated all of it, well…Well, Barnaby cared a good deal, and he had made it right.

Applause resounded within the Winott Point Tennis Association.

Griswolds, his children, belonged, and always would belong.

Ada was going to die shortly, most likely because of her heart.

Barnaby thought of that as he and Happiness walked Ada slowly but with swagger back to the master bedroom. Barnaby had an arm around her so that his hand reached under the loose flesh of her upper arm. His fingers cradled very firmly through the thin silk of her blouse to the stretched, heavier material at the side of her brassiere which she had allowed Happiness to remount for the walk. Through that tightness of the brassiere, he could feel the bones of her rib cage, and inside of her bones, he could feel the throbbing pump of her heart.

This was the first time in months she had walked more than a yard, and it followed all her exercise of the moments just preceding.

He had always assumed she was going to die, and now, maybe for the first time, he hoped that she wouldn't. He was glad to have his arm around her. He held her up to get her back to the bedroom, but he also hugged her. He liked to have her next to him.

And so there it was.

He did love her. Barnaby and Ada, sitting in a tree.

They got her into the bedroom and backed her knees against the bed and sat her down and lifted her feet and swiveled her to prone.

As her head hit the pillow, she said, "You can go now Happiness."

"Nighty night," Happiness said, and floated off and closed the door. From the other side she said, "Call if you need anything."

"We won't need anything," Ada shouted. "Go away."

Barnaby walked around the other side of the bed and kicked off his shoes (he had on real shoes for Christmas, for the goose) and lay down beside Ada.

Once, he assumed, she had had a larger bed, but this bed was not a hell of a lot bigger than his cot. It was a better quality than the cot, however, and so at least it could hold them both.

He put his arm around Ada, and rolled her to him, and she grappled an arm out around his stomach. He pulled a couple of surplus pillows out from behind their heads and tossed them off the deck and squeezed the edge of a remaining one under Ada's neck so that her neck looked more or less aligned as it reached onto his shoulder. Her arm that was not fixed across his stomach lay like a dead wing between them, but she didn't seem to mind. Barnaby squeezed part of the pillow under his own head and blew the scatter of hair on top of Ada's head away from his nose so he could breathe without that kind of tickling. Had Happiness put talcum on Ada's head? For some reason, it smelled like a baby. That was a happy barrier against Ada's breath, but even the breath didn't smell terrible this afternoon.

"I can smell you," Ada said. "You don't smell bad. Do I smell awful?"

"Actually," he said, "you don't smell bad either."

"Good," she said.

She rocked her head a bit as if she were nestling onto his arm and shoulder, and her arm and the claw of her fingers held tightly around the back of his stomach.

"You have fat, Barnaby."

"I still have fat back there. The gym doesn't get it."

"That's all right. You're not a boy anymore."

With her hand locked into its grip and her head settled, and when she had pedaled her feet a few times slowly, Ada was a sack of weight that Barnaby held against himself with both arms. It wasn't altogether easy to keep a strong grip on that kind of sack, and Barnaby was glad he had the strength of his time at the gym even if he did still have a roll around his waist. He could hold her for a while.

His cheek was against her temple, and he could feel her pulse against the edge of his lips. It seemed, under the fine, loose, polished thinness of tissue on her temple, a miraculous pulse.

Ada said, "I never thought I would have another man in my bed."

"Well."

"But I'm glad I did, and I'm glad it was you."

"Thank you," Barnaby said. "I'm glad it was me too."

"Our fathers would have liked one another."

"I think they might have."

"Your father loved you very much, and my father loved me." Through his shirtsleeve, Barnaby could feel her lips move against his shoulder as she talked.

"And now we love each other," he said.

"Yes. Don't ever forget that."

She let go her grip around his stomach, and Barnaby said, "I won't forget."

"Barnaby."

"Yes, Ada."

"I have to lie on my back now."

"All right."

"Will you make the pillows so that your arm can stay under me?"

"Okay."

"And stay beside me."

"If I didn't stay beside you, I'd fall off. Where did you find such a small bed?"

"Good," she said, and Barnaby let her roll back onto her back, and then he tucked the pillow up so that her head looked supported.

"Is that all right?"

"Don't take your arm away."

Then they lay like that as outside it got dark, as inside the night-lights in the sockets of Ada's bedroom came up to brightness.

From the living room there was the soft play of the Christmas music that Happiness had turned back on.

"I don't like Christmas," Ada said. "But some of the music is good."

Barnaby thought about his arm, until it went so numb that he either had to pull it out or forget about it.

In a while he looked at his watch, and Ada said, "I'm not asleep."

The breath of Ada's rotting body lifted up around them like a gentle breeze carrying low tide inland.

Barnaby must have slept in that, because he woke with a start and looked at his watch again.

"You were sleeping," Ada said. "You probably have to go now."

"I do have to go," he said.

"Thank you for coming to be with me."

"You're welcome. I liked it."

"Would you ever do it again?"

"I would."

"No, you wouldn't."

"I might."

"Are you going to come back from tennis?"

"I already promised that I would."

"Promise again."

"I promise."

"Promise that you won't let me die alone."

"I promise that too."

Barnaby slid his arm out from under her and stood up and walked around to the other side of the bed and bent down over Ada and kissed her lips. She kissed him back with a smack of her lips and a smile.

"This is the best Christmas I ever had," she said.

"I don't believe that for a minute," he said.

With the meeting still going on, but with the battle over and won, Barnaby sat by himself in the front row of seats in the Winott hut and wished he had had the taxi wait for him after all.

Coming into the hut, however, had demanded the sort of commitment that was incompatible with an easy escape. And then, when he was in the midst of preserving the Griswold name on the rolls, when he was himself bidding noble farewell to the association and the hut and the Richardson court and summers evermore, then he had almost felt as if he had the momentum of the wave beneath him again, carrying him, gathering the secret massive speed which meant he had a future.

And then, for some reason, Childs had begun speaking about the stock market. Childs had said, for Christ sake, that this was a market that could hurt people, and he hoped all the good people in this room would be safe rather than sorry by the first thing in the morning. What was that? Childs was now more than just a numbers geek who had run up one of the funds; Childs actually was now senior in the operations of the entire Fund Group for Fiduciary, which was the biggest mutual funds firm in the country. Jerry was not going to reveal which stock one of the sector funds was moving into. He wasn't going to tell people, not even Choate Winott, to go short in technologies. Was he? Because God knew Fiduciary, if it pushed, could move whole neighborhoods of the NASDAQ and the Dow both.

But what the fuck difference did any of that make to Barnaby at this point? None. The hell with Jerry Childs. There were no more waves for Barnaby, and there was no future.

Barnaby sat and felt the truth of his own farewells.

He felt the completion of what had happened last night: the last wash of his final wave had brought him here where he had all along been meant to say good-bye. His suspension had never been a pause or an admonition; it had been the limbo before final termination. The Griswold name would remain in membership and on the cup; people would sometimes shake a head or make an uneasy snigger at the mention of Barnaby. Maybe that would become a cautionary invective: you don't want to end up like Barnaby Griswold. But Barnaby the person, Barnaby who sat for a few dear minutes more on a cast-off chair in the hallowed preserve of his lost birthright, that Barnaby, this Barnaby, henceforth would walk in the American desert of homogenous banality hoping not for the police to like him but rather for the police to keep him safe. And he would not be safe. His farewell performance had been great for everyone else, but when Barnaby himself left the Winott hut and Winott Point, all walls would be down and every wind would find him.

Barnaby sat alone in the front row—everyone else was behind him—and he wailed inside himself like a little lost dog.

He went, "Ohhuuuuuuuu." He went again, "Ohhuuuuuuuu," in a high, puppy's yowl that would have broken his mother's heart except that his mother was out there dead in the freeway, a ghastly little throw rug for holiday traffic, and so there was nowhere anyone any longer to take care of her baby. "Ohhuuuuuuuu."

"Mr. Griswold? Are you all right?"

Holy shit. He'd been making his puppy noises out loud. He sat up and shook his head like an adult. Jesus Christ.

"Jerry," he shouted. "Forgive me. It's the God damned sinuses when I've been away from weather like this. The only thing that helps is to make noises like a whale record. I don't mean to interrupt. I'll hold my breath. Please. Go on."

Oh, fuck, fuck, fuck. He'd made his noble good-bye, and now everyone behind him would think that he'd been weeping.

He had been weeping.

Oh, fuck, what a state of affairs. He wished he was already gone out into the netherworld. He wished he was on his way back to Ada. He would be near her for a couple more months until she died. That would be the next watershed to anticipate now that the suspension was as good as history.

He held himself erect and tried to concentrate on what Jerry Childs was saying, had been saying. He remembered Marian, but he was not going to concentrate on that. No wonder she had kissed him off. She was the late and treasured daughter of fucking Choate Winott. The wonder was that, knowing who Barnaby was, she had ever gone to the zoo. Except that was the sort of grace those people had; they would go to the zoo with the lowliest scab. Once.

No, he concentrated on what Jerry Childs had been saying after the market horseshit, something about the theft of seaweed from the Point's kelp beds.

Christ, no wonder Barnaby had drifted off. Maybe everybody behind him had lost the thread too. It might have been only Jerry who had heard the puppy. Barnaby thought that was the case.

All right, he'd wailed aloud and been caught at it. Now he forced himself to concentrate on the last minutes of his last meeting. He followed Jerry out of the kelp and into evidence that off-Pointers had been using the Point's rocky little beaches even though the big town beach was sand. Barnaby had always favored the town beach, but now, as was being made clear, he had to use that sandy beach whether he wanted to or not.

He wondered what on earth Marian had thought when she heard him yowling. He wondered what she had thought when he fell to his knees before the empty tiger world at the zoo. Though the tigers had bailed him out of that one. He wondered if Marian thought about him at all. Why should she? She'd known he was from the Point, and that was why she'd condescended to go to the zoo with him the one time. And then, Good-bye Tiger. He could not believe she was in the same room with him.

Had she ever touched his lips in Doug's? Had she actually kissed him?

No.

Don't allow that to be even a forgotten memory; surely that part never happened.

It was over.

All of it.

Childs was saying that the tournament would be played again at the end of August with the finals on the Sunday before Labor Day.

And everyone was rushing for the door.

Barnaby had thought that he would want to get out first, but he had no chance of that. Everybody else wanted to get out before Barnaby broke down into puppy tears again.

Just as well. Barnaby would be on foot down the Point Road anyhow, until he met his cabbie coming out to pick him up (if his cabbie was faithful—and Barnaby thought he would be, Barnaby a fireman and all).

Childs tried to time his exit to go out last with Choate Winott and Marian, and old Winott stopped and smiled with an embracing warmth and managed without saying a word to accept Childs's motion toward him and to use and guide that motion to keep Childs moving right out the door as if a conversation had been had and irrevocably finished until some future meeting which would be eagerly anticipated.

Christ, but old Winott was a man to admire.

No wonder Marian had been so efficient with her Good-bye Tiger to Barnaby.

Choate Winott and his daughter stood a moment more in the doorway to be sure Jerry got to his car, and then the door closed behind them too, and Barnaby was alone in the hut.

He got up and stepped through careless rows of worn-out summerhouse kitchen chairs and pulled the tiny cleat at the end of the light string to turn off the overhead bulb. He felt the salt pitting in the cleat and for the first time caught a whiff of the rotten, salt breath of low tide, joyously foul even in winter when nobody noticed except the fishermen like his cabdriver must have been, men who were going out in the cold and losing their fingers to the winches so they could drive Barnaby on the last errand of what used to be his life.

He couldn't bear it, and he kicked through the chairs to the door and ran out, and with the unlikely, for him, aptitude of a natural athlete, he instinctively balanced to accept the slide of his thin shoes on the slick that had caught him before.

He called, "Mr. Winott," and had such momentum that he was upon them with the sliding instancy of a cartoon. And Marian was already smiling with mischief before he stopped, though it was he who came sliding. Had she been in mischief from the beginning, even at the gym? Barnaby stopped as close to her as when she had kissed him at the zoo, and even in an old loden coat and corduroys (the same corduroys from the zoo?), she was as beautiful as if she were wearing one of the evening gowns she had had to have worn to the Christmas dances of earlier years.

He could imagine, could absolutely see, her shoulders bare but for thin satin straps. She was almost bony, she held herself so straight in a long dress—with hardly any breasts, and not ashamed of it, and no bra beneath the dress. She had kissed him. She had, and as if it were just the two of them again, he could see her with her evening gown fallen to the tracked, snowy floor of this second-growth wood at the edge of harbor at the end of daylight on the day after Christmas. He could see her with no clothes at all and with her nipples right away stiff from the cold. He could see her with her wonderful posture and with her commanding, teasing curiosity about what he would do. She smiled at him with her green and brown eyes and with her eyebrows like an eagle, and all that he could think of was to fall down to his knees as he had at the zoo. And press his cheek against her warm, firm, naked runner's belly. He felt the curling bristle of her pubic hair against his chin and felt his penis getting hard again.

Oh no, not again.

In a lifetime of deals this had never been remotely a problem. Now that all the deals were done, he was an adolescent between racks of dirty magazines.

He pulled his chesterfield closed across his front and looked violently to Choate Winott.

"How do you do," he shouted. "I'm Barnaby Griswold. Mr. Winott, I think Fiduciary is going to dump a ton of stocks before the year end. They may wait a day to see if the market gives them a reason, but they're going to sell enough to move things even if nobody else comes along. Did you hear Childs in there?"

Christ, what a thing to say to a real human being. Even if it made any sense, Winott was a banker for Christ sake.

Barnaby thrust out his hand to shake, and the chesterfield flew open, and Barnaby stared at Choate Winott to hold Winott's attention. He couldn't do anything about where Marian would look, but it wasn't a full-blown erection; also his suit was too big (it was the first time he was glad of that), and then of course it was all gone with looking Choate Winott in the eye, Marian's father in the eye, his own father in the eye.

Not his own father, but close enough.

Winott shook Barnaby's hand and stared back, weighing whether to make any comment at all upon Barnaby's ridiculous market advice.

But Choate Winott had done more worldly things than Barnaby's father, and in his eyes was the possibility of humor. Winott had Marian's eyes, and suddenly Barnaby liked him just for that. Barnaby smelled low tide and tried to smell Marian.

Had the young, second wife drunk herself to death twice as fast as Barnaby's mother? Yes, she had, and still a sense of humor lived somewhere there in Choate Winott's eyes.

"I know who you are, Barnaby. I haven't seen you for a while, but you're still recognizable. I wrote to you after your father died. I admired him."

Barnaby did like Winott. He drove right past the Jerry Childs crap. He was a banker, but a tolerant banker.

"Yes, sir."

"And I loved your mother. We dated when we were kids; did you know that?"

"No, sir."

"I wish somebody'd watched over her a little more at the end."

"Yes, sir. So do I."

"Drinkers are hard work. She loved you."

"I think she did"

"I know she did. I kept in touch. Your father on the other hand thought you were a fluffmeister."

"He told you that?"

"It wasn't something he said to everybody. What he said was that if you'd been a fluffmeister lawyer and he'd had more sense he could have used you to save the law firm. He took a summer off to make you paint the house with him. Didn't he?"

Barnaby nodded.

"I would have shot my sons before doing that. So he must have loved you, whatever he called you."

Barnaby nodded again.

"He would have been proud of you for looking after your mother-in-law."

"I beg your pardon?"

"News of your activities precedes you. Aren't you in Oklahoma, taking care of your ex-wife's mother?"

"Actually, I don't have anywhere else to go."

"As an alumnus of Fort Sill, I can say with certainty that everybody has somewhere else to go. Except my own daughter. Naturally." Winott looked at Marian with a mixture of fake and real irritation.

Barnaby did not look at Marian. He said, "I took Marian to the zoo."

"Yep. The zoo. Marian told me. The zoo with Barnaby Griswold. Why did you do that?"

"You mean the zoo?" Barnaby said.

"I'm just asking a question, here."

"I didn't know she was your daughter."

"What's that supposed to mean? And why the hell are you getting beaten up?"

Marian laughed, and punched her father's shoulder hard. He raised his eyebrows at her and then looked back to Barnaby.

"Marian takes these things lightly, but she is my only daughter, and my youngest child by a long shot even if she is twenty-eight, and she has been in trouble since the day she was born."

"Thanks, Daddy."

Choate Winott raised his hands like a boxer in case she was going to hit him again, but he didn't look at her. He looked at Barnaby and said, "And you, Barnaby Griswold, are a creature of somewhat the same stripe only further down the road. A monster, some would say. A reforming monster by the look of things, by necessity, I'd guess. But still a monster. Am I right?"

Barnaby hesitated a second, but then went ahead.

He had to tell someone before he left.

He said, "I cheated once during the finals of the cup."

Marian said, "Actually it was out. The ball down the line? But you were going to cheat anyway."

Barnaby said to Winott, "I was going to cheat anyway."

"Well, I don't give a shit about that. I'm a banker. Do you know why Marian and I are here today?"

And with that, Marian lunged at her father and pushed him so hard his feet went out from under him. God Almighty. He was a solid old man, but he was an old man, and his arms flew up and he pitched back toward the stone wall at the end of the pea vined boat racks. Barnaby had no time even to move, and Marian, as her father went headfirst for the stones, laughed.

Choate Winott spun, in a much more elegant version of Barnaby's earlier move, and bent his knees (it was probably always in the knees), and put a hand out to the wall to steady himself. Then he stood up straight and said, "This is what you're in for if you hang around her for any length of time."

What?

"He's not hanging around anyone," Marian said. "He doesn't even know me."

"Then why did you drag me here to see that the Griswolds weren't thrown out of the sacred Winott Point Tennis Association?"

She stood straighter and held her chin higher and stared back at her father defiantly. "I thought the association needed to keep up a connection to one serious cheater."

Good God.

Barnaby said, "I thought you told me, Good-bye Tiger."

Twenty-eight. That was no child. And she'd known it was Barnaby all along, even in the tennis match.

"Good-bye Tiger?" Choate Winott said.

"Nothing," Marian said to her father.

Marian Winott liked Barnaby Griswold.

Old Winott said, "Forget the association, Barnaby. Do you need a job?"

"Daddy," Marian said. "He doesn't need a job, and you don't have to bribe him. He's already asked me out once."

Christ Almighty. She liked him.

"Of course he needs a job. And if I were going to bribe him, Marian, it would be to stay away from you."

Was Winott offering him a job now? Barnaby tried to feel through his wet and freezing feet whether some sort of wave had come back up beneath him, but no. Could a job ever be a wave? No, but he needed a job, and he wasn't sure he could find one. A forty-six-year-old fluffer with a bad record. Barnaby said, "Would you give me a job?"

"No. I admired your father, and I haven't forgotten his saying essentially that your sort of foolishness might have served his law firm if he'd been able to embrace it. But no. On the other hand bankers are now by definition speculators, and along with every other kind of expert, some of us like to have intuition people around. Dowsers, as my own father used to call them, people who look for money with a bent stick. No insult intended. I've always considered myself something of a dowser which is why I don't need you. But I could call one or two guys, in Oklahoma of all places, who might put you to use."

Marian looked at Barnaby and shrugged.

Barnaby said to Winott, "Why would you do that?"

"You see, Barnaby, this is one reason I admired your father. I never would have had the patience to raise you. Why? Because if my daughter's going to go to the zoo with somebody your age, I'd like to know that at least he has a job."

Barnaby said, "Oh."

And Marian said, "Great, Daddy."

"Well, God damn it, Marian," Winott said.

And Marian grabbed hold of the sleeve of his parka to tug him away from Barnaby.

"The other reason I'd help you," Winott said, ignoring Marian's hold on him, "aside from my fondness for your father, is because you're a monster, and I have a natural sympathy for monsters."

And now Marian pulled with determination on his sleeve and aimed toward their car. "When you get on the monster thing," she said, "it's time to go."

"I'm not really a monster," Barnaby said.

"No, you're not. You're a fool. I'm a monster. Marian will probably become a monster. But…"

Marian said, "Come on, Daddy. You're tired," and pulled harder on the sleeve.

Winott let her inch him backward, and said to Barnaby, "What's-his-name Childs is a horse's ass. Was there really anything more than that going on in there?"

Was this a quiz? Barnaby tried to think, and all he could think was that Marian liked him. He tried not to look at her as she dragged her father toward their ten-year-old Mercedes with battered fenders.

"Don't think, Barnaby. Christ. Nobody'd ever pay you to think."

"Fiduciary," Barnaby said in the large voice of a pitch from the old days. "Fiduciary," he said again, trying to conjure whatever it was he was about to say. "Fiduciary is going to sell the farm before the end of the year."

And actually, it was true. He said it, and he believed it. Could he feel the motion of a wave beneath him? No.

The market was going to dive. That he knew.

If he knew that, there had to be a wave somewhere.

"Did you know the market was down sharply this afternoon?"

Barnaby shook his head.

"So you think right now that the Fiduciary traders are ready to dump in Japan?"

Barnaby nodded. Somewhere a wave was going on past him. A job. How would he ever know who he was if he had a job? Yet he should be glad. He had to be glad. He was glad.

"Just for fun, I'm going to go home and call around. Talk to me after the holidays, about the work. Come on Marian. Maybe Barnaby Griswold's made us all a lot of money."

She said, "Offer Barnaby a ride. He's wearing gigolo shoes and his feet are freezing."

"Get in, Barnaby," Winott said. "Where are you going?"

But if he got in with them, they'd never get him out. He had to catch the train back to Boston and then get himself to the airport; he was planning to spend the night in New York and then on to Ada tomorrow. He would blow all that if he got in the car. He'd try to buy them dinner and he'd forget where he'd checked his suitcase at the airport. Besides, he had his taxi coming, and he would hate to pass that cabbie in a Mercedes, even an old one, not when he'd become a cop and a fireman for a few minutes.

A job. God only knew he needed a job.

He needed Marian, and she knew that. Why didn't that horrify her as much as a job horrified him?

He said, "I better walk. I'm going to meet my taxi on the way. My feet are fine."

Marian smiled.

Could he have kissed her?

In front of Choate Winott? Get a grip, Barnaby.

Winott said, "They'll offer shitty pay, but if it worked out, I bet they'd find money for you to hedge with some percentages at profit breaks. And Tulsa. That might be where they'll offer the best deal. It ain't the big time, but it would be work. You don't have a constitutional aversion to a job, do you, Barnaby?"

Marian rolled her eyes and got in and closed her door.

And as the Mercedes started away, Barnaby yelled, "Marian. Are you coming home?" and she looked back over the seat and held out a fist with her thumb up, just like the cabbie, although Marian had all of her fingers.

He had never made the calls because he had not wanted everyone else to know; he had not wanted to know for sure himself. Though he had himself known even before he apologized for his life to Peterpotter and a room full of strangers. He had known as surely as his father had expected him to. When he'd first lost it all, he had been ashamed of the loss, and then somehow he'd managed to become ashamed of ever having had it; there was the secret, and he had been afraid if he called anyone they would hear that shame in his voice. Because a fluffmeister cared about the money, the money most of all, and Barnaby Griswold had forever before cared about money with a glee that had transported him and everyone around him. Shame had no place in that party. Shame was opening the oven door; shame was a cold wind on fluff. So he'd hoped that a championship would stand in for glee, would reinstall the ruthless innocence which had always been his happy trademark. Then he had hoped for the goodness of a pilgrimage to turn the reflections of the world back into reflections of himself the way they'd always used to be. Had he been ashamed even before it all went away? Had he made too much too fast on the Old Ladies Bank deal? Barnaby Griswold, for whom too much had never been nearly enough; one way or another he had made more than he could digest, and the fun had leaked out, and how could a man like Barnaby call colleagues and victims without fun in his heart?

When it was gone, he'd wanted it back, but so what? Money was drawn to a fool by foolishness, by larks and play periods involving other money, by hats with wings. Money had come to

Barnaby in the past for the fun of it, but never again would there be the same sort of fun. It would be earnest fun now, when it happened. He would laugh at the jokes of kind people, people who helped one another and maybe even helped him. God knew he was going to need help. He would laugh at the jokes maybe of people who went to church on days other than Christmas and Easter. He hoped he would know when to laugh, because he wanted to get it right. He had changed, and he had a lot to learn, and he would learn. He had changed, and he was as grateful as any man could be. He was forty-six and he had lost everything, including the nature that had always been his greatest resource, and yet somebody had just given him a job. Winott wouldn't have said it if he weren't going to produce. Barnaby Griswold had a job, and thank Christ. He had been swinging into the true abyss, and now he had his own tiny, precious corner of safety in Tulsa. God Almighty but he was grateful.

He sat in the back of his Portuguese friend's taxicab as they inched along the Point Road which was freezing up, and he said, moving his lips but not making any sounds that would lose him his new friend's confidence, he said, "Thank you, God, for bailing me out this one last time."

There wouldn't be another bailout, he knew that. But he would never need another.

In the back of his cab, leaving a place he'd loved, leaving a place he'd thought was everything to who he was, Barnaby Griswold was more grateful than he'd ever been in his life.

In Tulsa, the assignment would be to recognize and recruit fools and their foolishness, and he could do that. He could make banter from the old days when he had to. But that was hardly the same as living it. Once you'd put foolishness in your job description (and Barnaby meant to learn what a job description was), you could never pretend to being the real thing. Good.

His father had won. Which was to say, his father had stuck with him and pulled him through, gotten Choate Winott to give him a job. Of course his father had loved him. Winott had seen it.

And there was even Marian, though he hardly dared let himself think of that. There was Marian too. Good-bye and good riddance to money. Hello (he hoped) to love.

Barnaby sat in the back of his taxicab, exhausted with relief and numb with joy. He could have wept (Christ what a weeper he'd become, though this was more in the old style) for all he had been given and for the loss finally, finally, of his own foolish nature. Even as he sank low in his seat and felt ecstatic tears of welcome and farewell pump up through his diaphragm, the spirit of foolishness separated itself from him and lifted away out of the taxi into the early winter night on Winott Point.

Barnaby chose to think that spirit would stay near the old Griswold house and watch over what had been his family.

As it happened, the taxicab was just then passing the house, and Barnaby looked over the hedge at the dark clapboard bulk and realized with a start that it wasn't dark at all. The lights were on.

Barnaby sat up and told the cabbie to stop.

The girls had come for Christmas. It had never occurred to him they wouldn't stay in the city. He wondered if they had a tree.

Should he go in? What would they say if they opened the door and found their father?

He thought about Marian and Choate Winott and he wondered if it were possible at this late date to become a better father. He had always said that one day he would, and perhaps this was the day to begin. Everything else was beginning, the good and important things. Perhaps he already was a better father.

He handed another twenty over the cabbie's seat back and asked him to wait. Then he got out and walked up the driveway and across to the front door that nobody ever used. He kicked his numbed feet into the snow up the steps and could feel individual bricks teetering. It hadn't been cold enough yet to freeze the bricks in place. He pressed the rusted door bell, and heard (no sure thing) the bell ring inside.

He was going to say Merry Christmas to his own children whether they liked it or not.

He was going to spread his arms and bellow it. "Merry Christmas, girls."

He wished he had come with large boxes from Bergdorf's under his arms. That was how he had handled things in the old days, especially if the deal had come in. Or, for that matter, if the deal had gone away—all the more reason to drop a bundle on presents. Oh, Barnaby had often been a great Christmas soul. He'd taken the girls to the *Nutcracker* two years in a row for mid-week matinees, though the second year, after a particularly persuasive lunch at La Cote, the shift to ballet had been less than perfect; the whole afternoon had been less than perfect, which was the kind of thing that always baffled Barnaby, because if the afternoon had been spent on business, the lunch would have led with perfect seamlessness into the business of dinner. Anyhow, that had been a year when the presents (from Bendel's, if he remembered rightly) had been even more splendid than usual.

He dug his soaked shoes, slippers now for all intents and purposes, into the snow on the front porch so that he wouldn't lose his balance when he threw his arms wide and bellowed and strode forward to hug his girls.

Though maybe something other than the bellow would make more sense.

"Hello, girls," he could say quietly, with his arms at his sides. "Merry Christmas. Remember your father?" And then if they had the tree lit, if they had some Christmas feeling inside them, as he knew they did, they might come out onto the snowy, night porch themselves, and hug him, their father for Christmas.

He wished it were not already after Christmas Day, especially since they wouldn't recall that Christmas went on for twelve days. No, the girls were certainly not the theologians Barnaby was, and so even though it was only the day after Christmas, he wondered if it might not be better to say Happy New Year. That didn't have the same wistful ring of love and family and forgiveness as Merry Christmas, but if he wanted forgiveness, no matter how much he had changed, no matter how much better a father he'd become, he would have to be patient. He wished he had sent them something, but Ada had insisted on no presents and no tree in Oklahoma and it had been all Barnaby could do to get a Christmas check to Happiness. Which had made things seem other than seasonal inside the tiny world at Picadilly Manor. And of course there was no Bergdorf's in Oklahoma City. What could he have gotten them that they would have wanted? That he could have afforded?

Was it too late to run into town in the cab for something? He'd rung the bell already for Christ sake.

He rang it again.

He was their new father, and they could damn well learn how to say Merry Christmas when they didn't have any boxes from him under the tree. There were enough boxes that first Christmas after the Old Ladies Bank deal to make a lifetime of presents for an army of anybody else's children. So what if he hadn't arrived with them?

Relax. That was nothing like the note he wanted to strike.

Besides, they were hardly children now.

Had it been ten years since the *Nutcracker* fiasco? He hated to think. Twelve years? Which would have been long enough for them to forget the *Nutcracker* if there hadn't been all the other fiascoes. Long enough certainly to become young women. Ladies. Merry Christmas, ladies. How did that sound? Would he recognize them? There had been an awkward afternoon some years ago when he had passed them on the street and not even noticed them, but those had been the years when their appearance changed by the hour. He would have known them then if he hadn't been distracted. He would know them now; they would be who opened the door. Who else would be in the house?

But would they recognize a father who no longer occupied all of a suit, who was no longer even a fool?

Maybe they were distracted themselves.

Christ, it was cold. The bricks in the steps would freeze up tonight. He turned to be sure his cabbie was holding steady.

He rang the bell again.

He pulled his keys out and unlocked the door and opened it.

He raised one bold arm into the house and prepared to bellow (without question it was best to bellow for this sort of invasion) Merry Christmas and Happy New Year.

But between raising his hand and taking a breath for the bellow, he realized that the house was empty. They were up from the city for Christmas all right, but they were out. They'd turned on every light in the house except for the tree and gone out. Well, who was he to gripe about that kind of thing?

He waved a don't leave me here to the cabbie and went on through the front hall and into the living room. At least they hadn't left the lights burning on the tree, but there the tree was, where Barnaby had always put it, or where he'd had Win have the guy from the tree place put it, since it was rare that he'd ever gotten up before Christmas Eve. He stood and looked. There were packages still open. The ornaments on the tree were ornaments that he recognized. Some of them were ornaments from when he was a kid. He felt as if he hadn't seen a tree there since then, but as a kid they'd never come out here for Christmases. It was Barnaby who'd wanted to, and now that he looked at that tree he was proud of having wanted to. A successful domestic instinct if ever there was one. Barnaby was not without virtues of the home. It was just that the tree had not been in its place for the last several years; that was why it seemed a tree from long ago. Despite all the panoply of presents he'd had his secretary assemble, he'd missed Christmas Day altogether the year the Old Ladies Bank deal came in, and Win had packed the girls and everything else up and come back to the city the day after. He had not forgotten the date, but he had celebrated with other people and he had thought that the celebration could just continue. Twelve days of Christmas. And then the next year, it had all been unraveling, and it was not clear to him just at the moment how one year went at all, and then Win and the girls were off on their own with another family, for God sake, twice. The seasons after Barnaby became a full-time resident of the house on the Point, those years had seemed without need of a tree, though Barnaby did not think of himself as a Christmas hater like Ada. He loved Christmas, but Christmas had not been a part of all that. He was surprised the girls had found the ornaments. He might not have found them himself.

He had always closed off some of the house when he was running the furnace, but that wasn't his bill anymore, and he was glad of the warmth for his feet.

He could smell the Point damp baking out of the walls like a swampy saddle. Through the windows behind the tree, if it hadn't been dark, he would have seen over the brackish pond toward the cove and the ocean.

He thought about looking to see what the girls had gotten, but he didn't want to get caught bending under the tree with his paws in their stuff.

Had Ada sent something? She always had in the past. Checks, recently. But Barnaby would have seen the checks. How had he not arranged that? How had he not sent anything himself? He had sent checks from here on the Point before Oklahoma. And gotten no thank-you notes, which had hardly seemed fair when those checks were expensive for him to write. Had their mother sent something from wherever on the face of the earth she floated? It looked as if she must have. It was all he could do not to go root around under the crusty, gold-gone-black ornaments of his childhood for precious wrappings from Tobruk. Was it this house, and at Christmas, that had let Win keep thinking Barnaby would change? Barnaby thought that it was, and now of course, too late, he had changed after all.

But that was history; it was all history now, and he preferred to keep up the sense that he was moving forward with his just-recent beginning. So he backed away from the interrogation of a lifetime of Christmas trees.

He backed right out of the living room and ran up two steps at a time to the phone in the upstairs hall.

He glanced only for one fearful instant into the glaringly lighted girls' bathroom at the head of the stairs. The thick spread of cosmetics and underwear was so molten it could have been alive. No one spoke about women anymore as "the other," but by Christ they were.

He sat at the phone and looked out the window over the front porch. His cabbie's headlights held firm at the end of the driveway. Good. Barnaby was not stranded, and the girls would have a warning when they arrived. He wondered what they were driving. He dialed, and Happiness picked up on the second ring, and he said, loudly and gaily, "It's me."

Happiness said, "Hello?"

"It's Barnaby. I'm calling from Winott Point to say that everything went fine at the meeting and I'm coming back. Don't bother to put Ada on. I'm just checking in. So you'll know."

"Do you want to talk to Ada?" Happiness said.

"No, no. I'm running. But tell her I called."

"I'll tell her you called."

"There's snow outside. Beautiful. Have you ever been in real snow?"

"I come from eastern Montana, Barnaby, and the Lord brings more snow to Montana some years than people want."

Montana. How the fuck had he never known that?

"Happiness?"

"Yes?"

"I want to tell you something. Marian is actually here, was here. I saw her. She likes me after all, and she's coming home. How about that? And you know what else? Somebody, her father actually, who is a big-shot banker, is going to help me get a job. In Oklahoma. Which means I'll still be back before New Year's Eve. The day after tomorrow, actually, just like I promised. We don't want Ada to worry about that. I'll be back. And I'll tell her about everything else myself. But isn't it exciting? Things are turning around for me. Aren't you glad, Happiness?"

After a long moment, Happiness said, "I'm going to sing you a little song, Barnaby. Are you ready? Here is a song especially for you. It goes,

Wonnnn day at a time, SWEET JEEEEEEEsus,
wonnn day at UH tiiiime.
Wonnnn day at a time, SWEET JEEEEEEEsus,
wonnn day at UH tiiiime.
Wonnnn day at a time, SWEET JEEEEEEEsus,
wonnn day at UH tiiiime.

Barnaby said, "Thank you, Happiness."

You get what you deserve, when you ask your mother-in-law's companion if she isn't pleased for your successes. You would have thought Barnaby could have learned that much after all the years of au pairs and maids and, for a brief time there, real cooks.

"It's a good song, Barnaby. You can sing it yourself if I'm not there to sing it for you. Would you like me to do it once more?"

"No, thank you. It is a good song. But I have to run. I've got to make the train and catch a late shuttle back to New York so I can be sure to get my flight out tomorrow afternoon. If I miss that, I'm stuck. Tell Ada I called. Tell her I haven't forgotten and I'm on my way. There's the cab outside, so I'm going to go. Bye-bye, Happiness."

"Good-bye, Barnaby."

He hung up and stared out at the cab's headlights. Was it beginning to snow? He was sure he could feel the girls approaching, and he was equally sure that he did not feel as much up to managing them as he wanted to feel. He wished he had someone else to talk to. He looked to the Point phone sheet on the wall and dialed Dicky Kopus.

And it was Kopus who answered.

"Richard. Barnaby Griswold here. Didn't get a chance to talk to you at the meeting. Just wanted to say Merry Christmas."

"Griswold. You put on a fucking movie this afternoon. Great. So what else are you doing? Watching over your ex-wife's mother? Is that true? You get paid for that? There any money in that, Barnaby?"

No, Kopus was not going to be what he'd hoped for.

"Nope," he said. "No money."

"What are you going to do? You're broke, aren't you? You just giving up?"

"Actually, I have a job offer, but I'd rather not talk about that right now."

"Hell, if you want a job, I can offer you a job. I might be able to use you. I drive my guys pretty hard, but if you hustle, there's bucks to be had. You're a good bullshitter."

Enough. He could feel the girls approaching. They'd probably gone out for a video.

Yet he couldn't help himself.

He said, "Actually, Kopus, as well as Merry Christmas, I thought I'd offer you some free advice. I'm not telling everybody, but I did just get some very reliable information to the effect that the stock market is going to take a real hit tomorrow. I don't know if you're in the market, but if you are, it would be worthwhile doing something first thing in the morning. This is going to be a big move. Who knows; if you sold short before the ball got rolling, it might not be too late to actually make a killing. Just thought I'd mention it. In the spirit of the season."

"Are you crazy, Griswold? Yeah, I'm in the market, and now that I've talked to you, I'm buying more. You flunked, Griswold. You're broke, and you're changing your mother-in-law's diapers. So either you're kidding me, or you're wrong. And nobody who's broke kids me about money. Who paid for your ticket back here? The mother-in-law? See, that's me kidding. Merry Christmas, Griswold. I hope your new job works out. Now I've got to go. Janice has caterers downstairs and I've got to write some checks. Bye."

Barnaby waved out the window in the hope that the cabbie might be watching and know that everything was fine.

Car lights came down the Point, but went on past. It was beginning to snow.

Barnaby dialed Tom Livermore's home number from memory and got a maid who was indecipherable.

But when Tom came on, he said, "Barnaby. Great to hear from you. Another Christmas without Barnaby Griswold is another Christmas down the drain. Where are you? In town? Can you come over? How are you doing? Somebody is having fun somewhere around here, but I don't know them, and I just get duller and duller. I need your help. The world needs your help. What can I do for you?"

Just like that, Barnaby was going again. Tom Livermore liked him and missed him. The letter about staying away was ancient history, once necessary and now forgotten, as it deserved to be. "The world needs your help." That was gushing for Livermore. It was Christmas, and nobody had teased Tom.

"How about a job?" Barnaby said. "You want to give me a job?"

Silence.

Christ. Had nobody teased Livermore all year?

Barnaby made a laugh and shouted, "No, no. Tom. That's a joke. You can tell it to your directors. Barnaby Griswold asked for a job at the Crenshaw Foundation."

Small laugh from Tom. "I'm sorry Barnaby. I knew that. I'm just a little, you know. Market's got me uneasy just when I'm trying to put together year-end results. Also, Penny left me again this Christmas, but of course that's not much of a distraction anymore."

"Tom," Barnaby said. "Listen. I think Fiduciary is going to dump enough stocks that if anybody else comes along with them the market will go off a cliff. Tomorrow. I think they're probably selling tonight in Japan, and I'll bet they're going to sell fast enough that it shows."

Silence.

But a good silence this time. Barnaby let it go on.

"What are you doing with it, Barnaby?"

"I'm not doing anything. I don't have a nickel. You know that, Tom."

"Any particular reason for thinking it?"

"I'm up at the Point and I heard a guy from Fiduciary talking to people while he kissed their asses. I'm the only one whose ass was not being kissed, so I'm probably the only one who caught the drift. Pure hunch, but I'm right."

"I'll see what I can find out. Are you at your old number up there on the Point? I'll get back to you and let you know."

"It's not my number anymore, and actually I've got to catch a train and a plane. Coming down to the city tonight so I can fly out late tomorrow afternoon. If I'm feeling flush, I may go have an appetizer at La Cote for old time's sake. Think Michel will let me in during friends week? Want to come?"

"I might look in. Call me tomorrow. Did you tell any-one else?"

"I told a local jerk who wouldn't really make a splash if he did anything, but he won't do anything. I also told Choate Winott, the banker, and actually he was going to call around. Less than an hour ago."

"Choate Winott's an unlikely victim, Barnaby. You really haven't taken a position for yourself anywhere?"

"Goodness of my heart, Tom. Merry Christmas. But you want to know something? I may have a job in the works, and I'm in love. Well, I like her. If I really thought she liked me, I would love her. She talks to me. I think she will love me."

"A job? What do you mean, a job? Don't do that, Barnaby. You're the only crazy person I know. I don't think you'd like a job."

"Hey, Tom. Come on. I'm broke."

"I'm sorry. I know your suspension is up this week. But you don't want to become like me. Give it a month, and I'll see if I can't find you a desk and a secretarial pool and some kind of stationery. You didn't really call about a job to begin with, did you?"

"No, Tom. I didn't call about a job. Forget the job. How about love? Doesn't love sound like a good thing for me? She's a pretty girl."

"Does she know you, Barnaby?"

"No. Not really. But I'm not myself anymore. No booze. I'm so healthy from the gym that my suits will never fit again."

"Is she twenty-eight?"

"Yes, she is twenty-eight. God damn it, Livermore. What does that have to do with anything?"

"All the girls in the jokes are twenty-eight this year. Don't you know that? I thought you were going to tell me why it was funny. Anyway, here I am, day after Christmas with Penny gone again. What do I know? Listen. I'm going to check on this other thing. That's where I do my best. It used to be where you did your best too, in your own way. Maybe we should both forget love. Call me tomorrow, and I'll tell you what there is to tell."

"So long, Tom."

And that was that. Barnaby's last deal.

Barnaby Griswold was finally going to live a life like everybody else, and that was a good thing. It was the very best thing. Soon he would be fifty for Christ sake.

And if all he was doing was judging and sorting the Tulsa soy skin entrepreneurs, that was better than competing with them. He would take home a paycheck like a human being.

Already his father was relieved at the news. Was it possible that one day his father might actually be proud? Would his mother cease weeping in her grave? Would his daughters remember who he was?

He wondered if his daughters knew who Marian was. They might. They might be able to tell him what sort of hell she had raised. Did Marian already know that he had lost his foolish-ness? Was that why she liked him, might like him?

But clearly the girls were not coming back right away, and Barnaby had to get going if he was going to make his train.

Out the window, it was snowing heavily.

Snow was pouring down.

Was the cab moving? Oh shit.

Barnaby sprang away from the phone and ran down the stairs and out the front door and sprinted to the cab in his fine English shoes with the snow covering him as he went, covering his tracks as he made them.

The week between Christmas and New Year's was a week of French perversity at La Cote. They took no reservations, and the coach light under the awning was dark, and on the door was a discreet little sign saying the place was closed. But the door was not locked, and if you were a favored soul you could go in and have lunch off an abbreviated menu, a lunch prepared by, of all people, Michel's three crooked cousins. There was cachet to it, despite the cousins, but it was never crowded because most people of style were out of town, or out of midtown, and the tourists were easily brushed off if they chanced in. When very occasionally someone arrived who was known and not liked by the establishment, which was to say Michel, then that person was told that only invited friends were in the restaurant which was closed and please, please come back in the second week of January with a reservation of course. Michel delivered the words with such exquisite ease that rarely did anyone try to push past him into the restaurant. Nobody wanted whoever was inside, the friends, to see and remember who it was that was not a friend. Only once, apparently, had someone from a time before Barnaby's era in fact pushed past Michel, someone, perhaps not unlike Barnaby, who had once been a friend and disqualified himself for awful behavior. When that deluded soul had brazened in among the tables of real and desirable friends, having pushed Michel, tiny, revered Michel, then men had risen from their seats prepared to thrash the offender. Women, so it was said, had thrown cutlery and even one of the cousins' weighty custards, which would itself have been cause for de-friending in any other circumstances.

Barnaby, needless to say, had (before his fall) been a friend. The Christmas after the Old Ladies Bank deal came in, he had essentially spent every daylight hour of the entire friends week in La Cote, much of the time with his sleeves rolled up and washing dishes. It was one of the most cunning things he had ever done; people came back to look at him and to have him call, "Bonjour. I hope that was not you who didn't finish the soup." The fact that his alternative quarters in La Cote were a good part of his escape from the firestorm in his own house was also cunning.

When everything came undone, he was never actually refused entry. He only was looked at by people, customers, never Michel, until he didn't have the heart to come anymore.

The heart or of course the money.

Although, during friends week, Michel often refused payment. The week Barnaby washed dishes, he ate for free all week long and told everyone that he was working for board, which was considered as charming a thing as could be said because everyone knew that Barnaby was closing in on the kind of money that endowed real libraries at good boarding schools.

Really, there was no reason Michel would not let him in. Barnaby had never actually set fire to anything.

Except that if you weren't around for several years, what kind of friend were you? Were you a friend at all?

Was ruin alone cause for de-friending? Barnaby didn't know. He figured a friend came in for at least a half-dozen lunches a month, but couldn't there be exceptions?

Last night he had stayed in the residential hotel where he had used to go when domestic uproar dictated. Instead of the comforts of the old days, they gave him a cubicle fit for addicts, but the town was full and Barnaby was lucky that one of the guys he had over-tipped all those years before was still around.

So he'd slept until noon and had a shower and shaved. He was clean when he got to the door of La Cote, but his other suit did not fit any better, and he didn't know the rules about that either. Did an ill-fitting good suit disqualify? With the English, presumably a well-tailored but now ill-fitting suit, even with a measure of gravy, would be a recommendation. But with the French, such things were not sure.

Barnaby stood tall, holding his suitcase in one hand (to be ready to go on to the airport) and put his other hand to the door knob.

It was after one-thirty, and his itinerary to Oklahoma was routed in a way that allowed him to spend several sleep-allotted hours on plastic chairs in Dallas rather than Atlanta, but the originating flight didn't leave La Guardia until early evening, so he had time to kill. Instead of going in here, he could go to a museum. He could go to another restaurant. He could go to a movie for God sake (though a suitcase at a movie would be awkward). But those were all options in other people's lives. If Barnaby Griswold was in town during friends week he would go to La Cote for lunch if it was the last thing he did. It wouldn't be the last thing he did— Michel would not shoot him. But it would probably be the last time he went in, tried to go in. La Cote had been the headquarters of the pinnacle of his earlier life, the only life that anyone would ever want to speak about, the life before he had to learn what went in the drawers of his desk. Oh, God but he didn't want to have to learn those kinds of things. He didn't want to have to learn to work anything more complicated than a quote screen.

No. That wasn't fair.

He was curious. What it would be like to have a desk he was supposed to use and a room in which he could be expected to be found? Would his new, young office mates in Tulsa call him Barnababy?

He stood tall, turned the knob, and walked in.

"Who is this?"

Michel was there in the vestibule and looked at Barnaby with alarm.

The restaurant was quiet, but Barnaby could tell by the click of silverware against good china that people occupied some of the tables beyond the gilt partition.

Barnaby held out his hand to shake, and Michel stared at him.

"Who is this?"

Did Michel not even remember him?

Barnaby said, "Can you use a dishwasher? I could start right away."

Michel threw himself at Barnaby, and the physical understanding inside of Barnaby was that this was how Michel got rid of the most contaminated of the un-friends, drove them with the fury of a 130-pound pulling guard right back out onto the street where they belonged and then hurried in again to wash his hands.

But now Michel was no longer pushing.

He was hugging.

Oh God.

Barnaby's heart swelled almost to bursting.

Michel was hugging him. Tiny arms wrapped around and tiny head pressed hard against the placket of the chesterfield below Barnaby's collarbone.

Michel was hugging and not letting go. Shaking? Was Michel crying for Barnaby's return? Barnaby's heart did burst, and tears came out of his own eyes.

By God. He was still a friend. He had been away to the furthest reaches of cold waste outside the pale—he was still away (why not be frank) and would be away forevermore. But he was remembered. Oh God, to be a friend.

He dropped his suitcase and brought his own big, now stronger, arms around Michel's tiny, exquisitely tailored shape, and hugged in return.

When they both let go, and Michel stepped back, Michel's cheeks and eyelashes were indeed jeweled with tears, and he looked up at Barnaby to see if Barnaby too had been crying, and when he saw that, yes, Barnaby too had wet his face, then Michel threw himself at Barnaby once more. He hugged with the force of a tiny bear and then once more stepped back and stood to attention and faced Barnaby with the formality of an honorable soldier meeting a comrade who had been given up for lost and yet just now had made it back by grace and courage from apocalypse.

"You are the only American I have known who is all American and also truly French. I salute you."

With which he began ripping at the buttons of the chesterfield in a frenzy, and when they had in continuing urgency gotten the coat hung in the unstaffed check room, and the bag tossed in there with it, Barnaby was pulled by his large and loosely sleeved arm around the palatially golden partition and into the dining room where Michel stood Barnaby like a hero at the head of the class and called aloud, most unlike Michel, called to the eminent souls arrayed down the narrow dining room in the informal sanctity that a shrine imposed outside of business hours.

Michel called, "Look. Look who is here. Barnaby Griswold. My brother of the blood. They have released him. They have let him out for Noël, and he has come back to us."

Barnaby stood and felt all of the surprised eyes turn on him and marveled about the releasing and letting out. He hadn't been sure anyone in this arena had known about him going to Oklahoma; that Michel should know, and should even understand that Oklahoma could hold you against your will, was wonderfully de Tocqueville.

And, there, another name from the crypt of Barnaby's education.

Fair enough. Barnaby lifted his arms out from his sides and opened his palms to the room and bowed his head. Why not?

There was quiet, and in the quiet Barnaby could hear the breathing of twenty or thirty of the world's fortunate sets of lungs, and Barnaby was suddenly not immune to the notion that Michel had gone mad and enlisted Barnaby in some expression of that madness.

Then they clapped.

They clapped, and there were voices. A few of the voices said, "Who?" But most of them said, "Welcome home," and "Congratulations," and "Thank God you're out."

Barnaby lifted his head and looked above them all, through the chandeliers at the ceiling which he noticed was a richer shade of gold than it used to be, almost a match for the partition. There had been a bathing or a burnishing.

And Barnaby too had been burnished. Just this minute. He could feel it shining out from within himself.

Before he left forever (left gladly, mind you), he was remembered and remembered fondly.

Michel shook his arm fiercely and said with sharp, soldierly command, "Stay right here. Don't move a step. Do you hear me?"

Barnaby let his arms drop, and the clapping and the other voices ceased, and Michel was running in his motionless way back to the kitchen for something.

Barnaby stood, and confronted again the eyes of all the other friends in town on this second day after Christmas. There were familiar faces: nobody he'd ever known, but people for whom he had bought bottles of wine in moments of pure exuberance or in moments of exuberant apology when he had spilled beyond the apron of his own table, people with whom he had toasted the occasional triumph or with whom he had joined, sometimes too passionately he was sure, in singing, to Michel's horror, a happy birthday at some cherub brought in for the occasion. The eyes, now that the applause was done, were subdued. There was in the place an air of suppressed misery which Barnaby supposed he evoked with his trailing vapors of Oklahoma. The eyes stared at him. The off-brand barracuda was in attendance. Barnaby knew her after a fashion. She was by herself, no boys, which seemed to Barnaby to be tastefully appropriate, and she too looked at Barnaby with a wonder behind which lurked something like horror. Surely it couldn't be horror. Grave dismay rather, at the truth brought into everyone's midst, the truth of the other, darker side of life, a side that had claimed Barnaby who was once one of their own. They were all glad with compassion that he had dropped by, and they were also terrified by the possibilities he represented. But weren't they also thrilled?

He thought, as he had thought often before, of saintly people like Mother Teresa and the rest of them who came away from their regions of misery periodically to raise money, or to accept awards that they would then translate into money, for the amelioration of that misery to which they gave themselves. The awards and the money raising always took place in splendor, and the saint's passage through that appreciative, applauding splendor had always seemed to Barnaby to be the sort of thing for which he himself was made. He would so liked to have been graceful and humble in the eye of royally terrified admiration. He could so easily have allowed himself to have dessert because it was best to do so whether he wanted it or not. He could have moved quietly and beamed. He could have swathed himself in splendidly wretched clothing for exhibition to the public at larger events. What he could not have done, and what he could not conceive of the Mother Teresas as ever having done, was go back to the misery. How could anyone do that? Safety pin the wretched rags back around your waist for real, and head away from the palace to live—not to visit but to live—again in the swamp, in the slum, in the chemical waste with all of those people who were so unhappy in so many all-too-imaginable ways. Barnaby had always wished that Mother Teresa would not ever have to go back. She looked like agreeable company. Why couldn't she make that her life? Why couldn't she go from award to award and from fund-raising to fund-raising, and just mail the funds and the awards to wherever they were needed?

But there you were, another reason why retiring from pilgrimage had been the best course for Barnaby.

And here, everyone else had gone back to their lunches, and Barnaby had almost gotten to the point of wishing that, holy or otherwise, he himself might not have to go back to Oklahoma. When he noticed the wallpaper.

The wallpaper was new.

They had put up new paper, and the tigers were gone.

Christ Almighty. His heart heaved in his chest and he was dizzy. He put out a blind hand for support.

There was movement near him, but he could not make it out. Michel had him by the arm again, but Barnaby could hardly stand even with Michel for support.

For God sake. The wallpaper. How could he go away for-ever knowing that the tigers were gone too? This, he thought, as the universe seemed to melt, was what pregnancy or menopause must be like.

He reined himself in. He turned himself as sensibly as he could to Michel, and Michel was holding before him a framed something. A testimonial? Wasn't that going a little far? Had business fallen off for them? Had there been a poisoning? That they welcomed every vagrant off the street with a testimonial?

With a piece of the old wallpaper?

It was.

"You see? We saved you your tigers."

Barnaby took the glassed, framed, swatch of old wallpaper from Michel and was amazed, touched, terribly disappointed. It was not a small piece. It was eighteen inches square, anyway. But how could anyone think that the tigers would still be there? Michel might as well have given him eighteen square inches of jungle.

And yet, here was Michel at his side, swooning with pride and feeling and generosity and all other things that were French when the French were at their best.

And so who was Barnaby, here on his last visit, admitted only by grand dispensation, who was Barnaby to express anything but the most gracious appreciation?

"Are you glad?"

"I am glad, Michel. Thank you. Merci. You have saved my tigers, and I am most glad. May I keep it?"

"It is for you. It has been waiting for you."

And as if they'd been waiting for that cue, a pack of dangerously uncivil creatures burst from the kitchen and rushed up through the tables.

"Señor Barnaby. Hasta la vista, baby."

"Barnaby, mon ami. You look fantastic. The jail is good for you."

It was Michel's three hoodlum cousins, and they swarmed at him covered in tomato paste and reeking of garlic as if they had become Italians in the kitchen. All of them were holding open bottles of wine, and thrusting them at him. Jesus, good Bordeaux.

Did they say jail?

"You lost weight, monsieur, and it looks like you have muscles. In jail you lifted weights. And now you have the fashionable suit also. You come from jail and you are a là mode."

They thought he'd been in jail?

He held off the Bordeaux (bottles he'd paid for?), and said, "No. No, I was never in jail."

"We know. Everybody knows. To be an American of style and to go to jail is fabulous."

Barnaby glanced out over their heads which were lowish despite powerful shoes. Some of the other friends were eating again, some watching the action around Barnaby; all clearly knew—as evidently as one knows a lock from a key—that Barnaby had been in prison.

"You are a gangster."

"Where do you get a suit so perfectly too big? In this country? In prison?"

Michel moved them all in a troop toward an empty table alongside the barracuda who managed to look up and see Barnaby without at all noticing the busy, vulgar surround of the cousins and Michel.

"How do you do," Barnaby said. "You may not remember me, but I'm Barnaby Griswold."

"Of course I remember," she said, and it was Barnaby who had forgotten that she had a voice as hoarse and liquid as a movie star under water. She reached out and touched the back of his hand so quietly and forcefully that he felt he had forgotten about hands. "Did you come out with your prison clothes? I would love to see you in them. Have you come straight from a cell?"

"No," he said.

"I understand," she said with significance past anything Barnaby could make of it.

The cousins would not let Michel hustle them away, though Michel was trying.

"Monsieur Barnaby. We are going to get you a woman tomorrow."

What?

"After prison, you need a woman. Tomorrow. We'll bring a beauty."

"No, I'm leaving this evening. I'm going to Oklahoma to look after my ex-wife's mother. She's expecting me and she's not well, but thank you."

"Then we bring her to you right now. Sit and we find her."

Over the cousins' heads, Barnaby could see the eyes of the other friends again, the men especially, attending this conversation with interest. An appearance by the cousins was not the usual event for La Cote even during friends week, and loud promises of women delivered to the premises were even less usual. For that matter, Barnaby's stature as a veteran of prison and a man who needed to be plied with women was new even to his own extravagant imagination.

But instead of wishing for a scar and a revolver, Barnaby wondered at the gloom in all the friends' eyes.

Really the whole room breathed an unstated gloom. Even the most prurient of the men who were thinking of a woman in the hamper for dessert were much more gloom than appetite. Why was that? It couldn't still be Barnaby himself.

The cousins weren't gloomy, and neither was Michel (regardless of his fluster at having let the cousins too far off their leash).

There was routinely the tired affect of wealth and jaded disinterest here, even in the spring and fall when seasonal hilarity could overtake anyone, but that disinterest was only a Tiffany shade over the fire of appetite, which burned in everyone who could afford to come often enough to La Cote to warrant status as a friend.

Yet today, as far as he could tell, Barnaby was the only friend who was not genuinely blue.

"No," he said to the cousins with a burst of rashness and a furtive rap of his knuckles for luck against the wood of a chair back. "I am on my way to see a beautiful young woman of my own."

"You have a lover already? This afternoon?"

"She waited for him."

"She waited? They never waited for me."

"And now, Monsieur Barnaby, you go with your lover to your dying mother."

"Mon Dieu."

"A gangster from the old style."

One of the cousins lifted his bottle of Bordeaux, and the others did the same.

"To America," the one said.

"To America," the others cried, and all three drank from their bottles and then slammed the bottles down on the barracuda's table and grabbed chairs from other tables and sat.

The barracuda too had an air of powerful dismay about her, but she looked like she would be able to distract it. She smiled at the cousins and patted the banquette beside her for Barnaby.

Barnaby was honored, but he said, "One minute." He wanted to share all this with at least one actual colleague from the old days. He handed the wallpaper to the barracuda and asked, "Would you hold it for me?" To Michel he said, "May I use the phone?"

The barracuda said, "Yes of course, darling."

"Use it. Use anything," Michel said to Barnaby, and then to the barracuda said, reluctantly, "Madame. My cousins. May I pour?"

Barnaby went out to the phone in the coatroom, and when Livermore got on the line, Barnaby said, "I'm here at La Cote, and it's great. They think I've been in jail. I'm a paroled gangster. I always knew I should have let them put me away. I didn't even know if Michel would decide to remember me, and they love me. Come on over and have a laugh before I have to catch my plane back to Oklahoma."

"Where have you been, Barnaby?"

"What do you mean? I'd been traveling almost thirty hours by the time I got to bed last night. So I slept to noon. Hey, I'm still sober. I just said everybody loved me; I didn't say I was accepting drinks. Come on. The barracuda is here and I told her Penny was out of town."

"You can forget about Oklahoma, Barnaby."

"What?"

"You're back."

"I'm back?"

"The Dow is down eleven hundred and thirty points."

Eleven hundred and thirty. Amazing. He'd called it.

"You called it."

A free fall. No wonder the rest of the friends were gloomy. Some of them were probably suicidal. They had their sell orders in and were waiting out the day at La Cote.

"Barnaby? Are you there?"

"I'm here."

"Well listen to this. I told a few people. We made the calls. Wasn't hard to track Fiduciary overnight with the kind of moves they were making. Here at the Fund we took some hits, but a lot less than we would have. And we got in on short contracts that more than made up the difference. You made me money Barnaby. And you made other people money. The people I told knew it came from you. They'd been telling me for the last couple of years that they missed the Barnaby component in their portfolios. Hell, we missed the component here at the Fund."

"Am I really back?"

"It's stabilized now; careful money is returning. Actually, Fiduciary has already come in again here and there. But it was the edge of chaos for the first few hours after opening. A lot of folks lost a hand or a foot. And the word is out that you called it."

He was back.

"I'm back." He whispered it, and listened to the sound.

"You're back. Don't, for Christ sake, spend anymore time in Oklahoma. Your sanction is up on the first, and people are waiting for your call. I'm waiting for your call. If you need a place to live the next couple of months, you can bunk with me. I won't hear from Penny until the end of May; that's the usual pattern."

Barnaby said, "So you probably can't come over and say goodbye." Because of course he wasn't really back. He was leaving.

"You come over here. You're persona grata at Crenshaw. Not only can I be seen with you in the light of day, I want to be seen with you. And I have one more little surprise to tell."

"I've got a plane to catch in a couple hours. I haven't had lunch yet." There, that was the note to sound. It was also the truth.

"You can have lunch, but don't get on the plane. The guys I called had made money on you before, and some of them felt they still owed you from the Old Ladies Bank. They never had to give up anything, and they worried about you. There but for the grace of God and whatnot. The first thing we did was buy a few short contracts with you in mind. We figured if you were wrong, we'd eat it just enough to feel we didn't owe you anymore. You've got spending money, Barnaby. Listen. Eleven hundred and thirty points. You've got more than spending money. Come over tonight and we'll talk about it. Hell, you could probably have your old secretary back."

"I have to watch over Ada." Yes, the truth. Perfectly simple.

"Don't do that. Ada has a support system in place. You put it there. Actually, isn't Win coming back soon?"

"She'll be back on the first," Barnaby said.

"Just like the old days. Blind timing. You've been hiding down there, Barnaby. You've done your duty. Anything more would be crazy. You're back, now. You're back and people need to see you. If people hear you're in Oklahoma, they're either not going to believe you called it or they're going to think it was a fluke. You're not an Oklahoma guy. You're no stock picker with a screen. Everybody who knows you knows that. You have to show up. Now. Tomorrow. The day after tomorrow. Get some deals going. If you saw anything down there, bring it back, but not now."

"I'm in love, Tom, and she's going back to Oklahoma too. I think I have a job. I can have one if I want it. A real job. Friends of Choate Winott. And it'll be a better job with this call. I have to stay in Oklahoma until Ada dies, but I think that's where I belong for the long run as well. This is it, Tom. I'm going to begin a new life. I'm going to live like real people." It did feel good to say it out loud.

"God bless you for pleasing a twenty-eight-year-old. I always knew you had it in you, but this is not the moment to get carried away with it. And it sure as hell is not the moment for a job. From buddies of Choate Winott? You'll be the Tulsa freak in charge of the Tulsa freak fund. Winott's a good guy. Bless him, I say, for finding you a job when it looked like you might need one. But you don't need one now. And that's not you, not buying for a fund, not buying for anything. You're a seller, a finder and a seller and a fluffer. You're also a player again. You're a player here. You make the best fluff in the business, and now things are churned up, and everybody will be scared, and the only fluff anybody is going to buy for the next couple of months is going to be yours."

Barnaby said, "Come off it, Tom." Because, after all, what difference did it make? He was going.

"All right, maybe I'm going overboard. On the other hand, maybe I'm not. Anyhow, this is the moment for you. You're in the zone. This is a market tidal wave, and you're the only guy riding it. Get yourself seen and find a dozen deals; you could place them all by Washington's birthday. I'll take you to the cabin for celebration and you can fly your girlfriend up with one of her classmates for me."

"I can't do it." Be frank with him. "I like Ada. I've got a responsibility." There. He'd finally even said that out loud.

"Don't be a fool, Barnaby. Of course you can do it. Are you afraid? You sound afraid. That's not the Barnaby Griswold I know, but I can understand that you'd be gun-shy after what you've been through. Well, the time for afraid is over, Barnaby. And it's over forever. We've all missed you. Nobody has had any fun for longer than I can remember. Come by the house once you've had something to eat. Stay. Tomorrow have six lunches and three dinners. Be large. Be Barnaby. Bring me a deal. We have money to burn over here."

"I'm going back to Oklahoma, Tom." Say it, and be done with it.

Livermore laughed and said, "Don't be a fool, Barnaby," and hung up.

Barnaby hung up himself.

He came out of the check room and out around that opulent partition, and everyone was looking at him again. He had gone to the phone, and today, for them, the phone meant only one kind of information.

He said aloud to the room, "Down eleven hundred and thirty but stabilized. Fiduciary is buying back in. The worst is over."

A woman looked at the man beside her, and the man stood up and walked out. The woman followed.

Nobody else moved. The rest of the friends must have survived, though Barnaby was sure some of them were already thinking about selling the Paris apartment.

"Everybody else alive?" he said.

They all looked around the room to see if there would be more blood. Michel looked too, with great, great sympathy. The cousins looked with enough eagerness and hunger to make you think they would follow any other casualty out onto the street and eat the back of his or her neck for fun. Barnaby saw them glance at the barracuda hopefully, and the barracuda looked back at them just as hopefully, and the cousins looked away. Barnaby had known she would be all right.

And what about Barnaby Griswold? Would he be all right? Was he really back, and was he glad? Could he feel the wave beneath his feet?

Truthfully, he didn't want to be Barnaby Griswold anymore.

He wanted to go home to Ada and Happiness, whether it was for another week or another year. He had promised Ada that she wouldn't die alone, and he meant to keep his promise.

For the first time in his life, he knew what would become of himself. He would have a real job, and he would kiss again—he knew it in his bones—the loveliest waitress on God's green earth. He would say her name, Marian, and she would be glad that he was the one who said it.

The friends began eating again, privately appraising their own lives again. The cousins stood and retreated to the kitchen.

Barnaby stepped back around the partition and dialed Ada's number.

And this time he could tell, by the rattle of the speaker and then the breathing, that it was Ada who picked up.

Before she could speak, he told her, "I'm coming home, Ada. Don't worry. Everything's fine, and I'm on my way."

"Barnaby?"

"Yes, it's me, and I'm going to see you tomorrow, just like I promised. Do you still want me?"

"Oh, Barnaby. I didn't think I'd ever see you again."

"Don't be silly, Ada. We'll have a party on New Year's Eve."

"But what if I die first?"

"You're not going to die before a big party."

"I might. I think the doctor is going to come by this afternoon."

"He is?"

"No, but you promised."

"I promised I'd be back tomorrow."

"Tomorrow is what they all say."

"I'm getting on a plane tonight. I'll be there tomorrow."

"Well, what do I matter? I'm so glad. I had hoped I'd see you one day, but thank you so much."

"Nebuchadnezzar and the Assyrian kings could not make it any sooner, Ada."

"But you promised, and I believed you."

"I know I promised."

"I don't want you to come back because you think you have to. I want you to come back because you love me."

"That's why I am coming back."

"Really?"

"Absolutely."

"All right," she said, and hung up.

So he hung up, too, and came back around the partition and hesitated before walking down the aisle to say his good-byes. The barracuda had the wallpaper balanced carelessly against the banquette, and she looked at Barnaby as if she could already smell his refusal of Livermore. Barnaby had disappointed her again.

Of course he had disappointed her. And that was for the best. He was leaving.

Yes. In fact, wouldn't it be best if he simply left right now without all the good-byes?

More than enough fond things had already been said.

And best, as well, to leave the disappointing wallpaper too. Michel would understand, or at least imagine leaving it to be noble.

Barnaby was going home. He was on his way back to Ada and Happiness. He was on his way back to Marian. He was on his way to a real kind of work. In Tulsa eventually. Tulsa would be best. Maybe Livermore had made him enough money to buy a house. Would Marian live in it? He thought she might, and one day his daughters would visit. He was a better father now. He was finally his own father's honest son.

What a wonder life could be.

Barnaby Griswold was going back to Oklahoma where he would do his part in all those invisible days outside history.

It was his last moment in La Cote, and he was sad, but he had some very happy things to look forward to. He wondered what it would be like to put his hand up under Marian's shirt. The small hard…Well.

The room was quiet again, and all of the friends looked at him again, and he nodded down the aisle to them and to Michel.

He nodded to the cousins back in the door from the kitchen, and saw that one of them did have an actual revolver sticking out the waist of his pants.

He nodded to the tiger there in the swatch of wallpaper that leaned against the banquette beside the barracuda.

And he turned away. Without another word to anyone, he stepped around the partition and walked into the coatroom and grabbed the chesterfield from its hanger and grabbed his bag.

Would it be snowing outside? The Boston snow had not hit New York last night, but there may have been the smell of snow as the one ruined soul had left with his woman a few minutes ago.

Well.

Wait, though. Barnaby took his hand off of the doorknob. He set his bag down, and stepped back around the partition and into the dining room so he could look at that swatch of wallpaper which he had no intention of taking with him back to Oklahoma.

From out of the swatch, a tiger, the great head of a tiger, returned Barnaby's look.

More than that, it was his giant tiger from the zoo in Oklahoma, come all the way here with his glorious sideburns to witness the farewell ceremony.

Even in a picture frame he was enormous, and he stared at Barnaby like everyone else did.

Barnaby went down between the tables after all. He went to collect the testimonial of his earlier life, a real tiger who could not be abandoned.

He didn't speak to anybody. He focused only upon the magnificent head of the tiger.

And the tiger focused back. That glorious tiger stared at Barnaby Griswold with such furious intensity that Barnaby wasn't sure now if he was meant to pick up the swatch or not, if it might not be better just to leave the thing after all.

Because the tiger stared now with fury explicit.

The tiger looked ready to reach out of the wallpaper and use its teeth.

Ridiculous. Barnaby grabbed up the frame.

It was warm to the touch, and he could feel growling come in a vibration up his arm. He held the frame against the side of his leg and could feel the heated growling vibrate threateningly against his knee and the outside of his thigh.

He walked with his framed swatch of wallpaper through the witnessing silence of the friends, and at the partition he turned back to face them a last time.

He said quietly and apologetically, "I called the drop in the market. I knew last night, and I called it on the money. I told a few people, and I'm sorry I didn't tell all of you."

Then Barnaby Griswold took a deep breath and said, only a bit more loudly, "I'm telling you now because you are my friends, and I want you all to know that I'm back."

Oh?

There was silence from the friends, but the tiger's growling took on the substance of sound, and Barnaby lifted the frame and looked into his wallpaper.

The fury in the tiger's face had been tempered by a mischief like Marian's, though suddenly Marian seemed very far away.

Barnaby said more loudly still, and more to his expectant tiger than to anyone else, "I'm back."

And the tiger's fury transformed itself, even as Barnaby watched, into furiously eager pleasure.

From one side of the dining room came the sound of a knife rapping against a glass as if for silence, though all was silent already.

Other knives joined the first. Every friend at every table, the barracuda too, picked up a knife and rapped on a glass, and because the knives were good ones and because the glasses were crystal, the sound was remarkable. It was a sound from Tolstoy or from Wellington after victory. It was a sound from known history, and it was appreciative in a way that went in through Barnaby's solar plexus and quivered him. It was a sound full of deeds done and libraries given after all. It was a sound not so different from trumpets and the voices of children at joyous hymn. It was a sound for a lifetime, and it was a sound for Barnaby Griswold.

He dropped his chesterfield to the luxuriously carpeted floor and he raised his arms, holding his tiger in one hand and holding his other hand in a fist.

"I'm back," he shouted,

And the knives to crystal rang on.

He said good-bye to Marian, and he was sorry to do that. He was also sorry about Ada. Deeply sorry, as men like Barnaby had to say when they were on the run in a fast game. Maybe she would still be ticking when he went down there to clean out the bungalow, but he wouldn't be doing that anytime soon. Ada was Win's mother, and it was Win's turn now. Livermore was right. Barnaby Griswold had to see and be seen. There were deals to be found, deals to be sewed up, deals to be fluffed. Oh, God, but there was work to be done. And Barnaby Griswold was the man to do it. Who needed a job? Who had time for a job? Against his father's scrutiny, Barnaby squared his own blessed-again, impervious-again shoulders.

For everyone else, he thrust his arms, his roaring tiger, his free fist, higher still so that there could be no question about this anywhere on earth. Lombardi's Packers and Ali with the heavyweight belt.

"Victory," he shouted, and he bent his knees to keep his balance as he ripped along the front of this monstrous wave.

"I called the Christmas Crash," he shouted, bellowed so that he could be heard above his tiger's bellowing. If it were not past Christmas Day, he would have added, Tra-la. And then he thought of the twelve days, and did add it.

"Tra-la," he bellowed.

And then why say more? He would see them all again soon. He dropped his arms to his sides and, holding firmly to his now-just-humming tiger, he picked up his coat and went around the partition and grabbed his bag and was out the door onto the surprisingly busy street, where it was in fact snowing.

Barnaby Griswold loved snow.

And there, by God, a taxi presented itself out of the traffic and the snow just for him. When you had a bag and good clothes, a taxi usually did present itself, for the chance of an airport fare. Even so, a dirty, yellow, available taxi in New York snow was a miraculous vision; it had almost the splendor of sunlight shafting through summer storm clouds to the ocean.

He threw his bag in and set his tiger on the seat, and he got in himself and closed the door.

The driver was an East Indian in a turban who half turned to ask over the seat back and through the bulletproof shield, "Where to?"

The man said it with the cheering lilt of a new arrival. He had to be new not to recognize Barnaby Griswold, not to know that instead of the airport, Barnaby was on his way to begin reaping the golden harvests of a resurrected career.

"Where to?"

The musical whimsy of once-British education on a foreign tongue sounded like an unfamiliar evening songbird. How charming, when Barnaby himself had just completed a posting to Oklahoma.

The driver's eyes now glanced in the rearview mirror, the eyes of another new friend who was ready to see Barnaby Griswold along to any destination on earth. Anywhere he wanted to go. Actually, if it weren't already late in the day, Barnaby would have gone downtown just to spread his once again ascendant, territorial musk.

As it was, the people in Livermore's building would let him into Tom's apartment, and a nap might be nice. Also a sandwich; he'd left La Cote without eating for goodness sake.

Of course the driver would not be happy with Tom's nearby address. The driver wanted one of the airports, La Guardia at the very least, and Barnaby had been away so long that it seemed important to try and please his new, turbanned friend. And, after all, what a wonderful sound it always made to say, La Guardia. Such marvelous words to spread out in the back seat of a taxicab after triumph on a snowy afternoon.

God Almighty. La Guardia was the wrong direction altogether.

"Where to?"

On the other side of the Plexiglas, the driver's turban looked not unlike Ada's hat. There were no earflaps, and it didn't tie under the chin, but with or without flaps and ties, this was no time to be thinking of Ada. Barnaby turned to the tiger on the seat beside him for support, and the tiger was there, gigantic, smiling. But, oh, unfair. The tiger, who had turned things around in the first place with all the snarling, now the tiger's eyes were as teasing again as Marian's. What kind of support was that?

La Guardia was the airport, and the airport meant going back to Oklahoma. Christ. Absolutely not. A few months back there, and Barnaby's window here would be gone forever.

Barnaby would be a fool to go back. Even Livermore, who wouldn't give most people advice on whether or not to breathe, had said so. "Don't be a fool, Barnaby."

Well.

Ah.

Don't be a fool.

Barnaby hadn't thought of it quite like that.

Thought of like that, of course, it all presented itself in a different light.

Barnaby held up one hand to stay the driver.

If he went back to Oklahoma now, it would be without question the most foolish thing he had ever done in his life—no need to try and document it; one knew in the gut. It would be throwing everything away, the unmatchable height of foolishness. He should be shot for even imagining it.

So. Yes?

Remember Barnaby Griswold?

Barnaby Griswold had called the Christmas Crash. He'd made it back. And walked away from it all.

They'd remember that Barnaby Griswold.

Oh, bravo.

"La Guardia," he shouted.

Were his mother and father watching? Of course they were, and both of them were proud. Ada could only die. And Marian must, probably sooner rather than later, come to her senses and pair off with someone her own age. But Barnaby Griswold would have done the right thing. Astonishing. Perfectly ridiculous.

"La Guardia!"

"Terrific, man. If it is no planes in the snowing, I can bring you here again."

Barnaby settled himself, waved the driver ahead, and lay an arm grandly along the back of his own seat. Barnaby Griswold's plane would be taking off. He could already feel the first of many new sorts of waves lifting his consecrated wings aloft.

And even as he felt the lift, he could smell the rank, city tide breathing from the very seat beneath him. Out the window was the whole furious chase of midtown slush, which he loved, which he was leaving. He wondered, for just an instant of longing, what had become of his tennis racket. He brought his arm down to let his hand rest for comfort upon the picture frame of his good friend the tiger. Thank God for friends. A light turned green in the pouring snow, and the taxicab inched ahead.

Good-bye. Good-bye.

Readers' Guide for

Fool

Discussion Questions:

1. Do you find Barnaby to be a sympathetic character? Is he an antihero? What happened in the novel to influence your answer? Do you need to like the main character in order to enjoy a book?

2. Did Barnaby ever succeed at being an athlete, lover, or pilgrim? How?

3. What is Barnaby's connection with the tiger? (There are several tigers in this novel, real and, presumably, imagined. Remember the wallpaper at the restaurant?) Does Barnaby wish he were the tiger?

4. What characteristics depict Barnaby as a fool and a fluffmeister? Is this title fair?

5. What is a fluffmeister?

Suggestions for Further Reading

For some readers, Barnaby Griswold is a good example of an antihero as a main character in a novel. If you'd like to read more fiction featuring antiheroes, try these:

F. Scott Fitzgerald's *The Great Gatsby* is about a man, born Jay Gatz, who builds his life on a series of lies and self-delusions.

Jeff Lindsay's *Darkly Dreaming Dexter* is about a serial killer who only murders bad people. The novels are the basis for the hit television series.

Mario Puzo's classic antihero in *The Godfather* is Michael Corleone, who finds himself in a situation where his desire to do the right thing can be brought about only by murderous deeds. Similarly, HBO's *The Sopranos* depicts the life of mob boss Tony Soprano—the man we love to hate.

Or, you might consider Barnaby to be simply unlikeable. Here are some other works of fiction with unlikeable main characters.

Tom Perrotta's black comedy *Election* follows the mishaps of two unlikeable characters: Tracy Flick, an annoyingly ambitious high school student, and Jim McAllister, the teacher who tries to orchestrate her demise.

It's not always easy to sympathize with Eva Khatchadourian, the narrator of Lionel Shriver's riveting *We Need to Talk About Kevin*.

The eponymous heroine of Elizabeth Strout's Pulitzer prize-winning novel *Olive Kitteridge* is often prickly, sometimes cruel, and probably wasn't either a good wife or mother. Yet it's these aspects of her character that make Olive so fascinating to read about, as they help flesh out her character as someone we will come to like.

If you're interested in reading more about the world of stocks and bonds, hedge funds and commodity trading, take a look at these novels:

A Week in December by Sebastian Faulks takes place in 2007. The narrative moves smartly among a large cast of characters whose lives are affected by the subprime mortgage mess. Don't worry if you're not up on the terminology of the finance industry. Faulks walks you through it without making you feel as though you're subprime for not already knowing it.

In *Capital*, John Lanchester offers a panoramic view of London society—high and low—through the experiences of a variety of characters, all affected by the financial crisis in 2008.

Anthony Trollope used much the same technique in his novel *The Way We Live Now*, set in the second half of the nineteenth century.

In Tom Wolfe's *The Bonfire of the Vanities*, we're introduced to Sherman McCoy, who has it all: a hot career on Wall Street, as well as a wife and a mistress, until a bad decision takes it all away from him.

And for excellent (and very readable) nonfiction on the financial industry, check these out:

Michael Lewis's *Liar's Poker* is an account of the author's three-year stint at Salomon Brothers, the prestigious New York investment company. And don't miss his *The Big Short: Inside the Doomsday Machine*.

Fool's Gold: The Inside Story of J.P. Morgan and How Wall St. Greed Corrupted Its Bold Dream and Created a Financial Catastrophe, by journalist Gillian Tett of *Financial Times* describes the events leading up to the financial crisis of 2008. (This is a good choice to read with John Lanchester's *Capital*.)

About the Author

Frederick G. Dillen is a Greenwich Village native who spent his formative years in a New England boarding school. He went on to graduate from Stanford University, putting his degree to minimal use at odd jobs in Palo Alto, Lahaina, Taos, and Los Angeles. He persisted at writing the entire time, and his short fiction appeared in literary quarterlies and *Prize Stories: The O. Henry Awards*. His debut novel, *Hero*, won *Dictionary of Literary Biography's* best first novel of 1994. Dillen and his wife, Leslie, are parents to two grown daughters and three dogs. After stints in California, New York, Oklahoma, and Massachusetts, they have settled for good (they hope) in New Mexico.

About Nancy Pearl

Nancy Pearl is a librarian and life-long reader. She regularly comments on books on National Public Radio's *Morning Edition.* Her books include 2003's *Book Lust: Recommended Reading for Every Mood, Moment and Reason*, 2005's *More Book Lust: 1,000 New Reading Recommendations for Every Mood, Moment and Reason; Book Crush: For Kids and Teens: Recommended Reading for Every Mood, Moment, and Interest*, published in 2007, and 2010's *Book Lust To Go: Recommended Reading for Travelers, Vagabonds, and Dreamers.* Among her many awards and honors are the 2011 Librarian of the Year Award from *Library Journal*; the 2011 Lifetime Achievement Award from the Pacific Northwest Booksellers Association; the 2010 Margaret E. Monroe Award from the Reference and Users Services Association of the American Library Association; and the 2004 Women's National Book Association Award, given to "a living American woman who... has done meritorious work in the world of books beyond the duties or responsibilities of her profession or occupation."

About Book Lust Rediscoveries

Book Lust Rediscoveries is a series devoted to reprinting some of the best (and now out of print) novels originally published between 1960–2000. Each book is personally selected by Nancy Pearl and includes an introduction by her, as well as discussion questions for book groups and a list of recommended further reading.

12/12
BUR
L

PORTLAND PUBLIC LIBRARY SYSTEM
5 MONUMENT SQUARE
PORTLAND, ME 04101

12/07/2012 $14.95